ALL OUR LIES ARE TRUE

A NOVEL

LISA MANTERFIELD

Published by Steel Rose Press, Santa Rosa, California

ISBN: 978-1-7373048-3-8

Library of Congress Control Number: 2023912646

For Jose, for everything

ONE

The police came on a chicken stew night. Dad and I were eating in silence, as we often did, the quiet broken only by the rhythmic *tap tap* of his knife and fork against his plate. That, and the thud of my heart urging me to speak.

I had promised Georgie I'd tell my dad about our plans.

"You have to do what's right for you, Abby," my best friend —my only friend—had said, when she dropped me at the bus stop earlier that afternoon.

"But with everything that's going on ..."

By "everything," I mostly meant my mother. If I went through with our plans, I'd be leaving just when my mother needed me most. That guilt had made me put off my application to the last possible date, voice my bold dreams only to Georgie, and keep making chicken stew like the good girl I was supposed to be.

The truth was, even if my mother wasn't ill—wasn't dying —getting my parents' approval for my plans would be a fight. And convincing myself I'd be okay out there in the world without my family behind me was the biggest battle of all.

"I don't know why they won't just let me grow up," I'd said to Georgie, pinning the blame again on the convenient scapegoat of overprotective parents. But I did know, and so did she. They were afraid something bad might happen, afraid they might lose another daughter. As if what had happened to Cassie could ever happen twice.

"At least they care about you," Georgie had said, pushing her sunglasses up into her silver-blonde curls to look at me. "In the end, they want what's best for you. Be glad for that."

She was mostly right. They did care and they'd always done what was best for me, protecting me in any way they could. But since meeting Georgie, who had managed to thrive in spite of neglectful parents, I wondered if keeping me safe had only made me more afraid. I needed to follow my own path, start my *real* life, but that didn't mean I was looking forward to breaking the news. Still, I'd promised us both I wouldn't put it off any longer.

"Dad?" I pushed a disc of carrot across my plate, circling it around a tiny blue flower on the forget-me-not design.

He didn't answer. Why couldn't he just look at me? Why couldn't he ask, "How was your day?" so I could tell him?

I'd tell him how Georgie drove the long way home with the windows down, the radio cutting in and out as she urged her little red Ford Fiesta over the hills and through villages tucked into valleys. How my hair blew all around my face and made me feel light and new. How the ivy-clad brick of the university buildings was bloodred, just like in the brochure. How I'd felt taller and older walking up the front steps, even in a too-big suit borrowed from Mum. How I was going to start my life, make a difference, right the wrongs. Be brave.

But he didn't ask. He *tap-tapped* his knife and fork, fed a piece of potato into his mouth. *Tap-tapped* again. And I sat trapped in his silence.

"Hmm?" he said at last. He looked up from his plate, but he didn't look at me.

I often wondered what went on in Dad's head, how many thoughts it took to keep him occupied all this time. Maybe he was thinking about Mum in the hospital, wired to machines, the pain-medication drip release clutched in her hand as the cancer marched on. Or about my sister Libby flying through the skies in a metal tube with wings, smiling and serving champagne as if there weren't forty thousand feet of nothing beneath her.

Did he think about me? Did he notice I was no longer a child? Did he understand I was ready for a life away from here?

Or did he think about Cassie?

We never talked about her. She'd been gone almost sixteen years now, but I still thought about her every day. All day long, I'd pictured her at the university with me, imagining for her a bright, shiny future. Was that what Dad saw when he looked at me? Did he always see what Cassie would never be? Or did he only see what I could never be?

Although Cassie and I were twins—had been twins, *were* twins, would always be twins, I suppose—we were not a bit alike. As the firstborn child, Libby had gone through our parents' gene pool and taken the best bits for herself—Mum's straight blonde hair, Dad's blue-green eyes, the flawless Kirkpatrick skin. When I came along five years later, I had sifted quietly through the unremarkable leftovers and come up with mousy hair, gray eyes, and pasty skin that my veins turned almost green.

Ten minutes after me, Cassie had burst into the world, all

lungs and demands. She'd looked at what was left of our family's genes and said, "Show me what you got in back." There, she'd found Grandma Kirkpatrick's exotic blue-black hair and our grandfather's mischievous blue eyes. She nabbed them and packaged them with skin so white it matched our great-grandmother's china. There was no way Dad saw Cassie when he looked at me. It had to be a big disappointment.

Dad's bristled jaw moved in monotonous circles as he chewed a piece of chicken, the fridge motor humming in sync. His dull eyes never left his plate. It was as if he were in the room alone, as if I wasn't there.

I pushed up from the table and carried my plate to the dulled stainless steel sink, overcome with a new wave of guilt, this time about Cassie.

"Tell me about your family," the university's department head had said that afternoon. "Do you have brothers? Sisters?"

"Just one, a sister," I'd answered without hesitation. It was easier than telling the truth. Easier to talk about Libby than to explain Cassie. That she'd disappeared, vanished, never been found. Easier than telling the rest of my family's story.

After our interviews, Georgie had dropped me at the bus stop two stops past my house because I'd wanted to avoid explaining who she was or where we'd been. "I need the walk," was the excuse I'd given her. It had also given me time to choose my words and just a few extra minutes away from the house.

"Don't talk to any strangers," Georgie said. She flipped the Fiesta into a tire-squealing U-turn and gunned it, lawn mower–sized engine screaming, back toward town.

The British summer had been hot and dry, threats of drought in every news report with pleas to conserve water. But with the late August sun on my face, I dreamed I could be anywhere in the world. As I walked the narrow path, the parched moors stretched out for miles behind me, a vast, lumpy quilt of yellows and browns without so much as a button of a house in sight. Except for ours, standing alone like a fortress, its heavy stone exterior and walled-in garden the last defenses against the real world.

I turned my back on it, focusing instead on the far horizon. A warm breeze blew through my hair, and the scent of Georgie's perfume lingered in my nose. It felt like the first day of the rest of my life. I shucked off Mum's suit jacket and picked up my pace toward home, the spongy peat beneath my feet adding an extra bounce to my step.

As I gathered the mail from the box in the wall, looking, as I always did, for news from the university, something at my feet caught my eye. On the ground was the purple, naked form of a little bird. Its skin, not even yet spiked with pin feathers, looked oily in the afternoon sun. Above its beak, round eyes bulged under the thin skin of its lids, and its neck was turned at an unnatural angle. It didn't move.

I crouched beside it, touching it gently with the tip of my finger. In the tree above me, a small brown bird twittered with fury.

"Poor little thing," I said to the motionless form. "You jumped too soon."

I pulled a tissue from my pocket and gently picked up the body. With the mother bird still twittering her warnings, I carried it into the garden and buried it under the dried-up hydrangea alongside the assortment of small creatures I'd failed to save over the years. A twinge in my gut said the bird was a sign. But I had to talk to Dad. I had to make my own leap.

"Rest in peace," I whispered, shifting a stone over the top of the tiny grave. "Nothing else can hurt you now."

I should have listened to my gut.

In the kitchen that night, I turned to face my dad, mustering my determination. "I have something to tell you."

He stood from the table and stepped my way. His gaze met mine for the smallest moment, and then he looked away. "What is it, Abby?"

"I've applied to university," I said with a flash of Georgie's boldness.

For a second, he was curious, and then his face darkened. He pushed his hand through his graying hair, the way he always did when he was stressed. "I don't like this," he said.

My resolve wavered, but I boosted what little fight I had left. "You can't keep me locked away here forever. I need to have a life!"

But Dad wasn't looking at me. He was looking past me, through the kitchen window, at the black car crunching up our long driveway and coming to a halt behind Mum's overgrown forsythia.

We never had unexpected visitors, rarely had expected ones, to be honest. Ours wasn't a house people dropped in on because they were in the neighborhood. It was a place people drove by on the way to somewhere else. But now, two dark figures moved from the shadows and approached the house.

I leaned closer to the window, just catching a glimpse of a woman before she rounded the corner to our front door. She was dressed in a stylish black suit and a tangerine silk blouse, her long hair falling in shimmering, inky waves down her back. She moved with purpose. Whatever the reason for her visit, I knew it was important.

Dad stretched his arm across my chest, but I was done being

held back. I pushed past him and ran for the door just as the bell rang.

Through the door's patterned glass, two silhouettes formed —the glamorous woman and a man, stocky and broad-shouldered. As he twisted, something flashed silver on the dark curve of his hat—a badge. A bulky shape at his chest crackled with words too garbled for me to understand.

Police.

My insides knotted, and my hand, recalling the childish nervous habit I'd broken long ago, reached to twist a strand of hair. The police never came with good news. For almost sixteen years, I'd imagined every possible version of the good or bad news they might bring about my sister. For sixteen years, they hadn't come with either. But they were here now.

When I opened the door, the woman had her hand raised, one copper-painted fingernail extended to the doorbell, her face leaning toward the square of glass. Her stern expression melted into a pained smile when she saw me, as if I was the last person she'd hoped to find. Her eyes were dark but friendly, lined with thick kohl and the lids smudged ocher. Gold hoop earrings swung against powdered skin.

"Miss Kirkpatrick?" she asked.

I nodded, unable to form a simple "yes."

The woman hesitated, and her companion took a slight step backward, his pale, freckled cheeks flushing, as if I were a dog that he wasn't sure was friendly. "I'm Inspector Siddiqi," she said, "and this is Sergeant Nowicki." She gave me a businesslike smile. This was personal, and the news wasn't good.

I set my body the way I'd learned from my kickboxing videos and waited for the blow.

She delivered. "It's about Cassie."

Two

The punch was swift. Two sharp left jabs and a cross, the muscles in my arms tightening on impact, the end of my glove powering into the spot right in front of me. Right between the eyes of my sister's killer.

In the cellar that Dad had converted, Bizet's *Carmen* pounded through my earbuds as I repeated the combo. Jab, jab, cross. Jab, jab, cross. Jab, jab, cross, uppercut, twist, and *boom*. A roundhouse kick delivered to the center of the bag, right to the solar plexus of the monster who had stolen my sister's life, the monster who had ruined mine. Again.

Above me, my dad talked to the police about the remains found in a dried-out lake bed less than a mile from where my sister had disappeared. In my mind's eye, I saw the girl they'd surely found—my lost sister—saw her glossy black hair, heard her infectious giggle. I saw her dancing, skipping, spinning, swimming—always swimming. I watched her pull in a breath and blow out candles on a birthday cake, my own cheeks puffed out beside her. Our sixth birthday, the last we'd shared together.

"Mr. Kirkpatrick," Inspector Siddiqi had said before I'd

been sent downstairs so the grown-ups could talk, "it's too soon to confirm, but we have every reason to believe this is Cassie."

In the cellar, I pounded the bag as the years of stories I had told myself unspooled—back through my teens, my childhood, back to the night sixteen years ago when my twin sister disappeared. All that time, I'd clung to the possibility that, someday, she'd come home. Now, everything I believed, everything I had told myself, tilted with the weight of a new reality, the pieces of my past slotting into unfamiliar places.

A sliver of moonlight shone through the high narrow windows that had once been ground-level vents, casting the whitewashed stone walls in an eerie light. A passing car hummed closer, and the headlights caught a row of bean poles in my mother's abandoned vegetable patch, throwing their shadows across the floor. For an instant, I was caught in their bars. And then the car was gone. On the wall, the round clock marked the passage of time, moving me forward when I wanted to cling to the past. I swung another punch, but the bag blurred through my tears.

I knew the body in the lake would be Cassie's. Ever since she went missing, I'd dreamed about my sister. She was always in water. Cassie had loved the water from the day we were born and some instinct—perhaps the twin sixth sense people talk about—told me that's where she had been all these years.

"I'm a mermaid," Cassie would say whenever she had a chance to swim.

"Well, just remember that even mermaids have to be careful," Mum always warned, cautious even back then.

The swimming lake by the vacation cabins had been the first place we had looked when Cassie went missing. I'd watched my sister a thousand times as she raced for the water, our mother calling her back, Cassie spinning in circles, desperate to be released, skipping to the shore and being called back again. Closer and closer until Mum caught up and deemed it safe to go in. Then Cassie splashing in, laughing, fearless, as if the water was where she belonged, while I hugged the shore.

At first, my parents worried that Cassie had gone to the water alone that night, creeping out, pushing the rules to see how far they would bend. We'd gone to sleep in our room in the cabin and when I woke up, she was gone. There had been no signs of a struggle, no doors or windows left open, no evidence that anyone had been in our room. It appeared that Cassie had let herself out and headed for the lake. The police divers had scoured the lakebed and turned up nothing. But the swimming lake by the cabins was not where Cassie had been found. She had turned up, more than a decade and a half after she disappeared, a mile away, too far for her to have wandered alone.

Someone took her there, I thought and took another swing at the bag. *Someone stole my sister from us.* Sweat poured down my body and my muscles screamed for mercy. But for the first time since I'd started boxing, my routine did nothing to calm my anger.

The police stayed an hour. After they left, I wiped my sweaty face and went upstairs to find Dad. I expected to find him slumped in his chair, head in hands. Instead, I found him in the kitchen making cocoa. Drinking cocoa together was a silly tradition we had, something we'd done since I was a girl. I didn't even like cocoa that much anymore, but tonight I welcomed the comfort of routine.

"Got to look after ourselves, now," he said, with a smile that did not reach his eyes.

"What did they say?" I asked.

He shook his head. "It's too soon to know, but ..."

"It's her, isn't it?"

"It might not be. We ..." But when he pulled me into a tight embrace, I knew.

"What's going to happen?" I said into his chest.

My dad shook his head. "I don't know."

"Do you think they'll find who did this?"

"I don't know."

"The police will want to talk to us again, won't they?"

"I'm sure they will. But try not to worry just yet."

Just a few hours ago, I had felt on the brink of flying free. I'd finally felt like my life was about to begin and I had planned to tell Dad exactly that. But there was no point now. The news about Cassie had clipped my wings, made the future uncertain again.

"In the meantime ..." He nodded toward the mug of cocoa.

Resigned, I took a sip. The familiar flavor I'd tasted every night for as long as I could remember was comforting. I hated to admit I needed it.

After Dad had gone up to bed, I went to my room and called Georgie.

"Did you tell him?" she asked. She was working the late shift at Coffee and Vinyl, and I could hear music in the background, something with a heavy beat that the student patrons could rock their heads to. Something that would never be played in my house.

"What?" I asked, my mind still on Cassie.

"Our plans. Did you tell your dad?"

Georgie was the first person I ever told about Cassie because Georgie was like the sister I wish I'd had. She didn't push to make me who she thought I should be or judge me for who I was. Georgie always saw what I could be and never let me stop believing it was possible. But Georgie still lived in a world where we would go away together, live the student life, reinvent ourselves. I lived in a world where my family would soon be the center of a murder investigation.

"No way," Georgie said when I broke the news about Cassie.

"You can't say a word to anyone until we know more, okay?"

"Of course."

I pictured Georgie pretending to lock her lips and throw away the key, crossing her heart in a solemn pledge to keep my secret, like we always did for one another.

"Are you okay?" Georgie asked.

"I suppose."

"How do you feel?"

I almost laughed. Georgie and I had met two years earlier at Project Talk, where we volunteered as mentors for at-risk kids. Her question was a standard opening we'd been taught. Still, I considered it. How *did* I feel? Angry? Sad? Confused? Torn. Mostly, I felt torn. I'd grown up as the sister of a missing girl, living in a sort of limbo. If they'd found Cassie right away, I might have had the chance to get over it, to talk to someone the way our Project Talk kids did with us. Neighbors would have rallied, tried to say the right thing and sometimes got it wrong. There would have been a manhunt—a real one, not just finger-pointing at my dad. With luck there'd have been an arrest, a trial, even a conviction. I would have had a face to picture, a target for my hatred, instead of a red vinyl bag to punch and kick.

And finally, there would have been a funeral, my family

burying Cassie in the cemetery in our hometown. I would have visited each year on the anniversary of her death, hung a wreath on her headstone at Christmas. On our birthday, just a few weeks away, I would have sat with my twin sister, the one who lived on and the one who didn't. And year by year, I would have grown a little more accepting of the fact that she was gone. I wouldn't have spent the time wondering if someday she'd come home. I wouldn't have dealt with my feelings in silence.

"I feel ... as if I've been turned inside out," I said to Georgie. "Like I have to start all over again."

"You have an ending now. Closure. You can finally be free of it all."

But I'd grown up as the sister of a missing girl—cautious, hopeful, moving forward with hesitant steps. Now I was the sister of a dead girl. The finality of that threw up a blank wall beyond which I could no longer see my future. I didn't know what would happen to us next, but I knew enough to be afraid.

THREE

Just before noon the following morning, a black taxi rumbled up our driveway. Keys jangled in the front door, and seconds later, a streak of teal tore into the kitchen.

"Christ Almighty," said Libby, straightening her suit. "There's a reporter outside the gate. Where's Dad?"

"A reporter?" I leapt to the window. Sure enough, a man in a royal-blue windbreaker stood at the bottom of our driveway, speaking earnestly into a camera. It had begun already.

"Where is Dad?" she repeated.

I ducked away from the window and locked eyes with my older sister.

Libby had come straight from the airport by the look of her, not taking the time to go home to her flat to change. Her knee-length teal coat hung open to reveal a neat teal skirt suit and a crisp white blouse. Her puffy feet were pushed into high-heeled shoes, also teal, and her blonde hair was pulled tight and arranged around a sponge donut to form an enormous bun. The whole ensemble was topped with a small hat—teal—and, as always, not a hair nor a mascaraed eyelash was out of place.

"He went out. He didn't say where, just that he wouldn't be long," I said. "What are you doing here?"

Libby parked her rolling suitcase and carry-on bag beside the table and surveyed the kitchen, looking at everything in it except me. "I was summoned."

"For what?"

Libby looked at me like I was the biggest idiot she'd ever met. "Because of Cassie. Every single thing we do will be watched and noted. We need to show a united front."

She said *show*, not *be*. She didn't say she'd come home so we could be together, so we could cry and hug together, so we could finally mourn Cassie together. That wasn't Libby's way. She'd come home to make sure everything looked normal to the outside world, to tell me what was best for me, when what she meant was that it would be best for her.

"Anything in the news yet?" she asked.

I shook my head.

"That won't last long. And you haven't talked to anyone else about it, have you?"

"I'm not an idiot," I said, spinning to meet Libby eye to eye. "I haven't told anyone anything," I lied. Georgie didn't count. Georgie could be trusted.

Libby sighed as if she found me exasperating, but her icy expression softened just a bit. "Then let's keep it that way." She shook her head. "What a nightmare."

Libby peered at her reflection in the kitchen window and brushed her little finger across something she apparently saw on her cheek. Sometimes I wished I could see what was going on underneath my sister's polished exterior. Libby huffed as if Cassie's discovery was all a big inconvenience, like a misplaced wallet or a broken heel, something that ran the risk of making her look bad.

"How was your flight?" I asked, trying for some sort of normal conversation.

"Fairly typical," said Libby. "Two terrified flyers in first, three screaming babies in economy, and another lost passport. All in a day's work." She gave me a polished smile.

I didn't think any of that sounded very typical, but that was Libby. She'd been trained to appear calm under pressure, to soothe nervous passengers and solve problems discreetly, all the while giving the appearance that everything was under control. Nothing ever fazed Libby. Not a frantic passenger with no documentation. Not even the discovery of her little sister's remains.

"I hope it's her," I said.

Libby turned on me. "What?"

"I hope it's Cassie. At least we'll know."

A look flashed across Libby's face. Fear? But then it was gone. "Yes," she said, her mask of briskness returning. "We'll know. And before we know it, everyone else will know, too."

The shard of Libby's bitterness always stung. But she was right. About a week after Cassie's disappearance, the police had taken Dad in for questioning. No official arrest was made, but the news reported that "Robert Kirkpatrick was helping police with their inquiries." It may as well have been a conviction. All the support we received from friends in our old neighborhood stopped. No one brought over dinners or offered to take me or Libby for playdates. All of a sudden, our tragedy became something we had brought on ourselves. My parents, and more specifically, my dad, were presumed guilty and the fact that they had suffered the loss of a child was suddenly forgotten. The media had camped out in front of our house and hounded my dad about his involvement. Even after the police released a statement that he was no longer a person of interest, the suspicion surrounding him never went away. The dark mark it left on "The Killer Kirkpatricks" was the reason we had been forced to move away, the reason I had grown up in a strange, isolated world.

I'd been too young to understand any of this at the time. Georgie found it all online after I told her about my missing sister. When she asked what it was like, I said it had been terrible. I didn't know I'd been sheltered from the worst of it. Now, it would start up all over again, and this time I doubted my parents could protect me.

"What are we going to do?" I asked Libby.

"We're going to keep our chins up and go on as normal." She tugged her suitcase back onto its wheels and headed for the hallway. "I've been on my feet since four in the morning Dubai time and I have *got* to get a shower. As soon as the hyena out there leaves," she said, indicating the reporter, "we're going to the hospital to be with Mum." She turned back to look at me. "And you'd better act like nothing's wrong."

Libby was still upstairs when Dad arrived home. His face looked as if the color had been scrubbed from it, and his eyes sat in deep hollows. He didn't have to say a word for me to know the police had called him about Cassie. After all the years of wondering, my sister was dead. I waited for my tears to come, waited for my dad to clutch me in despair, but all we could do was stare at one another and wait for the news to sink in.

"The police are on their way," he said. "You don't have to talk to them."

"I want to," I said.

He hesitated, and I was sure he was going to say no. I braced myself for a fight.

I was a daydreamer when I was younger, always lost in my own world. "You'll daydream yourself off a cliff one of these days," Dad used to say, smiling as if he was proud of me. As I grew older and realized how overprotective my parents had been, I imagined how it would feel to daydream myself off a cliff, to step into nothingness and fall—free fall—with the wind in my face. How would it feel with nothing to stop me, nothing to hold me back, just the power of gravity pulling me along my own unique path? There'd come a point, of course, where I'd hit the ground, when I'd feel the impact, the finality of it all. But I had the feeling that point would never actually come. When I pictured the leap, the plunge into nothingness, something always broke my fall.

Or *someone*.

A hand reaching for me at the critical moment. My dad clutching at my belt. My mother's arms catching me in the nick of time. Always safe—grateful, of course—but left wondering how it would feel to land on my own two feet.

Now, Dad sighed. "They're going to want to talk to you again eventually." He squeezed my arm. "Just remember, they'll be watching everything we do."

I wanted to tell him it shouldn't matter if we hadn't done anything wrong. But having seen the old news stories Georgie had found, I knew that wasn't true.

Four

People in the nearby town called our house "The Haunted House" because it had stood abandoned on the edge of the moors for years before we bought it. If they'd ever come inside, they'd have probably changed the name to "The Museum." My mother had hung the walls of our living room with patterned wallpaper when we first moved in, but over the years, Dad had covered it with his collection of obscure art. He had moody black-and-white prints that he'd found in charity shops and vintage posters collected on family trips. In between was a jumbled mix of miniature watercolors, framed objects, and bizarre works of modern art, all of them dark and strange. The floor-to-ceiling bookcases were packed with dusty leather-bound books, and any extra space was crammed with sculptures, ceramics, and found objects. Any trace of the old wallpaper had long since vanished under the cover of my dad's gloomy collection.

I wasn't sure what Inspector Siddiqi was looking for, but from the way her dark eyes narrowed and her scrutinizing gaze flitted around the room as she spoke, it was clear that, whatever it was, she hoped to find it here. In our home. In our faces. In the worn furniture Libby had quickly covered with blankets. In Dad's crazy mess. I understood that a detective's job was to detect, to build a complete picture of the case from all sides, but I felt as if I were wriggling in a petri dish under a microscope. It made me feel guilty and I had to force my squirming body to be still.

"I'm afraid I haven't got too many details at the moment," Inspector Siddiqi said, looking almost apologetic. She held up a report, sheathed in plastic, three gold bangles clattering at her wrist. "The medical examiner found evidence of a head wound."

I gritted my teeth to avoid wincing at the cold, clinical details of Cassie's death. I needed to hear this. I needed to know what had happened to my sister.

"The location of the fracture, just above the temporal bone, suggests impact from the side, not from above," Inspector Siddiqi said. "It was a neat, clean fracture on a relatively thin part of the skull. A blunt-force trauma, probably low impact."

"Were there ..." I stammered over the question I needed to ask and the words I couldn't bring myself to say out loud. "Were there other injuries?"

"Nothing we could see," she said. "Unfortunately, without tissue to examine, we can't say categorically, but in looking for evidence of violence, we found none."

"Except a blow to the head," I said.

"Which could have been accidental."

I looked away, trying not to picture what "accidental" might mean. Dad and Libby both sat in silence, their faces unreadable. I wished I could have seen what they were thinking, if they were imagining all the terrible things that Cassie might have endured.

The inspector flipped the pages of her notebook as if looking for something, but I could tell she was trying to decide whether to tell us more. "If it's any consolation," she said at last, "an injury like this would probably have resulted in instantaneous death."

She glanced at me as if knowing I had already pictured more. I braced for the worst.

"Given the proximity of the lake to the cabin, it's unlikely Cassie was taken farther away first. The most likely scenario was that whoever took Cassie killed her and disposed of her body quickly. It's unlikely that Cassie suffered."

My insides squirmed with a mixture of horror and relief. My sister, just a little girl then, had been murdered. And yet it could have been so much worse.

"We'll be reopening the case and making an official statement in the morning," Inspector Siddiqi said. "I'm afraid we can't release Cassie's remains at this point, but I will personally make sure we expedite our inquiries so that you can move forward with your arrangements."

Dad nodded, his face stoic. "Thank you," he said. "That will be a big solace to us."

No, it won't, I thought. A funeral for Cassie would be like slicing at a scar that had barely begun to heal. It would mean going through losing her all over again.

"Now that we have a little more to go on," Siddiqi said, "we're going to want to ask you some questions."

"Again?" I said, the strain of feeling more like a criminal than a victim's loved one finally getting to me. "We've been through all this before."

Dad glared at me, reminding me that we would always

cooperate with the investigation. I looked away, knowing I'd stepped out of line.

"I understand," Siddiqi said.

"I really don't think you do," I muttered.

Libby shot me a withering look and I clamped my mouth shut. I'd toe the line if that's what she wanted, but if I had to keep my mouth shut forever, I was going to explode.

Inspector Siddiqi cleared her throat. Her dark eyes turned soft, but her back straightened. "I understand this is very difficult for you," she said. "But given the recent discovery, it's imperative that we eliminate all of you from our inquiries as quickly as possible. I'm sure you can appreciate that."

I shrank down in my seat, backing down. *Eliminate us from their inquiries* as if we were the guilty ones. But if I wanted this to be over, that would mean doing whatever I could to help.

Inspector Siddiqi turned to my dad and gave him a warm smile as if she were a friendly neighbor who'd popped over for coffee. "I know this isn't easy," she said, "and I'm sorry to ask you all the same questions again, but I really want to do everything I can to find Cassie's killer."

"That's what we all want," Dad said, his voice flat.

"Tell me about the day Cassie disappeared."

Dad went over the story just as I recalled it. How he'd been out for an early morning run alone. How we'd eaten breakfast at the cabin and then had gone into the village to shop.

"We stopped at a café by the river," Dad said. "The girls liked to feed the ducks. After that, we went home. Theresa, my wife, packed a picnic and went down to the lake. We spent the whole afternoon there."

I'd forgotten about the river and the ducks. Hearing Dad recall that day made me wonder if I had even been there. How could I have forgotten? I supposed the memory had been eclipsed by everything else that happened that day. I glanced at Libby, wondering if she remembered the ducks, but her gaze was fixed firmly on Dad.

"In any of that time, do you recall anything unusual?"

"No," said Dad.

"Did anyone talk to the girls?"

Dad looked at us. "I suppose. There were other people around, tourists and locals. People were friendly, so I suppose some of them talked to us and the girls, but no one that particularly drew my attention as suspicious or strange."

"Do you remember anyone?" she asked, turning first to Libby and then me. We both shook our heads.

"And you were with the girls all the time?" she said to Dad.

"Yes. I mean, not by their sides. But we could see them, and Libby was with them by the water."

"And how old were you?" the inspector said to Libby.

"I was eleven," she said.

"And Cassie and Abby were six?"

I nodded. "It was our birthday right before we went away."

"Sounds like Libby was a responsible older sister."

My dad choked back a pointed laugh. "Libby was born grown up, I think."

The inspector smiled knowingly. "And so, you would have told your parents if anyone had approached you or anything unusual happened?"

Libby nodded. "I'm almost certain of it."

So would I, I thought. *I would have reported something strange, too. Wouldn't I?*

Inspector Siddiqi finally turned her full attention to me.

"So, you and Cassie went to bed that night. Around what time?"

"Early, I think. It was still light out."

"They were both tired that night," Dad said. "They were probably in bed by eight."

Inspector Siddiqi cocked her head towards me. I nodded. "I think that's about right."

"And you and Cassie shared a bedroom?" the inspector asked.

"Yes," said Dad. Inspector Siddiqi shot Dad a look and nodded at me to answer.

"Yes," I said, not looking at Dad. "Cassie and I had one room. Libby had her own."

"And where was Libby?"

My eyes darted to my sister as if seeking her approval. I pulled my attention back to the inspector and spoke calmly. "She was at a friend's, a girl she'd met at the lake."

"But she came home in the night, didn't she?"

"She had a bad dream," Dad said. "And she wanted to come home. My wife went to fetch her."

"Mr. Kirkpatrick," Inspector Siddiqi said. "I need to hear what Abby remembers."

"She was only six," Dad said. "And it's been so long, how can she tell what's a memory and what's a detail she's heard from someone else?"

"That's my job to separate the two," Inspector Siddiqi said. "For now, I'd just like to hear her version."

She gave me a reassuring smile. Without the frown across her forehead, she looked younger than I'd thought, perhaps thirty-five. "So, Abby, you're what? Twenty-two now?"

"Yes."

"Are you a student, or do you work?"

I glanced at my dad. His arms were folded, and his lips pressed tight. "I help with my mother's bookkeeping business," I said. "And I volunteer for a youth-counseling organization."

Inspector Siddiqi flipped through her notebook again. I had the feeling it was an act and that she already had her questions lined up. "Project Talk. And you're a great resource, from what I understand."

Heat rose into my face at her compliment. I stared at her notebook, not wanting to meet the gaze of anyone in the room.

"That night," Inspector Siddiqi said. "The night Cassie disappeared. Libby went to a friend's, but she came home?"

I nodded. I couldn't make eye contact with Dad. I was glad Inspector Siddiqi treated me like I mattered, but Dad had expressed one of my biggest worries. My story of Cassie's disappearance was a broken line. I had dashes of sharp images, words, a look, a face. But the details of the moments before I realized she was gone, and the things that happened after, were fragments of truth, snippets of things I thought I saw, stitched together with stories I'd been told, conversations I'd overheard. For most of my life, I had lived in the blank spaces in between, never sure which images were memories and which I'd conjured from other people. What if I said the wrong thing?

"Did you see Libby when she came in?" she asked.

"I don't think so."

"When did you see her next?"

"The next morning."

"After Cassie had been discovered missing?"

I nodded, but I wasn't sure.

Libby had been there that morning. I was certain of it, and yet the details had disappeared into the fuzzy edges of that day. I couldn't remember seeing Libby come home that night. I'd been asleep. But I knew she had because I'd been told.

Uncertainty twisted in my stomach. So much time had passed I was no longer sure what I'd seen or what I'd been told. I had been too young to be useful when Cassie first disappeared. I had neither seen nor heard anything. Like watching a clever magic trick, I had blinked, and Cassie was gone. The fact that I could tell the police nothing that would help find my sister was the biggest regret of my life and the cause of the guilt that rattled me now.

"Mr. Kirkpatrick, do you recall what time Libby called?" Inspector Siddiqi asked.

Dad nodded. "About half past one in the morning. We were about to go to bed."

"And your *wife* went to fetch her?" I winced at the way she emphasized *wife* and I knew what was coming next. "Because you'd been drinking."

In the initial investigation, Dad had admitted to having a couple of glasses of wine that night. The media had latched on to that fact, suggesting Dad's "drinking" had clouded his judgment and his ability to remember what had really happened, insinuating that he had been irresponsible and Cassie had vanished because of it. It made me sick. My work at Project Talk had taught me what a negligent parent looked like, and my dad was definitely not that.

"So, your wife drove to pick up Libby," the inspector said. "And where was this family's cabin?"

"Not far. Just the other side of the campground. But it was late, and we didn't want Libby walking alone, so Theresa drove over."

"And she went alone?"

"Yes."

"At half past one in the morning."

A suggestion of wrongdoing hung in the air for a moment, then the inspector sat back in her chair and nodded. "I have a daughter myself," she said. "Can't count the number of times she's begged to sleep over at a friend's house only to ring at some ungodly hour because she couldn't sleep or they'd had a falling-out."

She laughed to herself, but I didn't laugh. What had happened in our cabin was nothing out of the ordinary, at least not until Cassie had vanished. That fact changed everything.

The facts I knew were that Cassie and I went to bed in a cabin in the woods, my parents were in the living room, my older sister was spending the night with a friend. When I woke up in the morning, Cassie was gone. Everything in the room looked the same as before. Except that my sister had vanished.

Only one image was perfectly fused in my memory: My mother standing in the doorway of our room, a splash of red across her shirt. Wine. It had been wine ... hadn't it? And Cassie's bed, empty. The daffodil sheets were dented in the shape where she had last been, her pillow gone. Now she'd been found, I imagined that pillow had played some role in her death. I closed my eyes against the thought.

"Let's talk a minute about your brother," Inspector Siddiqi said, turning back to Dad again. Dad's face dropped and he visibly deflated. Uncle Dave had once been a fixture in our lives, but I hadn't seen or heard of him for years, not since Cassie had gone missing. "When did you last speak to him?"

"A few days after Cassie disappeared. When we notified family and friends that she was missing."

"But, at that point, you and your brother had already been estranged for some time?"

Dad straightened. "We'd had a falling-out years before when the girls were small. We never quite patched it up. But he's still family," he said, defiant. "For all our differences, I didn't want my brother to hear about it from someone else."

"Like the police?"

Dad looked the inspector dead in the eye. "I had my feet held over the coals. I was her father and they treated me like a criminal. I thought they might do the same to David. I wanted him to be ready."

"Did you ever suspect your brother?"

"What?" Dad said, genuinely shocked. "No. Dave and I didn't exactly get along like a house on fire, but he loved the girls. He would never have hurt them."

"Have you spoken to him since Cassie was found?"

Dad shook his head. "We haven't spoken for years. He worked overseas a lot. I don't even know where he is now."

"He lives about an hour or so from here," the inspector said.

My eyes shot up at the realization that Inspector Siddiqi was already steps ahead of us.

"I wonder…" Inspector Siddiqi said, and I knew that whatever had seemingly popped into her mind had been waiting in the wings for its moment. "We found some small remnants of fabric with Cassie, most likely clothing, but we also found this." She held up a small plastic bag containing a grubby scrap of green-and-blue woolly fabric. "We believe Cassie may have been wrapped in this. From the way she was positioned, we think someone took their time, took a lot of care with her."

My bones seemed to collapse, and I fought to remain still. I knew that fabric. I could picture it laid out by the water's edge, strewn with discarded flip-flops and half-eaten sandwiches. My back prickled with the memory of the scratchy wool against my sunburned skin as Cassie and I had stretched out to dry on the tartan picnic blanket. Kirkpatrick tartan, green and blue, with threads of red and white.

Dad took the bag and examined the scrap of fabric. He shook his head no. "Libby?" he said, passing the bag to her. My sister shook her head.

"Abby?" Inspector Siddiqi asked. "Is it familiar?"

I stared at the fabric, my mind trying to calculate the right answer, trying to guess if Dad and Libby had forgotten or if I was remembering something that had never been. The only thing I knew for certain was that I needed to stay close to my family. Together, we'd be safe.

I shook my head no.

Inspector Siddiqi took the bag. "Mr. Kirkpatrick," she said. "I have a few more questions I'd like to ask you. Alone."

"Of course," Dad said, glancing at Libby and me. "Whatever I can do to help."

"I wonder if you'd come down to the station with us. It might be easier that way."

"No," I said, propelling myself off the couch. "He's already been eliminated."

Dad reached out and squeezed my arm. If it was supposed to make me feel better, it failed. "It's nothing for you to worry about, Abby. I just need to help answer a few questions, that's all." He turned back to the inspector. "We all want to find whoever did this."

Dad gathered his jacket and followed Inspector Siddiqi out to her car. It was starting again. The life we had rebuilt, the quiet, secluded life we'd hidden behind, was about to be shaken upside down. We'd be The Killer Kirkpatricks again.

At the front door, Dad stopped and turned back to me. I held my breath, waiting for a word of comfort or a crumb of hope. But Dad looked over my shoulder until he found Libby. "Can you handle this?" he asked.

She nodded without looking at me.

And then my dad was gone.

FIVE

We argued all the way to the hospital, Libby driving Dad's Volvo like a woman possessed while I sat in the passenger seat, pleading my case over and over again.

"But something *is* wrong," I said. "We have to tell her."

"Now's not the time," Libby said. "We don't want to upset her any more than is necessary."

"But she'd want to know," I argued, remembering Georgie's comment about finally getting closure. "She *needs* to know."

"She's not strong enough," said Libby. "You want to kill her?"

I bit down on all the things I'd learned from my training at Project Talk about allowing people to voice their feelings after trauma. My mother ought to hear from us that Cassie had been found. But the more I argued my case, the harder I scrabbled for a voice in my family, the further I felt myself sinking into a once-familiar role.

Although I had been born only ten minutes before her, Cassie had quickly commandeered the role of the baby of the family. Libby, who was already five, going on fifteen, when we were born, relished her role as the big sister. She'd mothered us, focusing her attention mainly on Cassie, who had seemed happy to spend her time daydreaming, creating fabulous stories with her dolls and teddy bears, and being Libby's plaything. Libby had treated Cassie like a baby and I'd quickly become the odd middle sister. I suppose I'd been jealous of my sisters' closeness. I'd tried to compensate, to grapple for my share of attention. I once put on a play in which I was both director and star, giving my sisters bit parts to support me. But Libby had ended up taking over and Cassie had outshone both of us. I'd ended up on the sidelines once again.

But then Cassie had gone away, throwing off our challenging but established family dynamic. Libby had still acted like the leader, of course, but the baby of the family, the object of our parents' attention, had been a ghost in our house. The person everyone was supposed to nurture, my supposed ally against the power of Libby, had gone, leaving me untethered. I was the middle child by birth, the baby by circumstance, but had been forced to fend for myself while my parents struggled with their loss. And now, in a way, Cassie had come back, the focus of everyone's attention, and I felt myself slipping into my old role of the overlooked middle child.

As we turned into the hospital grounds, I changed my tactic, trying one more time to make my point. "How are we going to keep this from Mum?" I asked, crossing my arms across my chest. "She's bound to find out."

"I'll talk to the staff and make sure they keep the television off in her room," Libby said, not taking her eyes off the road. "I'll make her listen to music instead. Tell her it's good for her. It probably is, anyway, better for her mental health than that rubbish that's on all day."

"Someone's bound to blab it and then what? You want Mum to hear about Cassie from a stranger? How do you think that's going to make her feel?"

Libby shot me a look. The truth was, no matter how our mother learned the news that Cassie was really dead, and she would, sooner or later, the timing couldn't be worse. My mother was not going to survive this cancer, but no one knew if she'd make it six more months or six more years. She was a fighter, and any time a doctor offered a prediction, she set herself on a mission to prove the expert wrong. But the cracks in my mother's tough exterior had begun to show in the past couple of months. Her talk of fighting her cancer had changed. It wasn't that she was resigned to the disease taking her, but more like she had accepted that someday it would. She'd have days when the spark would come back and I would see the resilient Mum poking cancer in the eye and telling it to go bother someone else. But that feisty Mum had been missing lately and I was afraid the fight had gone altogether. Telling her about Cassie might give her some relief. Or it might finally tip her down the slope.

I didn't know which would be worse, allowing my mother to go to her grave, never learning what had happened to her daughter, or catapulting her there with the confirmation that Cassie had been murdered. Inspector Siddiqi had not used that exact word, had not confirmed exactly how Cassie had died, but as far as I was concerned, murder was the only way I could see for my sister to have gone from her bed to the bottom of a lake.

Libby parked the car in a small lot by the hospital's side entrance, hoping to dodge any dogged reporters. She led us through a maze of antiseptic hallways as if she'd been this way a hundred times. When we popped out into the main reception area, the first thing I saw was Cassie's face. It was splashed across a large TV screen above the information desk, the same photo that had been on every news outlet when Cassie first went missing. It was a school photograph taken by yet another photographer who had insisted we twins should be shot as a singular unit. Someone had cropped it so that Cassie was alone, but if you looked hard enough, you could see part of my arm down the edge of the frame, a wisp of evidence that I had been there.

"Great," muttered Libby, taking off toward the elevator. "We'd better hope Mum's asleep."

I tried to follow, but the familiar face on the screen drew me in and slid me back in time. I stared at the sliver of my arm, suddenly aware of my hands, my feet, my features, everything fully grown and mature, while Cassie looked just as she had when I had last seen her—a child, beautiful and untouched by life. Her innocence struck me hard and my breath caught in my chest.

"Abby," Libby hissed.

I blinked, my body back in the hospital reception, my heart stuck in the past with my six-year-old self and Cassie, with all the twisted years between us.

"Abby," Cassie seemed to call from the TV screen.

"Abigail," Libby snipped. "Hurry up."

I scuttled to the elevator, just squeezing in before the doors closed. Libby stabbed at the button for the third floor, muttering under her breath for it to hurry. I kept my eyes on the floor indicators above the door, not wanting to lock eyes with Libby for fear I wouldn't be able to stop myself from saying, "I told you so."

I wasn't an idiot. I knew my parents had sheltered Libby and me from the worst of the media's prying when Cassie had gone missing. We'd attended only one of the many press conferences during that time, but for the most part, they'd left us girls alone. But now that Cassie had been found, our family would be news again. My mother was in no position to protect me this time, and it seemed that we were already too late to protect her.

Libby took off like a scared rabbit the second the elevator doors opened. By the time I reached my mother's hospital room, Libby had already taken up her position on one side of the bed. A woman from my mother's book club, one of the regulars on her visitor roster, fussed with her coat and bag, making her excuses to leave. From the television screen hanging from a wall bracket, I heard the end of the early evening news transition to the local weather. We were too late.

My mother stared at the screen, her eyes wide. I didn't know the details of the news report, but I knew it would have gone for maximum drama. The news about Cassie had not been broken gently to my mother. I waited for her to react, to cry out, to break down, but she only stared, her tired face frozen in shock.

My heart tugged in my chest with a sudden desire to crawl into bed and wrap myself in my mother's arms, to cry with her, to have her wipe away my tears and tell me it was over now, to say we could finally all move on.

But that's not what we did in my family. We pulled together when things got rough, and things had been rough for as long as I could remember. We'd made it through Cassie's disappearance and my mother's long illness, and we'd make it through whatever happened next. We believed in sticking together, but that wasn't the same as holding each other close. Surrounded by my family, I felt strangely alone.

I fixed my face into a comforting smile and stepped into my mother's room just as the book club lady hurried past me. She looked from me to the TV screen, her wide eyes rimmed with tears. "We had no idea," she said. My mother had made a small group of friends through her love of reading, but the bonds had not, apparently, been strong enough for her to share her most terrible secret.

As I inched into the room, Libby was speaking gently to Mum, telling her about the police visit and the phone call confirming Cassie's death. My mother stared at her as if she were looking right through her, and she had been expecting this news to come someday. Shocked but not surprised.

Her expression changed when she saw me. Her shock turned to fear. Maybe she was afraid for me, living with the knowledge that my sister had been murdered; maybe it was fear that our lives would be turned upside down all over again. Whatever it was, it was clear she worried about me in a way she didn't about Libby. We were her two surviving adult daughters, but we were not equal.

"It's okay, Mum," I said, squeezing in beside Libby and reaching for my mother's hand. "It's over now. We can put it all behind us."

My mother stared at me, not blinking. Her lips quivered like she was going to speak, but then she closed her eyes as if she couldn't bear to look at me. She reached for the button that fed her painkillers. Clicked it once, twice, and then once more.

Click, click, click.

The fear fell away from her face, her expression growing lax. Her eyes softened and only then did tears push from their corners and a strangled cry leave her mouth. "It will all come out now."

It was too much for Libby. She hurried from the room, her

expression knotted in pain. I stayed and held my mother's hand until she slipped into a peaceful sleep.

Three clicks and she didn't have to deal with the world, didn't have to face the fact that her daughter was dead. Three clicks and she could disappear into a better world.

I wanted three clicks, too.

We stopped at the village bakery on the way home so that I could pick up Mr. Blackthorn's paperwork. My mother had been doing his books for years and I stopped by every week to pick up his receipts and invoices. Mr. Blackthorn always had a smile for me, not to mention the occasional custard tart or apple pie. I liked Mr. Blackthorn, and I enjoyed the order of bookkeeping work, adding up and balancing, everything making sense. But it was temporary work, and Mr. Blackthorn would have to find someone else once I left for university. Assuming my mother didn't get well again.

The bell jangled as I pushed open the bakery door to find Mr. Blackthorn chatting across the counter with a huddle of customers.

"Oh," he said when he spotted me. "I didn't expect to see you today."

The conversation stopped and the people at the counter put items in their bags and bid Mr. Blackthorn goodbye. I didn't need to be a genius to know they'd been talking about my family. "I've just been to see Mum," I said as if there was nothing more to discuss. "Do you have your paperwork?"

"I didn't get it ready," he said. "I didn't think ... with all that's going on. I am sorry to hear about your sister. We all are. Don't worry about the books this week. You've got more important things to worry about."

He didn't make eye contact with me the whole time, as if he couldn't find anything to say.

―――――

Cassie was on the news again that night. I gritted my teeth as the reporter rehashed my sister's case, making sure to highlight the biggest crowd-pleasing details. *Missing for sixteen years. A lake near where the family was staying. No evidence of sexual assault.* The media circus made me sick. Everyone clamoring to find the most enticing angle, planting sordid images in people's minds, forgetting that Cassie had been someone's daughter, a little girl who would have been—*should* have been—a grown woman by now. My sister.

"Bloody marvelous," Libby swore from her perch behind me, the venom in her voice making me flinch. "That's all we need."

The cameras cut from the studio to a reporter on location. He stood in the middle of nowhere, his jacket flapping in the wind. Behind him, a tall, imposing house towered over the road below. It stood in a coppice of spindly birch, behind which the moors stretched endlessly. It was the last place anyone would want to live. It was our house.

"They've been here again," I said, panicked that we were being watched even now.

"Vultures," said Libby.

The reporter stared gravely into the camera. "This is the remote spot where the family of Cassie Kirkpatrick has lived for the past decade and a half. People in the nearby village say the Kirkpatricks kept to themselves and never mentioned anything about their missing daughter. Most people we spoke to here say they had no idea of the tragic history of the Kirkpatrick family."

"Well, they know now, thanks to you," Libby muttered to the TV.

The scene cut to an earlier shot, and I instantly recognized the face of Mr. Blackthorn. "They're a nice enough family," he said, glancing at the camera. "Always friendly like, but they keep to themselves. Not real social like."

"Did you know about the disappearance of their daughter?" the reporter asked.

"Didn't know a thing about it. The wife and daughter came in here every week. Never said a word about it. Bit odd really."

I gasped at the insult. *A bit odd?* It was disgusting how people could turn like that, smile to your face one minute and call you "odd" the next. My breath quickened, my fists clenching as I listened to the report, trying to stop his sharp words from burrowing down to my most tender spot—that place where painful truths gather.

"Robert Kirkpatrick has been helping police with their investigations," the reporter said. "Does this surprise you?"

"Well, yeah, of course," said Mr. Blackthorn. "Whole thing's a surprise, really. He didn't seem like the kind of fella who'd harm anyone. But, like I say, I don't know him that well."

The reporter turned back to the camera. "Police say Robert Kirkpatrick is helping with their inquiries. They did not indicate if he would be charged in what now appears to be the murder of his daughter Cassie."

And there it was. My dad was damned by insinuation, guilty until proven innocent. No matter what happened now, even though he had never been charged, if Cassie's killer wasn't found, my dad would always be suspected. Our life here would never be the same again. I pictured the university admissions officer watching the news and deciding my troubles and I might not be such a good fit for their program after all. Unless the truth was uncovered, I would always be stuck, the sister of the little girl who vanished in the night.

"Oh, for God's sake," said Libby, turning off the TV as the shot went back to the studio and the next piece of news.

"What are we going to do?" I asked as Libby paced the room in a fury.

She spun to face me. "Nothing."

"Nothing?"

"We're going to act normal as if this is no big deal, and we expect it all to blow over. We're not going to give them anything to talk about, and when they find out—again—that it wasn't Dad, they can all go home and eat crow."

I wasn't sure what Libby really believed, but I knew it wasn't going to be that simple. Now that Kirkpatrick was a household name again, we wouldn't even be able to order a pizza without someone raising an eyebrow.

Six

Dad called early the next morning to say he wasn't being held, but he was staying close by the police headquarters to help answer questions. "Just go about your business," he told us, "and I'll be home before you know it."

Libby made the breakfast drinks that Dad had forced on us all for years. I took a slug of the smoothie, the bitter aftertaste of the vitamins turning my stomach. I pushed the glass away.

"Drink up," Libby said.

"I don't want it today."

"Don't be difficult, Abby."

I stared at the glass as if it had just insulted me. And then, for Dad's sake, I did as I was told. If they wanted me to act like my whole world wasn't caving in on itself, then that's what I would do.

"You're not serious," Libby said when I told her I was going to my weekly stint at Project Talk that night.

"You keep telling me to act normal," I said.

"I would have thought you had enough problems of your

own without trying to solve everyone else's," Libby said, wiping down the kitchen table for about the fourteenth time.

I sucked in a breath. Libby would never understand why Project Talk was so important to me. It was the one place I could come close to being myself, the one thing that gave me a purpose. And right now, it felt like a safe place into which I could escape. "I'm worried," I said, trying to keep my voice level. "Helping someone else will take my mind off things, at least for a bit."

Libby scoffed. She flitted around the kitchen, cleaning things that did not need cleaning, making a point not to look at me. Libby might fool other people with her image of efficiency and control, but she wasn't fooling me. She turned and gave me her "work smile," the one she used for difficult and demanding passengers, the one that made her *look* like she was being pleasant, even when she was acting like a total cow. "Do as you please," she said.

I was suffocating under Libby's watch. I needed to get out to see Georgie. Away from Libby's mothering. Away from the gossip and the media. And the sooner I did, the less likely I was to say something to Libby I might possibly regret.

"Maybe you should go home," I said.

"I'm not leaving you here," Libby said.

I held her gaze. I often wondered what my relationship with Libby would have been like if Cassie had not gone missing. Would we have gotten along better than we do now? It wasn't that Libby and I didn't like one another, it was just that we were so different. Cassie would forever be six years old, and my family treated me as if I hadn't aged either. Thanks to Libby, I had grown up in the shelter of two mother figures, one loving and protecting, the other organizing and smothering. And just as a plant can't grow in the shade, I struggled to find my footing in the shadow cast by Libby.

Libby thrived on organizing—people, things, time, me. The apps on her phone were strictly joy-free. She had apps to capture notes, to-do lists, and color-coded schedules. Her whole life synced so that no detail could get by her. When she still lived at home, Libby's wardrobe looked like one of those paint swatches at the D-I-Y shops. Her clothes were arranged with military precision, with tops on the top rail, bottoms on the bottom, and everything organized by shade. Now, she wore a uniform for work—the teal one provided by the airline—but anything else she wore was carefully chosen to present Libby in the way she wanted people to perceive her.

"I'll be fine," I said to Libby, refusing to back down this time.

She hesitated, no doubt picturing a hot bath, her own bed, anywhere but here. "Okay," she said. "But get a taxi home and don't talk to any reporters."

At four o'clock that afternoon, Libby dropped me off across from city hall. I did a quick check for news vans, then cut down the narrow cobbled lane to a small yellow stone building. Once inside, I exhaled, finally free of Libby's control, and made my way down the familiar carpeted hallway to a room where Georgie was already setting up chairs in a circle for the meeting.

Georgie was the first person I'd met when I started at Project Talk two years earlier. I'd seen an ad for the program in Dad's newspaper and hounded my parents about volunteering until they finally caved. Georgie had been like a beacon in that room, glowing with confidence I envied. Once we became friends, I discovered that her outward brashness was her armor. Georgie privately called Project Talk "The Sad Sack Club" but she said it with love, and she was a brilliant mentor. A graduate of the program herself, she once told me that she knew what it meant to have one single person acknowledge you when the people who were supposed to care didn't. She also got why I volunteered each week at the Sad Sack Club. Even though it was hard to hear the kids speak about what was going on in their lives, I felt like I was doing something constructive, something that could maybe make a difference. Just *something*.

"I saw the news," Georgie said as she tipped three kinds of cookies onto a plate, and I arranged them into a circle.

"He didn't do it," I said, nabbing a custard cream for myself.

Georgie raised her hands. "Never suggested he did."

"Libby says we need to act normal until it all blows over."

"Did she define 'normal'?"

I laughed. "No." Georgie had never met my sister, but my stories had painted a clear enough picture. Georgie thought Libby "had issues."

"Good. Then you'll be fine."

I munched at a corner of the cookie, my jaw working the crumbs to nothing. "What if the kids start asking questions?"

"Abby," Georgie said. "This is the last place you need to worry about people judging you. Just be honest. That's what we've been taught, right?"

I nodded. Georgie was right. I was safe here.

Claire, the group leader, arrived in a flurry, her wild hair wrangled into a ponytail and her sneakers squeaking on the polished floor. She handed us white business envelopes printed with the Project Talk logo. "Here are the reference letters I promised."

If Claire had seen the news, she either hadn't connected

Cassie and me, or she was a total professional. I clutched the letter tight, a little life raft that let me believe my future still stood a chance. Leaving Claire and my Project Talk family was the one downside of our plans to go away. Leaving my family was quickly becoming urgent.

"We're going to miss you and Georgie around here," she said. "You've done a really good job."

It was Claire who'd encouraged Georgie to apply for university and financial assistance, make a fresh start for herself. "The past does not equal the future," she liked to say. Georgie, in turn, had convinced me. "Who's going to keep an eye on me if you're not there?" she joked. Georgie was a survivor, and she didn't need me, but I liked that she saw me as someone solid and trustworthy in her otherwise unstable life.

"I wish I could do more with Danielle before I go," I said to Claire.

Claire squeezed my arm. "You can't save every kid, Abby. You have to focus on the good you've done." The way she said it let me know she knew all about Cassie. She was a true pro.

There were eight kids in the club, each with an assigned mentor. We had a core group of five who'd been coming for as long as I'd been volunteering. The other three spots were filled on a revolving schedule, with new kids coming in, staying awhile, and moving on. Mostly, I was glad to see kids leave because it meant they'd made progress, got what they needed, and gone back to their lives.

I'd been assigned to Danielle. She was one of those kids who really needed help, but whenever I thought we were making progress, she wouldn't show up the following week. Even when she did come, she was closed off, putting up a wall that was hard to break through. Then, the next week, she'd be loud and disruptive, filling the room with noise and boisterousness, trying to prove through bravado that she didn't need anyone's help. But I could see through her. I knew what it was like to be scared and uncertain, to know that you were different and that your life wasn't like that of other kids.

Still, part of me wished she wouldn't come tonight. If anyone was going to flat-out ask me about Cassie, it would be Danielle.

"Do you think Danielle will come this week?" I asked Claire.

"Danielle who?" purred a voice from the door.

My stomach flipped guiltily. There she was. She wore a top in a cheap shiny fabric that clung to her narrow body, showing flashes of creamy skin above the tops of her leopard-print leggings. She would have been a typical stringy preteen, tall for her age and maybe a tad overdressed, except that she oozed charm in a way that made me feel plain and frumpy. She reminded me a little bit of Cassie.

We formed our circle, and the kids took turns talking about the events of their week. Danielle was quiet, refusing to talk in the circle, so when the group broke for a snack, I took my chance to talk to her alone. She was perched on the corner of the snack table, one leopard-print leg crossed over the other, biting into a chocolate chip cookie like she was nibbling someone's ear. Her thick blonde hair hung over one shoulder and her glistening eyes were rimmed with dark lashes like the teeth of a Venus flytrap. She turned heads and flirted and spoke in a purring tone that might have been funny in any other kid, but in Danielle, it was terrifying. She was completely confident in her ability to beguile every person she came into contact with. But she was twelve years old and woefully ill-equipped to

46

manage the consequences. I could never say this out loud, but I was afraid for her.

"Hi, D," I said. "How's the cookie?"

She lowered her lids and flared her nostrils. "Orgasmic."

I reminded myself not to make a big deal about anything she said or did, not to give her any fuel for her seriously smoldering fire.

"You always choose chocolate chip. How come?"

She shrugged one shoulder without taking her eyes off the cookie, the way normal kids her age do when they're lying.

But Claire had told me Danielle's story. Her mother had been murdered, killed by her ex-husband, the father of Danielle's older stepsiblings. Danielle had been in the house when it happened, just like I'd been in the room when Cassie disappeared. No one knew exactly what she'd seen, and her story kept changing. But I knew one thing for sure. She was scared, and underneath her charm and bluster was just a little girl waiting for me to find a way to reach her. I'd made it my personal mission to gain her trust and hope that she would open up to me. I wanted her to know that she wasn't alone, that there were other people who'd had bad things happen to them, and that there were people who cared about her.

"Did your mum make chocolate chip cookies for you?" I asked.

She didn't answer.

In our training, we were taught to encourage bereaved kids to talk about their loved ones, because it was often the last thing people in their daily lives thought they'd want to discuss. I'd tried to convince Danielle that talking about her mum would help, that she could let people know it was okay to talk about her, that it wouldn't make them sad, but it would mean that her mother was real and still important. But Danielle didn't want to talk about her mother. Ever. That I didn't understand.

After Cassie disappeared, I'd asked my parents about her endlessly. I'd wanted to know my sister better, to fill the hole she'd left. But they'd never wanted to talk about her. Mum would get flustered and busy herself with suddenly urgent tasks; Dad would change the subject. It wasn't as if it made them sad, exactly, but Cassie's name was like a stick poked into the soft belly of a clam. My family closed around it, shutting down the conversations, shutting out Cassie as if she had never existed. And so my memories faded, but the feelings of loss remained. I didn't want that for Danielle. I didn't want her to forget her mother, no matter what terrible things she associated with her.

"Did your sister like chocolate chip?" she asked, not meeting my eyes.

I flinched. We both knew she didn't mean Libby. I glanced around the room. Georgie's mentee looked up at me, then looked away. She knew about Cassie, too. I caught another kid's gaze for the split second before he averted it. Everyone knew.

I braced myself. "Cassie liked Jammie Dodgers," I said, the memory filling my head again. "She'd take two at a time and hold them to her face like heart-shaped eyes, then she'd eat off the top layer and scrape out the filling with her teeth."

Danielle laughed. "That's disgusting. What happened to her?"

I shook my head. All these years, I'd wanted to talk about Cassie, and no one would let me. Now that I had the chance, it was the last thing I wanted. I was supposed to be helping Danielle with her loss, not talking about mine. But maybe I was missing an opportunity. My experience qualified me more than most. Maybe talking about Cassie would allow Danielle to trust me. It was worth a try.

"We don't really know what happened to Cassie," I said. "For a long time, we didn't know where she was or even if she was alive."

Danielle looked up from her cookie. I'd clearly piqued her interest.

"The thing is, I was asleep in the room with her when she disappeared. When I woke up, she was gone."

"Where did she go?"

"We don't know," I said. "I didn't see or hear anything. Some people didn't believe me. Some even said I was lying to protect someone. But I wasn't. I didn't see a thing, and I've had to live with that guilt ever since."

Danielle went back to her cookie, but I could tell I had her attention. She was waiting, I was sure, to hear what I would say next.

"The thing is, I hated that I couldn't help her, that I couldn't tell anyone anything to help find her."

"But you've found her now."

It wasn't a question. Danielle had seen the news. Or someone had told her. I glanced at Claire, who was circling the room, checking in on each conversation. She looked up, saw me watching, and gave me a compassionate smile.

"Yes," I told Danielle. "We've found her."

"Are you sad?" she asked.

I thought about my answer carefully, trying to turn the conversation back to Danielle. "When someone you love very much dies, it's hard. You're sad for a really long time, and it can take ages before you feel okay. And you never feel quite right again. Even if they were old or sick, it's still hard, but when someone dies who shouldn't have died, it's even harder. You try to make sense of it, but you can't because they shouldn't be gone. But the one thing that can help is closure. Do you know what that is?"

Danielle shook her head, and once again, she looked like a little girl, a little girl trying hard to act like a grown-up.

"It's when you get answers and start to understand what happened. It doesn't mean you like it or even accept it. But when you have facts, you can start to make some sense out of it. That's how you start getting back to feeling right again. And sometimes that just means talking about it with someone who understands."

Danielle was silent, her half-eaten cookie resting in her lap. She looked so small and fragile. She glanced up at me for a fraction of a second, and I held her gaze, silently willing her to speak. Then she pushed up from her seat. "I can't eat this. I'll get fat."

As she crushed the remains of the cookie in her hand and tossed it away, my stomach knotted. I'd lived for so long inside a family that never talked about what had happened to us. I'd swallowed down tears no one wanted to see and wrestled with questions no one wanted to answer. Meeting Georgie and confiding in her had freed me, and I wanted that relief for Danielle. But it would have to happen on her schedule, not mine.

When the meeting was over, Georgie walked the kids out to meet their respective adults. A moment later, she burst back into the room. "There's a reporter out there," she spat. "He's trying to talk to the kids."

"About what?" Claire asked.

I knew. "About me."

"I'll talk to him," said Danielle, wriggling her shoulders back.

"No, you won't." I pulled her to face me. "They will take anything you say and twist it to what they want to hear. You don't want that. Trust me."

"I'll deal with it," said Claire. She pulled a ring of keys from her pocket and handed one to Georgie. "Go out the back way and cut through the annex. You can pull your car up to the porter's entrance and get Abby out that way." She turned to me with a reassuring smile. "I did it once when I needed to avoid an ex-boyfriend."

I tried to smile, but my chin wobbled, and I was afraid I would cry. The world was closing in, suffocating me, and yet the closer it got, the more alone I felt, the further I drifted from safe ground. "Maybe I should stay away for a while."

Claire squeezed my arm. "Absolutely not. We're here for you, Abby. You know that, right?"

I nodded.

"This will all blow over soon," she added.

But it wasn't going to blow over, not for a long time. My past had caught up with me and it would hold on until it ruined my future. I wouldn't get closure, and no one would forget until we all had answers about Cassie. It was the only way I would ever be free.

SEVEN

Our house was dark. From an open upstairs window, a ghostly sheer curtain fluttered out in the breeze. The only sound, as I opened the door of Georgie's little red car, was the hum of the engine and the rustle of leaves as a breeze brushed over the trees. My home had never felt more like The Haunted House.

"Can I stay at your place tonight?" I asked Georgie.

She glanced at me, then at the house looming over us in the darkness. "I think you'd better," she said. I closed the car door.

Once the house was well behind us and the lights of the city were in view again, Georgie turned to me. "What in God's name possessed your parents to move to a place like that?"

"We needed to get away."

"To the middle of nowhere?"

Our neighbors in the town where we'd once lived had held a vigil when Cassie disappeared. Outside the neat brick house on our safe, suburban cul-de-sac, my childhood friends had lit candles while their parents held them close. *If Cassie could vanish without a trace, could it happen to their kids too?* My older sister, Libby, who was eleven at the time, had stood dry-eyed, barely blinking as her candle flickered. I had wanted to climb out of my own skin and run away from it all. No one knew what to say to me or how to behave around our family. There had been no flowers piled outside our home, no teddy bears and crayoned notes from Cassie's friends. Cassie had not been ill and died, had not been involved in a serious accident and fought for her life, only to lose. Cassie had simply disappeared, like a frame cut from a film, and left everyone hanging, our pasts freeze-framed in that moment, our futures unspooling on the floor.

A few months later, my parents had told us we would move away. I had assumed they were sick of the awkwardness, their friends struggling to act normal around them, our friends crossing the street to avoid us, no one quite sure what to say. I'd almost felt the neighborhood breathe a huge sigh of relief when the For Sale sign went up in front of the saddest house on the street.

"But how will Cassie find us if we move?" I'd protested when my parents sat me and Libby down to tell us the "exciting news."

"Oh, Abby," Mum had said, then smiled and added, "you worry too much." But the forlorn look on her face had told me the one thing no one in my family had ever said out loud: My mother no longer believed Cassie was coming back.

But I did.

The night before the movers arrived, I'd written a note to Cassie, telling her where we'd gone, leaving our new address and phone number so she could call. I'd given the note to my best friend, Paula, and made her swear to keep it a secret. No matter what my mother believed, I hadn't wanted to go without leaving some way for Cassie to find us.

"The past always bloody catches up with you," Georgie said as she pulled into a tiny parking space under a broken streetlight. Georgie's past was her parents. They'd been "chemically absent" from her childhood, as she put it, then suddenly resurfaced with their hands out when Georgie aged out of care and got herself a job. "But that doesn't mean you can't put on a spurt and outrun it," she added.

Georgie led the way up the concrete stairs at the end of her block of apartments near the city center. The light was out on the middle landing, and someone was yelling in one of the flats. A car alarm whined below us, and the drone of slow-moving cars and buses was interrupted only by the wail of a passing ambulance on its way to the hospital where my mother lay.

"How do you sleep with all this noise?" I asked.

Georgie laughed. "How do you sleep in the middle of nowhere?"

"Cocoa," I said.

Georgie turned and squinted at me. "You are such a grandma."

I shrugged. "My dad makes it for us, and I don't like to turn him down."

"Do you always do as you're told?"

She smiled as she said it, but I didn't answer. Georgie was less than a year older than me, but sometimes I felt like a late-blooming child around her, unsophisticated and out of touch, as if I'd lived life in a bubble. Other times, I felt like her elderly guardian, someone who'd lived seven lifetimes already and knew all the dangers life could present. Sometimes I did feel like a grandma, and sometimes I felt like a kid who couldn't even say no to a nightly routine of cocoa.

Georgie's kitchen looked as if someone had put a pizza in a

blender and flipped on the switch without a lid. Pans and dishes were piled in the sink and food was splattered over every surface.

"Frickin' Gary," Georgie muttered. "I just cleaned this."

From the next room came the sound of rapid gunfire and yelps of pain, followed by deep groans of despair. Gary, Georgie's roommate, was apparently playing a video game.

"I'm not dealing with this tonight," said Georgie. "I'll make us noodles."

As she pulled two plastic pots from the top of the cupboard, a Pringles can tottered and tumbled from the shelf, the lid popping off as it hit the counter. I lunged to catch the snacks before they spilled, but instead, a roll of cash bounced from the end of the tube. Orange tens, purple twenties, and a core of red fifty-pound notes, lots of them.

I stared at Georgie, not knowing whether to repack the money and say nothing or wait for an explanation. Even I knew it wasn't typical for people to keep giant wads of money in with their snacks.

"Jesus," she whispered, stuffing the money in the can and putting it back on the shelf. "It's Gary's."

"He should put that in the bank," I said. "It'd be safer."

Georgie looked at me sideways. "Yeah, I'm not sure Gary wants to answer too many questions about where this came from."

"Something illegal?" I asked, nervous.

"Probably," she said.

I had some vague ideas about where Gary got his money. He was Georgie's brother's best friend and had taken Georgie in after her brother went to jail. Georgie swore her brother was a good guy who had had one bad day. He'd fought hard to get custody of her as soon as was legally possible and done everything he could to give her a decent life, including dipping his hand into the mailbag at work and coming out with a couple of checks. Gary had promised Georgie's brother he'd watch out for her. "Honor amongst thieves," she'd told me.

"Are we safe here?" I asked Georgie.

She laughed. "Gary's as bent as a nine-bob note, but I'd trust him with my life."

Georgie's trust would get her into trouble someday, but if it hadn't been for Gary, she'd be living on the streets.

We carried our Pot Noodles to Georgie's room. It was like stepping into another world. The bed was neatly made with crisp white sheets. Against one pale-pink wall was a shelf stacked with folded clothes and two rows of books organized by height. On a low table, an electric kettle in bright chrome stood beside matching tea and coffee canisters. In the middle of her jumbled life and Gary's domestic bedlam, Georgie had made a life for herself. Maybe I could do the same.

I sat on Georgie's bed and poked a fork into my chicken and mushroom noodles, letting the steam hide my face. But I wasn't fooling Georgie. "You thinking about Cassie?"

I nodded. "She didn't wander off alone; someone took her."

Georgie swirled her noodles, but I could tell she was watching me. "Don't you remember anything about that night?" she asked.

I was about to say no, but that wasn't exactly true. "You know, like when you're on a plane?"

"No," said Georgie.

"Okay, well, when Libby first became a flight attendant, she actually did something nice, for once in her life, and got us tickets to go to Rome."

"Nice," said Georgie.

"Yeah, well, Mum had just finished her first round of chemo, and Rome was the one place she was dying to go."

"No pun intended."

"Right. Well, I'd never been on a plane before, so I got the window seat. I was scared but also excited about seeing the view. But no sooner had we taken off than we bounced through this thick cloud, and I couldn't see a thing."

"So unfair," said Georgie. "Is there a point to this story other than making me jealous that you went to Italy?"

"I'm getting to it. So, finally, we flew over the Alps, and all the tips of the mountains were jutting up, jagged peaks piercing a blanket of clouds. That's what my memories of that night are like. Mostly it's a fuzzy blank landscape dotted with the odd sharp image. All I want is to get out of the cloud and see the bits I'm missing."

"Jesus," said Georgie. "I can't imagine."

"I feel like I'm the one person who should have seen something. I'm the one person who should be able to help find her killer, but instead, I've got nothing but other people's stories."

"What if you went back?" she said. "To the lake?"

"The lake?" I asked, a cold wave passing through me and pushing up goose bumps. "What for?"

"It might jog your memory. You might see something that reminds you. I don't know."

"I already did that years ago."

"Not *that* lake though. You didn't know she was there then. I was thinking, maybe if you saw where they found her ..."

"But I never went to that lake. None of us did."

Georgie shrugged. "Did you ever go back to a place you'd been as a kid, and it wasn't at all the same as you remember it? Like, I once got stuck at the top of the climbing frame at school.

I was maybe six at the time. When I went back years later, the thing was barely higher than my head, but in my mind, it was enormous, scariest thing ever."

I laughed. "So?"

"You were just a kid when all this happened. You were scared and confused. You probably didn't even understand what it meant that Cassie had gone missing."

That was true.

"I don't know," Georgie said. "You seem frustrated and helpless, just sitting around waiting. Maybe nothing will come of it and maybe you'll be no better off, but at least you'll know you did all you could to help her."

This was definitely not what Libby had in mind when she told me to act normal and do nothing. But it was better than pretending nothing was wrong. I thought back to our trip to Rome. There'd been traffic at the airport and our plane had been put in a holding pattern. For half an hour, we had circled, banking left, over and over, until I felt dizzy and sick. With each turn, I caught glimpses of the terrain below—the coastline, a river, some ruins, a road leading into the city—but I was powerless to reach them. It had felt like the longest thirty minutes of my life.

And now my whole life was in a holding pattern, waiting to see what happened next. Maybe Georgie was right; maybe doing something was better than doing nothing.

"I should tell someone where I'm going," I said.

Georgie scoffed. "Why?"

"If I suddenly vanished ..."

"Fair point," said Georgie. "So, tell them you're with me. You don't have to tell them where we're going. Better to ask forgiveness than permission." As she got up and started pulling out blankets and pillows to make an extra bed, I took out my phone and texted Dad.

> Staying with a friend. Didn't feel like being on my own.

And then I sent Libby the same.

I didn't expect an answer from Dad, but when Libby still hadn't responded by the time we went to bed, I started to consider Georgie's idea. What if I could help prove Dad was innocent? What if, after all these years, I could help catch my sister's killer?

I pictured the newspapers then. We wouldn't be The Killer Kirkpatricks anymore; I'd be the one who caught a killer. Then I could finally get on with my life.

I couldn't sleep that night. All I could think about was Cassie. It's hard to explain to people what it's like to grow up with something dark and terrible in your past. My family was instantly not like other people's in a big way, and more like one another. We had a shared experience that brought us closer. We stuck together and took care of one another. People could be cruel about this sort of thing, especially when they didn't have the full story. They made all kinds of assumptions and filtered the news to support what they wanted to believe. Georgie understood this, and Danielle would undoubtedly face that cruelty if she hadn't already.

There would always be something missing for Danielle, too. And it was more than just the absence of her mother. When you lose someone, you sort of grow around the hole they leave. It never quite closes up and there's always a little bit missing that no one but that person can ever fill.

But it was more than that with Cassie.

I'd thought about it a lot and analyzed what that thing was, and here's what I came up with: It's like when my mother used to bake bread. She'd mix up the ingredients, but nothing happened until she added the yeast. That was the thing that enabled flour and water to turn into bread. That, and a bit of sugar. Grief was like baking bread. Someone dies and maybe at first you're in shock. Nothing happens. You're just numb. But then you see the body, or you have a funeral, or you get an urn of ashes and say a few nice words about it, and it's the yeast that starts the grieving process and starts the bread, so to speak, rising and building around the hole the person left.

But we never had that with Cassie. We never got anything final that acted as the starter to let us know it was okay to grieve. We never talked about her, never cried together, never reached a point where we could sit around and remember good times with her. We just moved forward, dragging that dark space behind us. Her absence was always there.

For all those years, I'd looked for some way to let go of the dark space left by Cassie, a way to heal but not to forget. I thought I could find it by helping Danielle. Now that Cassie had been found, I was afraid the darkness was going to hold on. Maybe if I could remember one detail, I could start to forgive myself. But it was as if those memories had vanished along with Cassie. Maybe now that she'd been found, the memories would come back, too. Maybe I needed to look harder.

When I woke up the next morning, my neck stiff from sleeping on Georgie's floor, there were no new messages on my phone.

"Georgie," I whispered. "Are you awake?"

A grunt came from beneath the duvet. "I am now."

"I'm going to go," I said.

"Home?"

"To the lake."

The duvet whipped back, and Georgie's rumpled face popped out. "When?" she said.

"As soon as possible."

Georgie blinked and a clump of dried mascara dropped onto her cheek. "And how are you planning to get there?"

I said nothing, hoping Georgie would take the bait and offer to go with me.

"An undercover mission," Georgie said, throwing back the covers and flinging her arms around my neck. "My favorite kind."

"I hope I'm doing the right thing."

"Sometimes," said Georgie, "even doing the wrong thing is better than doing nothing at all."

I hoped she was right.

EIGHT

We almost missed the turnoff. I got distracted and Georgie's phone had patchy coverage. I spotted a painted wooden sign just in time. "Shady Grove Cabins and Camping 1/2 Mile." The place was still there.

As Georgie followed the narrow lane, I kept my eyes peeled for the entrance. I needn't have bothered. It was clearly marked by a news van and several parked cars.

"Keep going," I said, ducking my head as Georgie drove by the white five-bar gate set between two stone pillars.

"Now what?" she asked, pulling over out of sight.

"We should go home. This isn't worth it."

"I thought you wanted answers," she said.

"I do. But I don't want to answer questions about why we're here."

Georgie sighed, not hiding her frustration.

"Okay, okay." I pointed to a wooden sign with Grove Trail etched into it. "Let's park out here and walk in. If those reporters spot us, just tell them we're out for a walk or scoping out accommodations for a future trip."

Georgie drove slowly down the lane until she found a grassy turnout where she could park. "Don't back out on me, Abby. Let's get in, see what we can see, and get out." I fumbled with my backpack, but Georgie caught my arm. "You can do this, Abby," she said.

Our plan was deeply flawed, but we were too amped up to see it. We would go to the cabins, starting with a look around the outside to see if that would jog any memories for me. Then we'd hike out to the lake where Cassie had been found. If I was nervous about going back to the cabins, the thought of seeing the spot where my sister had lain, waiting to be discovered for all these years, made me feel ill. I had no idea how I'd react when I actually saw it. I wasn't sure I could even get my mind around the significance of the place. There was only one way to find out, though, whether I liked it or not.

"Keep your head down," I said as we walked. "The place was crawling with nosy parkers and amateur Sherlock Holmeses last time. I don't want anyone to recognize me."

"We could just be direct," Georgie said. "Knock on the door, tell them who you are and that you want to see if the cabins jog any memories so you can help the police?"

"No way. The last thing I want to do is identify myself as Cassie's sister."

"Well, instead of shooting down everything I suggest, how about some ideas of your own?" Georgie snapped.

I felt the ground waver beneath me. Georgie was the one person I could trust. But she didn't understand what it was like to desperately need to remember and simultaneously want to forget.

"This is stupid," I said. "We should ditch the whole thing and go home."

Georgie grabbed my hand and gave it a reassuring squeeze. "It's not stupid." Her voice was gentle and encouraging. "But that doesn't mean it's not hard." She smiled at me, and my resolve strengthened again. I nodded at Georgie, who gave my hand a last squeeze and led the way to the little stile in the wall.

Shady Grove had been aptly named. The lane petered into a narrow driveway as it passed through the gate. It curved in front of a pretty stone farmhouse with "Office" carved into a sign hanging by the door, then wound up into a thicket of redwoods. Hidden in groups among the trees were the cabins where my family and I had stayed the year Cassie disappeared.

Georgie led the way, and I kept my eye on the reporters at the gate. If we could make it to the cabins without being seen, I thought we'd be okay. But as we crunched across the gravel, following the trail, a bark rang out and a black and white border collie scampered over, tail wagging even as he growled.

"Go away, doggy," I whispered. "Go home." My eyes darted to the gate. *Don't let them see me. Don't let them see me.*

"Jess!" a voice called, and a tall, slender woman appeared from behind the farmhouse. She was about the same age as my parents but with the clear, glowing skin of someone who spent plenty of time outdoors. I wondered how long she had lived there. Had she taken over Shady Grove in recent years, or had she been there when Cassie went missing?

She eyed us with suspicion. "Where are you girls off to?"

I faltered. She knew what we were up to. But Georgie was on the ball. "Just out for a walk," she said.

"Not snooping around, are you?" the woman asked.

"Snooping?" said Georgie. "Snooping at what?"

I ducked my head. Georgie lied like it was second nature, but I didn't share her wiliness. This might have been a small act of rebellion for her, but for me, it meant going against my family's wishes. Not doing as I was told. I was on unfamiliar ground.

The woman grabbed the dog's collar and led him back to the house. "Just make sure you stick to the trails," she called.

"Do you think she recognized me?" I whispered, my voice cracking.

"No," said Georgie. "Nosy old bat."

But I was uneasy. When the police had arrived at the cabin after Cassie disappeared, they took me with my mother and Libby to a farmhouse. I suppose they had wanted us out of the way in case they made any gruesome discoveries. Or, given that Dad had quickly become a suspect, maybe they had wanted to talk to him alone. I recalled sitting at a big wooden table in the farmhouse kitchen while someone made hot sweet coffee for my mother "for the shock" and mugs of steaming hot chocolate made with milk fresh from the cows of a nearby farm for us girls. It had been sweet and creamy and tasted like the outdoors, fresh and green. It was nothing like the bitter cocoa I drank with Dad every night. I'd never tasted anything like it before or since, and that thin slice of memory had stuck with me, even after all the rest had faded to white.

But the woman I remembered had been old then, at least in my memory. Had she been older than my mother, or had every adult seemed old to my six-year-old self?

"Anything familiar?" Georgie asked me, pushing on up the trail.

"Nothing. Is this even the right place?"

"Those reporters think so," said Georgie, climbing a set of steps carved into the hillside and edged with logs. "How many Shady Groves can there be?"

"Maybe they closed the old one and this one just happens to have the same name."

Georgie stopped at the top of the steps to catch her breath and gave me some serious side-eye. "I'm not being funny, but after what happened to Cassie, I doubt anyone would decide to name their fun vacation cabins Shady Grove. I'm kind of surprised they didn't change the name here."

"But that was years ago. People forget."

Georgie considered me for a moment, then she said, "Chloe Kubo. Sammy Rasheed. Sarah Louise Dawson. Mean anything to you?"

Every name was like a stab to my gut. They were all children who'd been murdered or gone missing in our county since Cassie. Their names had filled the news headlines for months, surging back into the limelight with every step of progress in the case. I had followed every story, somehow believing that if their cases were solved, Cassie's might be, too.

Perhaps more familiar to most people were the names and faces of the men—it was almost always men—who committed the crimes. While the victims slipped into oblivion with time, their killers, and even the suspects in some cases, lived on in infamy. Would people still remember Cassie Kirkpatrick if she hadn't been thrust back into the news? Would people still be able to picture her face? I had to give them another name and face to remember—that of Cassie's killer.

NINE

They say we die three times; once when we stop breathing, again when we're laid to rest, and the third and final time when our name is spoken for the last time, when there's no one left alive to remember us. I had made it a point to remember all those missing children and said their names to Georgie to make sure they were not forgotten. Now that Cassie had been found, she was moving through the progression of deaths. It gave me an uneasy comfort to know that the renewed attention she had gained might mean she wouldn't be forgotten either.

We walked in silence, following the trail through the trees. I had expected a sinister place, dark and gloomy, the air tinged with the knowledge that something bad had happened here. But, with the morning sun filtering through the trees and a gentle breeze ruffling the leaves, it felt idyllic, and images of our trip—of laughter and of Cassie—came tumbling back in. It was hard to imagine anything bad could happen anywhere on a day like this. But I knew it could.

Ahead of us, the trail veered to the left, but when we reached the bend, I stopped. Through the trees, I saw the glimmer of a small lake and a clearing dotted with picnic tables. I recalled laughter and the shock of cold water on my skin, the sweet tang of summer grass, a tartan blanket scratchy against my sun-sore skin. Memories of the swimming lake where we had played that summer rippled in my mind. Below us, the edge of a roof and the corner of a small stone building jutted through the foliage. From a thick oak tree, off to one side, hung a bright plastic swing. I stumbled to a halt. The seat and ropes of the swing were new, but the spot was achingly familiar. I saw Cassie squealing with delight, her tangled black hair rising and falling in damp ringlets, the ghost of her laughter somehow lingering. This was the cabin where we'd stayed.

Nailed to a tree above the trail was a faded sign that said Private Property, but there was no fence to stop us. We could step off the path and hike through to the back of the cabin. Anyone could have done that the night my sister was taken. Anyone.

The cabin looked empty. The curtains were drawn on the small square windows and there was no car in front or a row of muddy shoes or flip-flops lined up by the door.

Georgie glanced at me as if to say, "Shall we?"

I swallowed a knot of apprehension about the risk of trespassing and of what I might find and stepped into the low undergrowth. We hadn't gone more than a few steps when the sound of an engine reached us, and tires crunched up the gravel driveway. I grabbed at Georgie, and we ducked behind a tree. A dark sedan pulled up in front of the cabins and two people climbed out. Inspector Siddiqi and Sergeant Nowicki. The sergeant glanced up in our direction, just for a second, then opened the back door of the car. A man stepped out, his shoulders hunched, chin lowered. Hope and horror grappled in my chest as I strained to see who the police had brought to the scene. A suspect, perhaps the man who had taken my sister. And then recognition caught up.

I froze, tugging at the back of Georgie's jacket, begging her to run. She twisted away to look. I could barely breathe.

"What are they doing with your dad?" whispered Georgie.

"I don't know." They were taking him back to the scene of the crime, the place from which his daughter had disappeared. Maybe to clarify events, double-check the details they needed to solve this case. Or perhaps they were trying to destroy him with the memory, the cruelest way to get a guilty man to break. I shook away the thought. My dad was here to help, that's all.

"I can't let them see me," I said, turning back toward the way we'd come.

Georgie pulled me back. "It's too open that way. We need to wait until they leave."

"We can't stay here," I whispered. "We should never have come."

"It's okay, Abby." She glanced up the trail and pulled out her phone. She waited for what felt like a lifetime for whatever app she was looking at to load. I peered through the trees, trying to catch a glimpse of my dad, wondering where Siddiqi was taking him, wanting to learn what had happened to Cassie.

Eventually Georgie tapped the screen. "Biggin Tarn?" she asked. "Is that where they found Cassie?" I nodded. "We can get there on that trail," Georgie said, pointing back to the fork in the path.

The trail veered off to the left through the woods. My dad would kill me if he knew I was here. If we turned around now, we could be gone from here in a matter of minutes. But I doubted I'd get another chance to come back now that the police and the media were sniffing around. If I wanted to see the place on my terms, it was now or never.

"All right," I said to Georgie. "Lead the way but keep your head down. If the police see us here, we'll have a lot of explaining to do. And I'm not sure I could give them any logical answer."

"Except that you're looking for the truth."

But as we crept back through the trees and started up the trail, I wasn't even sure that was true anymore. I just wanted to do something—anything—no matter how harebrained, to help catch my sister's killer and bring this nightmare to a close. The police had had sixteen years to do their jobs and all they could do was keep hounding my dad. Now it was up to me.

I'd never been so afraid in all my life.

TEN

It was only a mile from the cabins to Biggin Tarn, but it was all uphill. Thanks to my kickboxing and the fact that I didn't own a car and so walked everywhere, I breezed up the hill. Georgie, on the other hand, wheezed like an old steam engine. I was glad for the noise as we got deeper into the woods. Our footsteps and Georgie's gasps helped to mute the debate swirling in my head.

There were people who believed my family had somehow brought this tragedy on themselves. They wondered how my parents could lose a kid from right under their noses, questioning how much they'd been drinking. Or if they were lying. Or if there was more to the story that the news outlets weren't telling. It was human nature to search for a reason because human minds didn't do well with randomness. When someone gets sick, we wonder what caused it or what they did to themselves to abuse their bodies.

Like my mother and her cancer. People asked if she smoked. If she was overweight. If she drank or ate junk food or did some other thing that could have caused this. Some even speculated that the strain of losing a child had done it. I had always chosen to believe that sometimes bad things happened to good people through no fault of their own. I didn't know what to believe anymore.

Should my parents have taken three little girls to a cabin in the woods? Plenty of families did. Should Cassie and I have been in a room on our own? Well, why not? We'd had our own rooms at home. Every day, there were kids who walked to school alone, who were allowed to play by the river, who came home to empty houses, all the things parents let their kids do as part of growing up. Millions of children had walked home alone, gone somewhere they weren't supposed to go, been lost and taken help from a stranger. A little girl in the town near where we lived had climbed over the garden wall and wandered away from home. Two men had spotted her making daisy chains at the edge of a field a mile from her house. They'd picked her up and driven her around until they'd worked out who she was and where she came from. That story could have had a completely different ending, but it didn't. She was lucky. Cassie wasn't. And neither were Chloe Kubo, Sammy Rasheed, or Sarah Louise Dawson. Tragedy didn't have to have a reason.

The top of the hill was just about in sight when we rounded a bend and found an orange barrier across the fork in the path. "Police," it said across the top. A sign saying "Trail closed" was fastened underneath.

"Oh well," I said, the words feathery with relief.

Georgie checked the map on her phone, following the dotted line of the trail with her finger, and stopped at the fork where we now stood.

"That's the path," she said, pointing beyond the barricade.

I had tried not to think about what we might find at the

lake. Now, I imagined the scene—the area cordoned off and a tent or barrier erected to cover the proceedings from the public eye. "I don't think we should go down there," I said.

"Neither do I," said Georgie. "So, let's go."

My fearless friend. She had pushed me to go to university, pushed me to stick it out with Danielle, and now she was pushing me to find answers. I didn't want to see the place where my sister's body had been found, but I did want to do *something*. I wanted to know that the whole thing hadn't been some terrible dream. Or perhaps I wanted to discover that it had. Either way, I needed to see the place. And if I got scared, Georgie would be there for me.

"There's an overlook here," said Georgie, pointing to a spot on the map. "We should be able to see the lake from there."

It was a tough climb around the rocks. The ground was overgrown with brambles that tore at our clothes and skin, but finally, we hauled ourselves up onto a flat area that overlooked the lake, just as Georgie had said. Below, the dark-blue water lapped up along the shore, but there was no sign of police activity.

"It must be down the other end, around the back of the crags," said Georgie, leaning out over the edge of the rocks.

"Be careful," I whispered, grabbing at her shirt.

"It's not a sheer drop. We can easily climb around."

"But we can't let anyone see us."

"I know," Georgie said. "Follow me."

My stomach roiled as we edged around the base of the rock protrusion, testing each footing for stability. My mind had cleared in the fresh air, and now it told me this was a bad idea. Still, I followed Georgie, keeping my eyes on my feet, not looking at the drop below us. I didn't look up until she stopped dead in front of me.

"What's wrong?" I whispered, but Georgie didn't respond. She didn't need to. I saw for myself what had stopped her in her tracks.

At the end of the lake was the scene almost exactly as I had imagined. A set of screens had been set up a short distance from the shore. Beyond was a police situation trailer and a cluster of cars and vans. Two canine unit officers skirted the shore, their dogs weaving back and forth with noses to the ground. A wooden boat dock, fringed with nubby pilings like two gappy rows of teeth, stretched across an expanse of rocky beach, stopping only a short distance into the water. The long hot summer had sucked away the lake, leaving the dock with no water to cross and the rocky lakebed below exposed. This was how Cassie had been discovered after all this time.

At the water's edge was a second screen. The back was open to the water and several people stood around an area marked with pegs and tape. That was the spot. That was where Cassie had lain, her little body frozen in time, while her twin—me— had continued to grow and age.

"You okay?" Georgie whispered as if someone might hear us.

"I think so," I said, the words belying my uncertainty. "Can you see ... can you see anything?"

"No," said Georgie, reaching back to squeeze my arm. "She's not there."

Of course, Cassie wasn't there anymore. The real Cassie, the sister I remembered, had never been there. But now even her body, her remains, had been taken away to be probed and examined by the coroner. What had she looked like? If I saw her, would I be able to recognize anything about my sister? I couldn't bring myself to imagine it.

As I peered around Georgie's shoulder, something in the water caught my eye, just a ripple at first that seemed out of place, then something broke the surface, a dark human head. I gasped.

I had a sudden image of Cassie in the lake, her hair falling like a sleek black curtain down her back as if it had been painted on. My vision wavered, the memory making me light-headed.

In the lake, the head emerged, attached, thankfully, to a black body. It took a second for the image of Cassie to fade and for my brain to recognize the shape of a diver emerging from the shallows. He handed his tanks and flippers up to a colleague on the dock, shaking his head. Whatever he'd been looking for, he hadn't found it.

The diver pulled himself onto the dock, his colleague hauling him out. He got to his feet, lifted his mask, and walked back toward the shore. As he did, a cloud passed over the sun, throwing the activity on the beach into shadow. As the diver strode into the shadow, I had a fleeting feeling of déjà vu. It was a wisp of an image—the dark shape of a man, the silhouette of the dock and toothlike pilings, a small shard of light cutting across the water—and then it was gone. I rummaged around in my mind, grasping for the image, trying to capture one more detail, one more clue before it disappeared. But it was already too late.

My knees softened beneath me, and I slumped against the wall. I had an odd feeling of vertigo, as if the ground, the rocks I was clinging to, were slipping away beneath me.

"Abby?" said Georgie, reaching to hold me up. "Are you okay?"

I closed my eyes and nodded, hoping the world would stop tilting. When I opened them again, my dad was standing on the dock staring at the water.

"We should go," said Georgie. She stepped around me, taking my hand and leading me back around the rocky outcrop. I stumbled behind, still trying to grasp the last thread of the image, trying to remember. I could see my dad, the dock, the darkness, but I couldn't form a concrete memory. It was like looking at a scene reflected in still water. It all looked real, but if I reached out to touch it, the picture distorted and disappeared, as if I had imagined the whole thing.

But now I knew I hadn't.

ELEVEN

"I know that place," I told Georgie as she pushed open the door of the pub by the river in Straitheswaite and bundled me inside. Despite her string of questions, they were the first words I'd been able to say since we'd left Biggin Tarn and Shady Grove.

"The lake?" she asked.

I nodded. I would have sworn I'd never been there before. And yet the lake and that dock, the toothy pilings so distinctive. I had seen a man on that dock, and I had seen what he had done. I had seen him there with Cassie. And the man was my dad.

Despite the warmth of the pub, I shivered as if I'd been standing outdoors on the coldest winter day. Georgie pointed me toward the fireplace and went to order hot coffees. As I slid onto a low stool at a table by the fire and watched the flames dance around the charred logs, the image of the police diver sparked clear in my mind, then faded. Sparked and faded as I grabbed for it, and it slipped away. His dark silhouette and the way he moved were seared into my brain as if it had been branded. The spot where Cassie had been found was uncomfortably familiar. I had dreams about a lake, a dock, a man, Cassie. I always thought they were just my mind spring-cleaning, piecing together a mix of the real and imagined. In some dreams, the lake had been familiar, the one where we'd swum. In others, it wasn't. Sometimes the man was familiar—an old neighbor, the occasional celebrity—often, it was my dad. The dock had always been made up, a place pulled from my imagination, not from memory. Until now.

I shook my head. Trying to make it all make sense. When Inspector Siddiqi came to the house and told us that Cassie had been found in a lake, I was shocked but not surprised. Cassie and I had been joined in water from the very start of our existence, twin sisters floating in our quiet, safe world, waiting to be born. In my dreams, Cassie was always in water. The small swimming lake was one of the last places I'd been with Cassie when she was alive, so it was no wonder Cassie and water were locked together in my subconscious. The water was our special place, and I didn't want to share that with anyone else. But now I wondered if my dreams held the answers after all.

"Drink this," said Georgie, sliding a thick glass mug of coffee topped with whipped cream towards me.

I took a sip, feeling the silkiness of the cream on my lips and the burn of hot coffee down my throat.

I had always savored my dreams about Cassie. They were a way to feel close to her again. We talked about dreams at Project Talk, how the mind mixes memory and imagination, how it substitutes images so that dreams become nonsense. Whenever I thought about Cassie in my waking life, my imagination often latched on to this ending.

I had one dream that haunted me, finding its way back to me from time to time. It was a dark, suffocating dream, the kind your body fights to escape even as it descends. The dream was murky and confusing, except for a few sharp images, always the same: a car, a shadowy figure in the trees, the faintest glow of moonlight on a lake, and the thing, a bundle, dropped from the end of the dock, discarded like rubbish that nobody wanted. And always, I woke up trying to scream because I knew the bundle was my sister.

But now that I'd seen the man on the dock by the lake, the jumbled images of my dreams formed into something else. More than imagination; closer to a memory.

"Better?" Georgie asked.

I nodded. But I wasn't better. There was something about the scene at the lake that was different from my dreams. Something more real. And now I felt it, another image. The man at the end of the dock, not dropping the bundle like rubbish, *placing* it, a neatly wrapped bundle, wrapped in a tartan blanket, I was sure, placed with care. "Someone took their time with her," Inspector Siddiqi had said. "Someone cared."

Georgie reached into her bag and pulled out a small silver flask. She sloshed a shot of amber liquid into my coffee, and a sharp smell of alcohol, mixed with the earthiness of the moors, tickled my nose.

"Try that," Georgie said and poured herself a slug. She took a long slurp of her coffee and leaned forward across the table. "What happened back there?"

I shook my head, not yet able to answer in case speaking my fear made it true.

"Was it seeing the site, all those police?" Georgie pressed.

I shook my head. Glancing to make sure no one had noticed Georgie's addition to my drink, I took a sip of the coffee and felt it trickle down my throat, the heat of the liquid warming its path and the soft burn of scotch whiskey radiating into my body.

"It was ... familiar," I said at last. "The lake, the dock, all of it. I wasn't expecting it."

"You've probably been there before. If you stayed at the cabins, you probably came up to the lake."

"No. We went to the swimming lake by the cabins. I remember that. Nothing there jogged any new memories. But the other lake, seeing that diver on the dock ..."

I closed my eyes, trying to relax and let the images seep back in. I was afraid to lose them and equally afraid of what else I might recall. Something dark was growing inside me, a feeling I couldn't blow away with boxing, a feeling I couldn't describe to Georgie. It had to do with my dad. I took a deep breath, pulling cool air and the scent of the spiked coffee in through my nose, filling my lungs, and blowing out the sense of frustration that had been building ever since my dad was taken in.

Before Cassie went missing, my dad had been a fun dad. I could remember laughing with him and him being goofy with "his girls." We had massive dad pileups, with the three of us, even Libby, heaped on top of him, all of us, including Mum, laughing.

But my post-Cassie dad wasn't like that. He was serious, a man of few words. He still loved "his girls," even though there were only two of us now. He hugged us and held us close and took us places, trying to give us a normal, happy childhood. But there was a thin protective layer that surrounded him, some-thing no one could ever penetrate. Libby had pulled away from him, but I had done the opposite. I overcompensated in my daughterly duties, always trying to break through that layer to get back to the dad I remembered. I could never tell if he was gone or just hidden.

"How can I help?" Georgie asked.

"Convince me my dad had nothing to do with this," I said, my voice barely a whisper.

Georgie frowned, quickly trying to twist her face into a reassuring smile. "He can't have," she said. "Not your dad."

"I know, but ..."

Georgie sloshed another shot into my coffee.

"I used to have this dream," I said at last and told her about the nightmare.

"It's just your subconscious putting together bits of information. Like it put together Cassie and water, two familiar things."

"And Cassie was found in water. So, if I dreamed about my dad on the dock, what was that, just coincidence?"

"Maybe it wasn't your dad. Maybe it was a man on a dock and your brain filled in the blank with something familiar. Think about it. The most familiar man for most of your life was your dad. It sort of makes sense, doesn't it?"

"I suppose," I said. But uncertainty squirmed beneath my ribs. "The thing is, the dock in my dream? It was *that* dock."

Georgie gave a half-hearted shrug. "A dock is a dock, no? It's a long narrow wooden path extending out over water. They're all the same. You've probably seen a million of them."

"It was that dock. I'm sure of it."

"There's no way you saw someone ..." Georgie winced, "... take Cassie to that lake. How could you have? You were asleep the whole time. And think about it. Whoever did that to Cassie, surely, they'd make certain no one saw them."

"But it's all so familiar."

"It couldn't have been your dad. Trust me, when it comes to men, I'm a good judge of character. Your dad would never hurt anyone. From what you've told me, he's gentle as a lamb."

That's what I'd told Georgie about my dad. But she didn't have the full story.

I had seen my dad lose his cool only twice. The first was the Christmas before Cassie went missing. Uncle Dave looked a lot like my dad, but he was much younger and funnier. Whenever he came to visit, he brought tales of his travels to faraway places. He said he'd been to Africa and the Far East and hinted that he moved in a mysterious underworld of intrigue and adventure. I imagined he was an explorer or a smuggler or maybe a spy. I imagined him in disguise, disappearing into crowds, slipping smuggled documents to strangers in cafés. The way Mum said, "Oh, Dave," about his escapades made me think his tales were of the tall variety. But Cassie and I loved them.

Uncle Dave had come for Christmas dinner that year. He'd clowned around, making us laugh, and it was fun at first. But he and Dad had drunk too much. After we'd gone to bed, I heard a huge row, with shouting and slamming doors. There was a crashing sound like someone had fallen, and then the house went quiet. Uncle Dave had visited only one more time after that, on our sixth birthday. After Cassie went missing, my dad stopped drinking.

Then one night, maybe a year later, I woke up to the sound of shattering glass. The noise was downstairs, inside the house. Terrified someone was breaking in to get me, I ran to Libby's room to wake her up, but Libby was already awake.

"What was that?" I whimpered.

"Stay here. I'll go down and see."

But I didn't want to be left upstairs alone, so I tiptoed down the stairs behind my sister.

In the living room, we found my mother on her hands and knees. She was crying, pulling framed photographs and bits of a china tea service from a sea of broken glass. The glass doors of the cabinet in the dining room were gone and a sharp, boozy smell hung in the air.

"Mummy?" I whimpered.

My mother turned at the sound of my voice. Her eyes were puffy and rimmed with red. Her left cheek glowed vivid red.

"Go back to bed," she said.

"Where's Daddy?" I cried.

"Daddy's fine and so am I. I just tripped, that's all. I didn't mean to wake you. Go back to bed and I'll come and tuck you in in a minute."

I didn't want to leave my mother alone, but Libby picked me up and carried me back to bed, stroking my hair the way my mother might have done.

Dad came home from work with flowers the next night. Within a month, a For Sale sign went up in our front garden, and shortly after that, we moved. In the new house, Dad started a healthy routine of daily walks, replacing our breakfast cereal with smoothies and our bedtime snacks with nightly cocoa. He'd still have a beer once in a while, at Christmas or maybe on a Saturday night. But I never saw him drink more than one, and I never saw him lose his temper like that again.

But I knew he was capable. Georgie was wrong; my dad *was* the type—he had just learned to keep his anger under control. But he had been drinking the night Cassie disappeared.

TWELVE

As Georgie drove, a swaying sickness came over me as if I were sitting in a small boat. A sort of gentle wobbling, one way toward sadness and the other toward fear. A strange anxiety hung over me; I was tired and fluey one minute, sparky and angry the next. Maybe this was how I was supposed to feel. Cassie wasn't just my sister, she was my twin. And even though we weren't identical—weren't alike at all, really—I had known Cassie before anyone else in my life, before we were even born. And despite the hope that I'd clung to that she would one day come home, I had known, at some deep, intuitive level, that Cassie was dead. I just hadn't allowed myself to believe it. Had my parents had the same intuition? Or had they *known* Cassie was dead? There were observations about my family that seemed normal, given what had happened to Cassie. But if I tilted them slightly, looked at them a different way, they didn't look quite right.

I rolled down the window and let the cold air blow into my eyes until they stung. As hard as I fought, the terrible truth wouldn't let me be. There had been two girls in the room the night Cassie disappeared. One was now dead and the other had survived. Now the face in the images in my head changed. I stopped picturing Cassie and started picturing myself. Because the truth was, whatever had happened to Cassie that night could easily have happened to me. Whoever had chosen Cassie might just as easily have picked her twin. And if my parents had somehow been involved, why had it been Cassie and not me?

"Do you want to stay at my place again?" Georgie said as we crested the hilltop and dropped down the long, straight road toward my house.

I didn't want to go home. We'd moved away to escape the past, but Cassie had followed us anyway. In people's minds, my dad never stopped being a suspect. I knew what they thought. How could a man let his daughter disappear from the room next door? How could he not have heard something? No decent father would have let that happen, and even if he didn't do it, he didn't stop it, and that, therefore, made him guilty. That suspicion had lingered over my dad long after the police had moved on. The public had a long memory, and the media loved a good mystery. Neither would let us go as long as Cassie's killer was still out there. And what a great twist to the story it would be if the killer turned out to be my dad.

I didn't want to be alone in the old house with the ghost of Cassie rattling through every room and the possibility of secrets behind every closed door. But I couldn't stay away forever, and if my fear came true and Dad was somehow involved in Cassie's murder, I needed to be there, at home, acting normal, just like Libby had said.

"I'm okay," I said.

But when the house came into view, it was lit from every

window and my trepidation about being alone changed to dread about being alone with my dad.

"Keep your phone handy, just in case," I added, and Georgie hugged me goodbye.

When I let myself into the kitchen, the air felt stretched like the strings of a tennis racket. Cutting through the tension came Libby. She was dressed casually for Libby—designer jeans and a silky tunic, feet bare—as if she were at home, relaxing. But her eyes blazed into mine like lasers. I wasn't sure if they were set to "stun" or "kill."

"Where the bloody hell have you been?" Libby said, her voice hard and cold.

"Out with a friend," I said, not able to meet Libby's hard stare. "I texted you."

"What friend?"

"Just a friend from group. Georgie."

"Out where?"

I busied myself filling the kettle and going through the motions of preparing tea, hoping it might calm my queasiness. I was tempted to tell Libby I'd been at the lake, just to see her reaction, to gauge if she had suspicions about Dad, too. But I was afraid of what I might discover. "I needed to get away for a bit, get out of this house."

"We've been worried sick about you." She sounded more angry than worried, but I knew better than to provoke Libby when she was in a mood like this. I was too weary to fight anyway.

I was just about to point out again that I had, in fact, texted her, but she hadn't bothered to respond, when my dad appeared in the doorway behind Libby. He looked like a boxer who heard the bell for the final round and would rather curl up in his corner and sleep than go back into the ring.

"You're back," I said, trying to hide my surprise at seeing Dad and my sudden guilt about going to the lake. "What happened?"

Libby cut in. "Nothing happened," she said. "Except for you disappearing."

"Libby," Dad began, but Libby cut him off.

"No, Dad. She has to understand; she can't go running around all over the place." She turned on me. "Everything we do is being watched right now. It's just like before. They have nothing else to go on, so they're looking at us. We can't put a single toe out of place, Abby. Do you understand?"

I looked from Libby to Dad and my anger sparked. All I could think was: *If we don't have anything to hide, what are we afraid of?*

"Libby," Dad said again, trying to soothe her, but Libby's fire had ignited.

"No, Dad," she spat, spinning around on him. "I'm sick of this. She's not a baby anymore. She can't do whatever she wants without consequence. She has to learn."

Heat rose in my face. Libby was always like this, always treating me like a child. My whole family behaved as if I had never grown up, as if Cassie and I were still six years old. Well, we weren't. I was a grown woman now, and Cassie? Cassie was dead.

"Learn what?" I said, glowering at Libby. But even as I confronted Libby, daring her to tell me, I couldn't look at my dad. As much as I hated the way my family protected me, I also feared being exposed to the terrible truth.

"Learn that we are not a normal family," shouted Libby. "We will never be a normal family." Her voice cracked. "Ever."

The flicker of sadness in her voice almost stopped me, but already my fists were clenched. "We're not normal, and we never will be because nobody wants us to be. We all go around pretending that what happened to Cassie isn't real. Nobody talks about it; nobody talks about *her*! You act like she never existed. And now you want to hide away until it all blows over. Well, guess what? It's never going to blow over. And not talking about her only makes it worse!"

Libby's face hardened as if she were ready to take me on. But then her voice dropped to a cool, low register. "You need to go downstairs and box," she said. "You're getting hysterical."

"I'm getting *real*," I said. "Our sister was murdered, and our dad is their number one suspect, so yes, I am getting a tiny bit emotional. The question is, Libby, why aren't you?"

"That's enough," said Dad, stepping toward me.

Libby ignored him as if he wasn't there. "Box," she said to me. "Now."

"I won't," I said, more petulantly than I wanted. "You can't tell me what to do all the time."

"Box."

My body tightened as if I might lunge for Libby. She was so self-righteous, so sure she was in control, but she couldn't see how she was running away. Flying away from the unpleasant aspects of her life. Putting on her uniform and showing to the world a woman who was pulled together and in control, her vision of normal. "The flight attendants are here for your safety and comfort." But if Libby's plane ever went down, the only thing the flight attendants could do was to tell their passengers to brace. They were as powerless as anyone else. Our family's plane was going down, and all Libby could do was point to the nearest exit. For me, that was boxing.

"Abby," said Dad, his voice gentle, tired.

I met his gaze, but in my chest, my heart pounded. He gave me a small nod. Dad, the peacekeeper, the bridge over troubled waters. Dad, who was the source of the silence. Dad, the number one suspect. *That which is not talked about cannot exist.*

Libby was right about one thing: my family was *far* from normal. How different things might have been if we'd dealt with our problems instead of masking them. Maybe Cassie would still be alive.

In the cellar, I wrapped my hands. I didn't want to box; I wanted to *feel*. I wanted my heart to ache, to tear myself open and let the pain out. Boxing was an outlet, a way to blow off steam, but I didn't want to blow it off anymore. I wanted to feel it build inside me until I might explode.

Kaboom!

I wanted to talk about Cassie, to sit with Libby and say, "Remember when?" I wanted Libby or Mum or Dad or someone—anyone—who'd once loved Cassie to wrap their arms around me and let me cry for my lost sister. I wanted to tell them about my terrible dreams and paranoid suspicions and have them soothe me and tell me that they weren't real. But that's not how my family did things. They dealt with Cassie's disappearance and now her death by stuffing it all in a cupboard and pretending it had never happened. I was supposed to deal with it by never expressing to anyone how I felt.

But sometimes, I couldn't hold it in. Libby and I would have these fights about nothing, all my pent-up emotions finding an outlet over spilled nail polish or a harsh word. Libby, who never allowed any ebbs and flows of emotion to break free from their tightly sealed box, always remained cool and hard.

There had been one argument that started over something stupid, as these things always did. I was about thirteen and going through a rough patch, my temper flaring at the slightest spark, sparks that Libby was happy to supply. But this argument escalated fast as each of our misunderstandings and misinterpretation of flung words built and spiraled out of control. I had snapped first. I threw a mug at Libby, having enough forethought to deliberately miss so that it smashed against the wall behind her.

And she laughed.

That laugh flipped a switch in me, and the next thing I knew, I was lunging for Libby, pinning her to the wall of our living room.

She hadn't laughed at that.

Later, when I'd calmed down, after Mum and Dad had intervened and separated us, I replayed the moment just before the good person, the good human inside me, took over. Libby had driven me to that point. But, just in time, common sense, restraint, a sense of right and wrong—whatever it was—had washed through me and made me stop. It was a relief to know I had the safety valve. It was the difference between a sociopath and a balanced person, that switch that said, "Stop!" I had it, but as far as I was concerned, it hadn't clicked on nearly soon enough.

Not long after that, Libby had brought home a set of used DVDs and a pair of boxing gloves and talked Dad into converting the cellar. After that, whenever my grief or anger threatened to overtake me again, I boxed my way through it. It made me feel powerful, the one thing over which I had control.

I joked once to Georgie that it was a lot healthier than throttling my aggravating sister, that I didn't want to add a murder charge to my family's problems.

The irony of that is not lost on me now.

———

When I went back upstairs to the kitchen later that evening, Libby was dressed in her uniform, hair and makeup assuming their perfect positions, luggage standing by the door.

"Dad made your smoothie," she said, pointing to a glass on the counter. "You missed it this morning."

"You're leaving?" I asked, my flushed face suddenly turning cold.

"Just for three days," Libby said. "I can't keep taking time off work."

I always resented that Libby could just fly away, leaving the messy parts of her life behind. I resented her, and at the same time, I was always glad to see her go. But not tonight. Not after what I'd seen at the lake. Or thought I'd seen. Or imagined I'd seen.

"That lake where Cassie was found," I blurted. "Did we ever go there?"

Libby turned, and for an instant, I saw a flicker of fear in her eyes. "Of course not," she said. "Why would you say that?"

If I told her about my dream, my suspicions about Dad, maybe she'd stay. Maybe she'd protect me. Maybe she'd be the big sister she once was. Like that time before we moved away from our old house. A rumor about me had gone around the neighborhood. Some boys said I was weird, and then someone started calling me names. I didn't really know what started it, but I do know that Libby stopped it right away. I don't know what she said, but I saw her march right up to those boys. I can still see her now, hand on one hip, jabbing a finger at each of them in turn.

One of the boys had snickered and Libby had turned on him. He shrank away like he was terrified of the sweet blonde girl. But those boys never said a wrong word against me again. In fact, they never so much as looked at me. Even back then, Libby was a force to be reckoned with. They knew it and so did I.

I wanted *that* Libby to step up and protect me now, but that brief glimpse through a chink in her mask told me she knew something I didn't, and she would leave regardless.

"I just wondered, that's all," I said. "Have a safe trip."

She hesitated for just a moment as if she was going to press me further, then she pulled on her jacket and dusted something off her sleeve. "You're going to have to help Dad while I'm away," she said.

"I help Dad all the time. I live here, in case you've forgotten."

"Don't get an attitude, Abby," Libby said. "We don't have time for that now. They're releasing Cassie's body, her remains, and we need to plan a funeral. I can't take time off to do that, so you'll have to help Dad."

"A funeral?" My mind reeled to catch up with this new information. Cassie had been gone so long, missing so long, and there had been none of the normal processes of death because Cassie hadn't been dead, or at least they hadn't known she was. There had been no funeral for her, no saying goodbye, no moment of collective grief from which we could all begin to heal. Cassie had just faded away, disappearing slowly into the distance, never quite gone but never fully there, either. I hadn't said goodbye, only left a note so she could find us. I had clutched at snippets of memory, held together the cracks that threatened to burst open and make me fall apart. But a funeral would make it real, a public acknowledgment that Cassie wasn't coming back. A second death.

"And stay away from that Georgie. We don't need strangers butting into our lives right now," Libby said. She yanked her suitcase onto its wheels and left. Left me alone in the house on the moors with the man who might be Cassie's killer.

THIRTEEN

Dad was so focused on his work that he didn't even notice me in the hallway outside his office door. He sat in a sea of papers peppered with islands of used coffee mugs. A sheen of sticky dust dulled everything to a sepia tone. If you could judge the state of a person's mind by the state of their room, my dad's head was a mess. He tore open his desk drawer, sending dust swirling into the air around him. Whatever he was looking for wasn't there, and he slammed the drawer shut so hard it caused a book on the shelf to topple and stir up another plume of filth. I pressed myself against the wall, an instinctive response to his angry outburst heightened by the doubts now swirling in my mind.

Through the crack at the door's hinges, I watched him. From beneath a dilapidated wooden chair, which had once sat at the head of our family dining table, he pulled out a cardboard box, kicking it into the room. He flung off the lid, rummaging through file folders, until he found one stuffed with slips of paper. As he pulled out a handful, I leaned in for a closer look.

They were identical slips, about the size of Dad's palm, printed with lettering across the top and scrawled with hand-written notes. Prescriptions. And there were hundreds of them.

Dad spun around then, calling out to me. "Abby?"

I held my breath, counted to three, then put on a Libby smile and popped my head around the door. Dad was already up, blocking my view of his office.

"What are you doing?" Dad asked.

I had the same question, but I thought fast. "Cocoa. I was going to make it. Are you ready?"

He squinted at me for a moment, then shook his head. "I'll do it in a bit. You should get to bed."

I hesitated, wanting to ask about the contents of the box. But Dad was already reaching to close the door.

I was sure of what I had seen in the box. Prescriptions, hundreds of them, too old and too many to be my mother's. My dad had always been strong and healthy, with no physical illnesses that I could recall. But he had changed after Cassie disappeared. He became measured, level. *Controlled.* My dad's personality had changed, and I was sure the reason was in that box. He had been medicated to keep something at bay.

I did as I was told and went to bed early, feeling like I might be coming down with a cold, but I couldn't sleep. With only a sliver of moon in the sky and no clouds to reflect the lights of the nearby city, the house stood in total darkness, the edges of the garden swallowed up by the blackness of the moors and disappearing into nothing. A sharp wind had picked up in the evening, and it blew through the coppice of trees behind the house, the rustle of leaves sounding like rain.

It had rained on the night Cassie had disappeared, the night

Cassie had been killed. Because surely that was what had happened. Cassie had been taken by someone. Cassie had been killed. Cassie had been dropped in the lake, a muddy grave well enough thought out that it had kept her hidden. And the rain had covered the tracks of whoever had taken her. Tracks that had led away from—and perhaps back to—our cabin in the woods.

In the darkness now, I recalled the sound of the rain that night. An old oak tree had bent its boughs over the cabin, and, in the wind, its branches scraped at the roof as if it were trying to get in. In a horror movie, the tree might have poked through the ceiling, snatching up Cassie in its gnarled limbs and spiriting her away. But that wasn't what had happened to Cassie. Someone had come into our room that night and taken Cassie from her bed. Someone who could move more quietly than the wind. I had slept through the storm that night, perhaps accustomed to the noises of the woods by then. So perhaps I had slept through the noises of someone breaking in. If someone *had* broken in.

I couldn't shake off the memory of the lake and the image from my dream that was now branded on my mind. What if someone had already been in the cabin that night? What if they hadn't broken in at all? What if someone had come into the room, as he had every night, to check on his girls? Someone whose familiar presence wouldn't have disturbed me.

I recalled my dad and "his girls." He had loved all three of us equally. Or at least he had when we were small. But in the darkness of my room, the outline of another memory began to form, an infinitesimal change I'd forgotten because it hadn't seemed significant at the time. It happened when Cassie and I were three or four years old. As soon as we could count to eight,

Mum had signed us up for dance classes. She took us to a shop in town and had our feet squeezed into shiny patent leather tap shoes that tied with ribbons. She picked out leotards and gathered together matching tights and headbands, and miniature tutus.

Libby had shaken her head, her nine-year-old lips already practiced at pursing in disapproval. "That tapping's going to drive me mad," she said as Cassie stepped into her tutu and clacked around the shop, to the delight of our mother and the saleswoman.

As it turned out, Cassie wasn't much of a dancer. I could watch the teacher's feet and commit the moves to memory, repeating them with perfect, if rigid, form. Cassie, on the other hand, would go left when she was supposed to go right, shuffle when she should have hop-stepped. But what she lacked in technique, she made up for in flair. And, when preparations began for the annual show, I found myself and my perfectly memorized routine on the second row, watching the back of Cassie's coiffed and sprayed bun bobbing to the beat of its own silent song and shining in the spotlight.

I wasn't jealous. It was just the way things were. But I stopped taking lessons and when Mum drove Cassie to her classes three days a week, I got to spend the time with Dad. But something else changed back then, something I had recalled only now. Dad and I grew closer during our time together, which I loved, but he and Cassie grew apart. When Cassie pushed people's buttons, he'd put a stop to it instead of indulging her. When she demanded his attention, he was almost cool. It was as if he saw something in Cassie that was less than perfect, and it changed the way he felt.

I sometimes wondered what Cassie would have been like if

she'd grown up. Would a girl who'd been the center of attention her whole life be oblivious to the power she held over people, or would it become like a drug that she continued to seek out? I imagined Cassie as a dangerous version of Georgie, a dark, powerful magnet pulling trouble toward herself. In my darkest moments, it made sense that Cassie was the one taken. If someone saw the two of us girls side by side, sleeping in our beds, why on earth would they pick Plain Jane Abby when they could grab the dark, mysterious gem that was Cassie?

What if there was another reason Cassie had been taken, a reason that had come to a head that night? What if he had been in the house all that time? That man who had done this to Cassie, a man who needed medication for an invisible illness, the man who would sleep down the hall from me tonight.

My logical mind could not reconcile these thoughts, could not believe my own dad was capable of murder. And yet, my subconscious would not let me sleep. Just in case the logical side was wrong.

The creak of the bottom stair jolted my eyes open. Dad was coming up to bed. I willed the blood to stop pounding in my ears so I could hear his approach. Every sound was familiar. The high-pitched squeak of the bottom stair, the deep moan of the second from the top. The creak of the floorboards at the corner of the hallway and the groan of the one outside my bedroom door. The one where Dad's footsteps stopped.

I held my breath, staring at the sliver of light beneath my door.

"Abby," Dad whispered on the other side. "Are you awake?"

I lay still. If I pretended to be asleep, what would he do? Would he leave me in peace? Or would he come in?

"I'm awake," I said, my voice small.

The door creaked open, and Dad stepped from the shadow into the triangle of light. "I brought your cocoa," he said.

I had a fleeting thought of poison. My imagination pulling out every horror cliché.

Dad set two mugs on my bedside table and perched on the edge of my bed. "You okay?"

I nodded. "You?"

"Been a long couple of days, but yes."

"What happened?" I asked. "With the police?"

"They took me to the station and asked all the same questions as last time," he said. His voice sounded tired, older. "Asked me all the same ones again today."

He didn't mention going to the lake. I was relieved he hadn't seen me, but his omission only added to my fears. "But they let you go?"

He looked at me as if surprised I'd ask this. As if he sensed suspicion in my voice. "For now."

I swallowed and tried to relax. "For now?"

"For now." He brought his hand to my face. I flinched. But he only brushed my hair aside in the gentlest of moves. Something my mother might have done, not a man who killed. "But they won't stop asking until they get better answers."

I nodded, suddenly exhausted.

Dad pulled the covers up to my neck. "It's going to be difficult for a while, Abby. Until it all dies down again."

"Until they catch whoever did it."

He nodded but didn't say anything more.

I didn't know what my dad was thinking, but I was thinking about Cassie. I was thinking about what sort of person would do what had been done to her. And for what reason? That was the part that always stuck with me. Bad things happened in the world. People killed out of anger, jealousy, revenge, even money. But who would want to hurt Cassie?

My throat tightened as I thought about what had happened to my sister, what she'd been through that night. Had she known her killer? Had she trusted him? And now this new question bubbled in my mind. Had that person been my dad? Was it one of the many things my family kept hidden behind their controlled veneer?

I shook the thought away, unwilling to let it take root. But the lake, the diver, the hidden prescriptions, the lie about the blanket—even dreams that always felt so real—put out tendrils that strangled my thoughts.

"Drink your cocoa," Dad said, handing me a mug.

I held it to my lips, the heat tickling my nose. I breathed in rich chocolate, smooth milk, and a hint of something bitter. I sniffed for something different.

Dad watched me. Waiting.

I looked into his eyes, looking for a hint of malice, a sign that his intentions were not good. But he smiled a dad smile, tired maybe, a little sad, but kind.

I took a tentative sip. The taste was familiar. Nothing new but the product of my overactive imagination.

"You should get some sleep, too," I said.

He hesitated as if he didn't want to leave.

"Will you be okay?" I asked.

"I'll be fine," he said, waving me away. "Don't you worry about me."

He wasn't fine, none of us were, but worrying was the only useful thing I could think to do. I needed to find answers. I needed to see those prescriptions. I would wait until I was sure Dad was asleep and then I'd go down and find out some truth.

But sleep overtook me, pulling me into a dark but restless slumber.

In the morning, the box in Dad's office was gone. Whatever secrets he kept in there, he did not want me to know.

Fourteen

"We want a simple service," Dad told the funeral director after explaining the circumstances of Cassie's funeral. "Something intimate and quiet, just for family mostly. As little fanfare as possible."

A nervous laugh caught in my throat just in time. "As little fanfare as possible" was never Cassie's style. A carriage pulled by six white horses, a box of butterflies fluttering into the sky, petals scattered, balloons released, a pure white casket all but buried under cascades of flowers. Even at six years old, Cassie had done everything with fanfare.

At our sixth birthday party, twenty of our school friends had gathered at our house. When Mum brought out the cake—strawberry, Cassie's favorite—Cassie had stood on her chair and conducted everyone while they sang "Happy Birthday." I had been part of the chorus. When my parents had adults over, Cassie would announce herself as she entered the room, then dance, sing, and tell corny jokes. I would hide behind my mother's knees. According to my mother, Cassie had been that way since her noisy entry into the world, practically screaming down the walls of the maternity unit for the first forty-eight hours of her life. I'd once heard Mum tell another mother that I slept through the night from being two months old, but Cassie was two before she allowed them a good night's sleep. The way she told the story always made me feel like Cassie, the problem child, was the one she admired the most. In her short life, Cassie had done almost everything with fanfare, everything except leave. That she had done quietly and without ceremony.

"We don't want to put on a show," Dad said.

No, I thought. *We always want to make things look* right, *don't we?*

The funeral director pushed a glossy sheet across the small round table where we'd been offered a seat as if we were having coffee and discussing travel options. The cold I'd worried I was getting hadn't materialized and now the perfumed air of the funeral home had a clear path to my nose. The smell made me nauseous. The muted colors, the soft music, the gentle, compassionate smiles of the funeral home staff seemed like they belonged in some bizarre alternate world.

"We offer a range designed especially for young people," she said. "What would Cassandra have chosen?" I wondered if the funeral home had a standard package for sending off a loved one who'd been dead for so long. How did you say goodbye to someone whose face you struggled to picture? How did you honor a person whose memory was a scrapbook of images pieced together from stories and imagination? The truth was, no one really knew what Cassie would have wanted because Cassie would have wanted to live. Of that, I was the most sure.

I looked at the images of an oak casket, a miniature version of the traditional adult kind. It looked like a Halloween decoration, something you'd fill with gummy skeletons, marshmallow ghosts, or licorice witch's hats. A more ornate version came in white, baby blue, and bubble-gum pink. There was even an environmentally friendly willow one that reminded me of my grandmother's sewing basket. *A tisket, a tasket, my sister in a basket.*

"The white one," I said.

The funeral director glanced at Dad, who nodded his consent.

The funeral director shuffled her papers as if about to veer from the usual script. I felt bad for her having to have such awkward and uncomfortable conversations, but she was a professional.

"I understand that some considerable time has passed since Cassandra's passing."

"Cassie," I said. I wished the woman wouldn't keep referring to her as Cassandra. It was her given name, of course, but she'd never been called anything but Cassie. Cassandra was the name of an adult, an efficient businesswoman in a tailored gray suit, or perhaps a star of the West End stage. Cassandra Kirkpatrick, Attorney at Law. Olivier Award-winning actress Cassandra Kirkpatrick. Cassandra Kirkpatrick wasn't someone who would be buried in a miniature white coffin. Cassandra Kirkpatrick would have gone out with a bang. "We called her Cassie."

"Cassie," the woman said, scribbling a note on her form. "Do you have any personal items you would like to be interred with Cassa ... with Cassie?"

"I don't think so," Dad said.

"Ollie," I said.

When the funeral director gave me a questioning look, I added. "Her favorite teddy bear. Ollie."

"Ollie's long gone, Abby," Dad said, throwing the funeral director a tight smile as if apologizing that I'd suddenly come unhinged.

But he was wrong. Cassie and I may have been separated by fate, but Ollie and Bear, our matching teddy bears, had always been together—my secret—and I knew exactly where both of them were.

"I have him," I said.

Dad narrowed his eyes as if assessing if I was telling the truth. But then he nodded at the funeral director, and my long-held secret was out.

When we'd moved from our old house, Mum had me pack my clothes and favorite toys into boxes marked with a big purple *A*. She worked beside me, silently putting Cassie's things into separate boxes.

"You forgot to put her letter on them," I said when I noticed the boxes were blank. I took the purple marker and drew a big, neat *C* on each box. My mother said nothing.

As she took the sheets off Cassie's bed, which had remained made up since Cassie had gone missing, she put Ollie in the box.

"Ollie and Bear have to go together," I said.

"Just for the journey," Mum said gently. "I'll put him right here where he'll be safe."

I said that would be okay, but when Mum went downstairs to get more boxes, I smuggled Ollie out of his box and tucked him in one of mine next to Bear, hidden among my other toys.

I forgot about Ollie and Bear during the move. The new house held no sad memories—at least not at first—and I was so excited that I had my own room with a view of the garden. Better still, Libby had taken the room at the top of the house, so our bedrooms wouldn't even be close together. I felt very grown up, unpacking my own things and arranging the room just how I wanted it. When I came across the bears, I sat Bear on my bed next to my pillow, where he could keep an eye on me. I hid Ollie in a special box that had once held a Christmas ornament and placed him carefully on the top shelf of my wardrobe, where I was sure he'd been safe. I never told anyone I had him.

It wasn't until a few days later that I realized I hadn't seen Cassie's boxes.

"They're safely in the attic," Mum said.

"For when Cassie comes back?"

"That's right," she said without meeting my look.

"Which room will Cassie have?" I asked.

"Not now, Abby," Mum said, looking harried.

I assumed the room next to mine would be Cassie's, but by the end of the summer break, Mum announced she was looking for bookkeeping clients and that I would do school at home from now on. She turned the room into a study, and I stopped asking where Cassie would sleep when she came home. No one else talked about Cassie, so neither did I.

It was a few years before I plucked up the courage to look in the attic for Cassie's things. Thanks to Libby's delight in telling me ghost stories, the attic had become a mysterious corner of the house and I was afraid of it. But I was worried I might be forgetting Cassie. I wanted to touch her things to remind myself that my sister had been real. Unable to carry Dad's step ladder upstairs, I looked for some way to climb up. My mother had placed an oak chest of drawers under the small landing window and used it to store extra bedding for the winter, but it was too heavy to shove under the attic trapdoor. Finally, I dragged a chair from the bedroom, stacked a wooden ottoman on top, and clambered up the precarious tower to the little trapdoor in the ceiling.

It was hot in the attic, not a climate for ghosts, I decided, so I plucked up the courage to poke around. There were several boxes stacked in one corner. They were marked "Xmas Decos," "Photos," and "Bob Misc," which I assumed was Dad's. One labeled "Private Keep Out" in Libby's handwriting all but dared me to lift the lid, but it contained nothing more than some old postcards, a few photos of her old friends, and odds and ends she'd collected. None of the boxes were marked with the purple C. All traces of Cassie were gone. I couldn't remember the boxes being taken away, but the truth was, I had no recollection of them ever arriving.

I asked my mother where they had gone. "Stay out of there," she snapped. "It's not safe." I assumed she meant to warn me of the dangers of the ladder, the low rafters, the trapdoor. It hadn't crossed my mind then that my parents had given up so quickly on the idea of their daughter ever coming back and that they might not want me to know.

At Project Talk, I learned about coping techniques and came to believe that my parents had been protecting themselves by not clinging to a foolish hope that Cassie would someday come home. But thinking back to my mother's insistence that they pack Cassie's things separately, even her determination to pack Ollie, I wondered if my mother *knew* Cassie wasn't coming back. What if it had been more than a mother's intuition, more than just a suspicion that her child was dead? What if she knew because she had been involved?

As the funeral director wrapped up the details of Cassie's funeral service, I couldn't meet Dad's eyes. This was my *dad*! A man dealing with the death of his daughter, the way I was dealing. Or not dealing. How could I even think these things about him?

And yet, everywhere I turned were things that didn't add up about Cassie's disappearance. I was afraid that the truth I so desperately wanted to uncover would not be what I wanted to know. I needed someone to be honest with me, for once.

FIFTEEN

"Make sure you let your mother get some rest," Dad said when he dropped me outside the hospital on his way back to work. "This is a lot for her."

It's a lot for all of us, I thought, but I promised that I would be considerate.

I waited until he pulled away, then turned away from the main entrance and set off into the nearby neighborhood. I needed some air. I needed to think. These memories of Cassie kept emerging from the fog. Viewed in one light, they were sad reminders of a lost sister. Viewed in another, they were evidence mounting against my parents.

I crossed the street and walked past a row of formerly grand houses, now converted to the offices of dentists and lawyers. On a stone gatepost, a sign caught my eye. Along with the words "Atlas Private Investigation" was an image of a globe made to look like a magnifying glass, the kind an old-fashioned detective might have used in the stories I'd once loved to read.

I'd started reading mystery stories a few years after Cassie went missing. I discovered them when Mum took me to the library, and I must have read every single one the library had. They were tales of kids like me heading out on adventures to solve the mysteries that the grown-ups around them refused to acknowledge. I had pictured myself defying those grown-ups and setting out on an adventure with nothing but a hunch and a trusty companion—not Libby; she thought the stories were stupid—determined to uncover the truth of my sister's disappearance.

Even after Mum had insisted that I read other kinds of books, I'd written pages and pages of clues in a notebook and listed imaginary suspects.

Eventually, my mother found the notebook. "What is this?" she asked, waving it at me in a way that said she already knew.

"It's mine," I said, grabbing for it.

"What is this, Abby? Is this about Cassie?"

"Nobody else around here cares about what happened to her anymore. But I do. I want to know."

"The police are doing everything they can, Abby. Everyone is."

"Then why haven't they found her?"

"I don't know!" Mum yelled. "I don't know why they haven't found her. But you have to stop this. You have to let it go."

That night, Dad had built a bonfire to burn some garden waste. When I asked to help, he sent me back indoors. I watched the flames from my bedroom window, mesmerized. And when my mother came out and dropped my notebook onto the fire, I didn't even flinch. After that, I stopped trying to find Cassie. I suppose the book had just been my way of processing what had happened. It was less about solving the mystery and more about needing to *do* something, to talk about it to someone. But my mother hadn't wanted to talk about it. She was dealing with her grief in her own way. My way had been to write about it; hers was to try to forget.

But now I wondered. After the way she hid Ollie, the way Cassie's things had disappeared after we moved, the way she'd reacted to my trying to find answers. Had my mother been trying to protect herself from grief, or was she removing reminders of what she and my dad had done?

I turned back to the hospital. There was only one way to find out.

———

I nodded to the nurses as I marched down the familiar hospital corridor, determined to get answers. But when I saw my mother in her bed, my resolve crumbled. She looked worn out, paler and thinner than she had a few days ago. I slid into the chair beside her bed and watched her sleep. She was a shell of the woman who had once been my mother, smaller, more fragile. But inside that delicate shell, she clung to her secrets. A thought struck me, twisting my insides until I bent double. What if I was too late? What if she took her secrets with her before I could find the truth? Would I keep my promise to my dad and let her?

"Abby," she said, opening her eyes and lifting her fingers off the bed in a weak greeting. "What's the matter?"

I forced a smile and took her hand. It was cool and fragile, and I was afraid to hurt her. "Nothing."

"How did the plans go?" she asked, her words slurring. "For the funeral."

"It was fine." Mum's other hand gripped her drip release. I had to move fast. "I have something to tell you."

She narrowed her eyes, looking worried. "What is it?"

"I've applied to go to university."

Mum pushed a weak smile onto her face. "Your dad told me. When will you know?"

My dad? I'd barely had a chance to mention it before the police arrived that day. He hadn't said a word about it since. But he'd told my mother. "I have a conditional offer and as soon as I get my exam results, I'll know," I said. "But maybe I should wait, defer another year."

"No," she said with surprising force. "All this with Cassie. You need to get away and start your life. It's time."

I wasn't convinced, and yet that's exactly what we had done after Cassie disappeared. "Is it getting away or running away?" I asked.

"People can be unkind," she said. "We moved to a place where people didn't know all about us. I thought it was the right decision for you."

"And was it?"

She didn't say anything at first. She stared past me as if she were watching the past unfold. "We make a lot of poor decisions in our lives, Abby, but we can't go back. We have to live with our choices and do the best we can."

"You always knew Cassie was dead, didn't you?" It was out before I could stop myself.

My mother looked straight at me, her old ferocity flaring in her eyes for a moment. "I'm her mother."

"That's not an answer."

"Mothers know these things."

"No, they don't," I said. I thought about Chloe Kubo,

Sammy Rasheed, and Sarah Louise Dawson, their anguished mothers pleading for help. "Mothers never lose hope that their children will come back."

"Maybe on the outside, but on the inside, they know."

"Is that why we moved? Because you knew she wasn't coming back?"

"We moved because I wanted to protect you."

"From what?"

"I didn't want you to have to live with the shame."

"Shame?"

"People talk."

"Were you ashamed of what happened?"

"Of course not," she said, but she looked away again and I knew she was lying.

I had to ask what I'd really come to find out, even though I was no longer sure I wanted the truth.

"Did Dad hurt Cassie?" I asked.

She exhaled loudly and clicked her drip-release button.

"Did Dad ever hurt you?" I asked quickly before she faded away.

"Your dad loved you girls, loves you still. His intentions were always good. His intentions are *still* good, Abby. You need to remember that."

I had asked her two questions and she had answered neither. But I already knew the answer to one: My dad had hurt her once. And maybe he had hurt Cassie, too. His intention was to keep lying and my mother's intention was clearly to keep avoiding the truth.

In the mystery stories I'd read as a child, the most likely culprit was always the grown-up telling the kids not to meddle. So, what did that say about my parents?

When I arrived home, Dad was pacing as if he'd been waiting for my arrival. He didn't even ask how my mother was.

"Inspector Siddiqi called while you were out," he said. "She wants to speak to you."

"About what?" I said, panic rising instantly in my chest.

"I imagine about Cassie's case," Dad said as if I'd asked the most stupid question.

I swallowed. Had Sergeant Nowicki seen me at the cabins that day? He couldn't have. Had the police discovered something new? The image of the diver flashed across my field of vision again. What if they wanted to trick me into revealing something that would point the finger back at Dad? What if I said the wrong thing? What if I said the *right* thing?

"I'll go with you," Dad said.

I shook my head. My mother was right. I had to start looking forward and standing on my own two feet. I couldn't let my family protect me forever. "I'll be okay," I added, trying to reassure Dad.

He gave me a tired look. "Just tell them what you've told them before," he said. "Just tell them the truth."

The problem was the truth—or my memory of the truth—was getting murkier. I no longer knew if I believed the truth that I had told back then.

Sixteen

"Tea?" Inspector Siddiqi said, offering me a seat. "Coffee? I have some very nice chocolate biscuits."

I shook my head. I didn't want to spend any longer than was absolutely necessary here and I certainly hadn't come to socialize. I had expected Inspector Siddiqi's office to be a neat, organized space with color-coordinated files in regimented racks, a few bright prints on the wall, and a healthy potted plant on a corner of her desk. Instead, I found myself in the office of a madwoman. Dangerous skyscrapers of files teetered on every surface and pale-yellow sticky notes flapped from the walls and cabinet doors. The potted plant was there, but it looked like it was hanging on for dear life to its last few days. Her desk was covered in so many papers and notes, I doubted she'd be able to find a pen and notebook to write down anything I said. It gave me little faith that the inspector was capable of solving Cassie's murder. Given my recent suspicions, perhaps that was a good thing.

"Don't worry," said the inspector. "I'm not here to rehash the story about the night Cassie disappeared. Goodness knows you've had to tell that enough times and I can't imagine you'll tell me anything new, right?"

I forced a smile. The image of my mother, lying and hiding, flashed in my mind. I thought about my weird dream—the lake, the dock, my dad. Surely, they were nothing more than a meshing together of scraps of memory, things I'd seen on TV muddled with people I knew. There was no way I was going to tell Inspector Siddiqi about my dream. She'd think I was a weirdo, not to mention I couldn't see what good it could do.

"I saw you at the lake," Inspector Siddiqi said, yanking me back into the room.

I stammered, trying to replay the day and wondering how she'd known we'd gone from the cabins to the lake. Was she bluffing? "I ... It wasn't me."

"It's okay. You're not in trouble, although you might have been if your dad had seen you."

The shock must have registered on my face because she added, "I didn't tell him."

She gave me that smile again as if we were in on this together. Part of me thought this was an act to trick me into talking and the other felt I could really trust her and I should tell her everything, no matter how sketchy it might sound.

"What were you doing there?"

"I don't know," I said, thinking how stupid I had been to go. "I just felt so helpless, like I wanted to do something, you know?"

"But why there?"

"I thought if I saw where Cassie was found, maybe I'd remember something important. Maybe I had seen something that was too horrible to deal with and so my brain had stored it away or something."

"A shadow memory."

"What?"

"Shadow memory. It can happen sometimes with trauma. The brain segments the events and, for all intents and purposes, hides them so the person effectively forgets."

Claire had mentioned this once at Project Talk, suggesting that Danielle had locked away the worst of what she'd seen that night. "So, the memory isn't gone, it's just hidden?"

"Exactly. Assuming you have something to remember. Do you?"

I shook my head. I didn't, not anything concrete, anyway. I couldn't tell her anything unless I was sure it was a real memory, not just a scared child's dream.

"Can they be retrieved, these shadow memories?" I said, anxious to know and terrified of the answer I might hear.

"If a person is in a particular physical or emotional state when the memory is formed, say high stress or a loud environment, then the memory stays hidden until they're in that state again."

Claire had said the same, explaining how fireworks could trigger memories for soldiers with PTSD. "I was asleep when Cassie was taken," I said. But a terrible thought struck me. My dreams. Was that how this worked? When I was sleeping, in the same state I was in when Cassie disappeared, was I then recalling a shadow memory? But that didn't make sense, did it? If I'd seen something that night, I couldn't have been asleep, could I?

I wanted to tell Inspector Siddiqi all of this, let her help me understand. But always hovering just beneath my desire for answers was just enough doubt about my parents' involvement.

If they'd done something bad, I didn't want Inspector Siddiqi to find out from me.

"Do you think," said Inspector Siddiqi, "that maybe you *weren't* asleep when Cassie was taken?"

My senses prickled with the anticipation of being caught in a trap. "What do you mean?"

"What if you *did* see someone take her, but you've hidden that memory as a defense mechanism. Do you think that's possible?"

I hesitated. Now she'd said it, I wondered if that was why I'd been back to the lake, why I was determined to uncover what had happened to Cassie. That perhaps I did know something, did see someone. And now Inspector Siddiqi had determined who that person was, and I could no longer be certain she was my ally.

"I was asleep," I said. "I don't remember seeing anything until Mum woke me the next morning when she found Cassie missing."

Inspector Siddiqi stared at me for an uncomfortable length of time. I held her gaze with a neutral smile until she finally looked away.

She took a long drink from a mug with "World's Best Mum" stenciled on the side. "What was it like being Cassie's sister?"

I froze at her odd question. I wanted to trust her, but she hadn't called me in here to talk about my feelings. She knew something and this was her way of chatting me toward it. I just didn't know yet what it was. "Being Cassie's sister was all I ever knew," I said cautiously. "So, I don't know how to tell you what it was like. It was like being me."

"I have a sister," she said, reaching behind her for a framed photo that was part of a huge collection on the far corner of her desk. She held it out for me to see the photo of her younger self with two serious-looking men and a laughing woman. "Baheerah," Inspector Siddiqi said. "And my two brothers. We aren't a bit alike."

I looked at the woman and could see for myself all the ways they might be different. Baheerah was soft and curvy where Inspector Siddiqi was straight and slender. The laughter on her face and the way she hugged her siblings close contrasted with the serious smiles of the others.

"What about you and Cassie? Were you alike?"

"Not really." I imagined a picture of us three siblings together. Libby, intense and serious, Cassie posing for the camera, and me, always looking like the odd sister out.

"Did you have hobbies as a child? What did you and Cassie like to do?"

I shook my head. "We were kids. We played."

"No sports, music, dance classes?"

Now she had my attention. I had the feeling she already knew the answers to all her questions, baiting me to see if I would tell the truth. "We took tap classes," was all I said.

She slid a photograph across the desk.

I felt the bottom of my belly hollow out and an icy sensation flooded in. The photograph was of a shoe—black patent leather, satin ribbons for laces, a squat heel edged with a thin silver tap. I opened my mouth, the words "Cassie's shoe" catching in my throat. I bit them back.

"We believe Cassie's wounds were caused by a shoe similar to this," Inspector Siddiqi said. "Did Cassie own tap shoes?"

"I think so."

"Would she have had them with her at the cabin?"

Another flash of memory came. Cassie dancing on the cabin's tiled kitchen floor. *Tap, tap, tap.* Libby whining that the noise was driving her bonkers. Dad yelling at her to stop.

I swallowed. "I'm not sure."

Inspector Siddiqi didn't so much as blink at my answer. She held my gaze until I squirmed in my seat. "I have a daughter," she said, the change in tone catching me off guard. "Kayla. That's her in all the other photos."

I leaned in toward the group of silver frames carefully arranged in the chaos of the office. Kayla as a tiny baby, cradled in her mother's arm. Kayla as a toddler, all dark curls and mischievous eyes. Kayla in a school uniform, a leotard and tutu. Kayla with an older couple, probably grandparents. Kayla with a man that must have been her dad. Kayla's life documented in black and white, a happy life full of love. I blinked at the dampness that pooled along the rim of my eyes.

"Kayla loves her Auntie Bah," Siddiqi said. "My sister has a way with her, and she can talk to her in a way I can't. You know what it's like talking to your parents."

I smiled, uncomfortable. I didn't know why the inspector was giving me her whole life story, but it felt like bait for a trap.

"You and your family moved away not long after Cassie's disappearance," the inspector said. "Was that hard?"

"Kids can be mean, and my parents thought we'd do better if we moved."

"Did you stay in touch with your old friends?"

"I stayed in touch with my best friend for a while, but it was hard. Eventually we lost touch."

Paula and I had cried and hugged one another on the day my family moved away. She had been the one thing that didn't change after Cassie went missing. Our neighbors and my other friends acted as if there was something wrong with us or that they might catch our family's tragedy if they got too close. But Paula had just carried on being my friend.

After we moved away, we phoned one another every day at four o'clock. She would tell me everything about her life and I'd tell her everything was fine with mine. Then one day, she stopped. Whenever I called, her mum said she was out or busy.

"People move on," my mother had said, stroking my hair. "Why don't you help me bake a cake for tea instead?"

My mother covered over the pain with baking or gardening, even then. I missed Paula almost as much as I missed Cassie. She was the last real friend I had until Georgie came along.

"I bet she missed you," Inspector Siddiqi said.

I shrugged. "I doubt she remembers me."

"She does. Believe me. I had a friend who moved away when I was about eight years old. Neil. A boy, much to my mother's great displeasure. This is him." She handed me a photo of two little children, a dark-haired girl and a cute blond boy, their front teeth missing and their arms flung around one another. "His parents died suddenly, terrible story, and Neil and his sister were sent to live with their aunt and uncle. I never got to say goodbye to him, but I still think about him, even after all these years."

"Did you ever look for him?" I asked, wondering if Paula had given me a single thought since we left.

"A perk of my job is that I have access to a lot of information," she said, giving me a conspiratorial smile. "I know where he is, what he does, what he looks like. He's doing well, as far as I can tell."

"Have you tried to contact him?"

She shook her head. "I've thought about it a lot, just

sending a quick note to his work email, saying, 'Remember me?' I suppose I want him to know I've never forgotten him, that while he was going through that terrible time, someone was thinking about him."

I imagined how I'd feel if Paula contacted me out of the blue. How would I feel if I knew she'd never stopped thinking about me? My eyes stung suddenly, and I blinked to stop the tears. I would have loved to know that I hadn't been forgotten. Danielle needed to hear that, too. "I think he'd be happy to know that."

"But," Inspector Siddiqi said, leveling her gaze on me. She was about to get to the crux of this conversation. "I've worked with a lot of people dealing with trauma, and I know how they compartmentalize things to get through it. I've always been afraid that contacting him might do him more harm than good."

I waited.

"I worried I might loosen memories he'd shut away to protect himself. I'm connected to perhaps the worst period of his life. Maybe he doesn't want to remember me. Maybe he'd rather forget."

I swallowed hard. Was she suggesting I had compartmentalized Cassie's disappearance? Did she truly believe my dad was involved and that I had seen something I would rather forget? Had she uncovered some piece of evidence that suggested I had been there when Cassie's body had been dropped in the lake? I shook my head. I couldn't have been. I'd had a dream about it, that was all. Just a dream.

I steadied myself and met her gaze with a confidence I didn't feel. "I don't think he wants to forget. When someone you care about dies like that, you don't want people to forget."

Inspector Siddiqi gave me a warm smile. I glanced at the photographs of Kayla and wondered if Inspector Siddiqi really was the world's best mum in her daughter's eyes. I had always believed my mother had done everything she could to protect Libby and me after Cassie disappeared. My parents had made a lot of difficult decisions, but I assumed they had done what they thought was right for us. Just as Neil and his sister had been yanked away from their lives and sent to start again with their aunt and uncle, we had been taken away from the place where everyone knew us.

I understood much later that we had to move away from our old neighborhood. We would have been hounded every day. We would have been stared at and whispered about. And that was only the well-mannered people. Some kids would have gossiped or asked probing questions. The rest would have made up lies, called us worse names than The Killer Kirkpatricks, taunting us about Cassie.

But I missed the house where Cassie and I had been born. There was a park at the end of the street where we'd lived. Mum would take us every day and catch up with the other mums. Under their watchful eyes, I had played and laughed and taken risks. Or Cassie took risks, daring me to climb, pushing me to go higher. But at least I had felt free there.

After we moved away, my mother decided we would be schooled at home. I was even more timid after Cassie went missing and staying at home with Mum sounded okay to me. But Libby would have no such thing. She had demanded to go to regular school and threw an almighty tantrum until she got her own way. My parents often caved with Libby. It was just easier that way. This time they compromised and sent her to a small private school in town. When I asked to go, Mum said she'd see when I was old enough, but by that time, I'd settled into the rhythm of homeschooling. I didn't have the fight in me that Libby had.

Libby never talked much about her school. She said she had friends, although she never brought any of them to the house. She disappeared into school and left to start her job as soon as she could. I threw myself into my studies, finally taking the opportunity to shine in my mother's eyes. I attended a few clubs and events to help me become "socialized," but they were "activities," scheduled play. I couldn't remember playing recklessly after Cassie went away. I understood why my world was so protected, why my parents kept me so close. But now I wondered. Was it for my protection or for theirs?

"Well," Inspector Siddiqi said. "I think that's all for now." She stood up and reached out to shake my hand. "I appreciate your coming in."

"Happy to help," I said without conviction.

"One last thing," she said as I turned to leave. "I understand you've applied to university."

"Yes," I said, warning alarms sounding. Of course, she had dug into every corner of my life. She already knew all she needed to know. Had she known that day she came to the house? Did she know I had lied?

"Child Psychology, right?" she asked.

I nodded, glad I hadn't trusted her with my suspicions. She might put on a good act of being on my side, but she didn't have my best interests at heart.

"Good for you. I'm a bit of a fan of that head stuff myself. Had to take a course for my degree. Criminal psychology, of course. Fascinating stuff, the human mind."

"It is," I said.

"My mother was mortified, of course," she went on. "She didn't want me to be a detective, you know. Didn't think it was an appropriate job for a woman. Of course, my mother didn't think any job was appropriate for a woman except being a first-class wife and mother." She sighed and shook her head, the sheen of her bouncing waves mesmerizing me.

I glanced at the door, wondering if it would be rude to get up and leave before she got to the point I sensed she was heading toward.

"I became a detective because of Neil, I suppose. My parents didn't want me to do it. They were dead set against it."

"Mine think I want to be a psychologist because of Cassie," I blurted, realizing too late that I had fallen into her trap.

"Do you?"

"Maybe," I said.

She smiled at that. "For the most part, our parents want what's best for us, but sometimes what they think is best isn't what's actually good for us. We have to make our own decisions."

I nodded. I knew she was trying one last time to gain my trust, but this time she'd hit my soft spot. "I should be going."

"Of course," she said. "Good luck with your studies."

As I turned to gather my things, my eyes flickered over the collection of photos of Kayla, of Inspector Siddiqi's family memories. Our living room walls were covered in pictures, too. I had stopped seeing any of the individual images in Dad's collection long ago and barely even noticed when he added anything new. But now I pictured every frame in the room, looking for something I already knew in my gut wouldn't be there.

There was not one single family photograph on display in

our house. There were no pictures of Cassie and no pictures of Libby and me. It was as if we had never been children and as if Cassie had never existed. Inspector Siddiqi had never forgotten her friend Neil and I had never forgotten Cassie. But my parents had done everything they could to keep my memories of her at bay. As if they had something to hide.

I wasn't sure if I was safe anymore. Was I standing on solid ground, or had I leapt onto the higher ground only to have it float out to sea? I had so many questions. Why had we really moved away? To protect us from gossip or to protect us from the truth? Why were there no pictures in our house? To protect us from the memories of Cassie or to make us forget? And why had my friend Paula stopped calling me? Because she didn't want to remember me, or because my parents didn't want me to remember her? Something was out of balance in my world, and I struggled to pinpoint exactly what it was.

My brain hummed in the aftermath of my interview with Inspector Siddiqi, and little pricks of worry sparked where an unpleasant truth had poked at my beliefs. A muddle of emotions swirled around me; my sense of duty to my family, the horror of what had happened to Cassie—both the known and the assumed—the questions left unanswered, and the suspicion that clung to my family like the smell of heavily spiced cooking. It left me with the sort of sickness that continued long after I should have felt safe.

Most of all though, I envied the photos of a little girl adored by her mother. There was no collection like that of me.

SEVENTEEN

"This came for you," said Libby, thrusting a letter at me the moment I appeared in the kitchen the next morning. She was still in her uniform, her jacket thrown over the back of a chair and her dangerously high heels kicked to one side in a most un-Libby-like way. Dad had said she'd be home for Cassie's funeral, but I didn't realize that "home" meant *here*. I needed some time alone to answer a niggling doubt, and I wasn't in the mood for her grilling me about everything I did or said.

"What is it?" I asked before spotting the university logo and kicking myself for not realizing that, of course, Libby would now get to see my mail first.

"As I don't have X-ray vision, I really couldn't say," Libby said, but she looked away from me and I knew she was lying. She'd seen the logo, too. "Well, open it," Libby snipped.

"It's a private letter addressed to me. So, I'll open it in private if it's all the same to you."

I stuffed the letter into my pocket and made a big show of making tea, hoping Libby would leave me alone. But the letter burned hot as if it might burst into flames if I didn't open it right there and then. It was a thin envelope, just a letter, and not something I was expecting at this point in the process. The admissions administrator had given every indication that I'd be a welcome addition to the program, but maybe she'd connected me to Cassie—or more to the point, my dad—and had a change of heart. Maybe the university had decided it would be too disruptive to have me on campus. Or worse, that I wasn't the right sort of person to be around people in need. Maybe, like Libby, they thought I had enough of a struggle managing my own baggage, never mind helping other people with theirs.

My throat tightened and I gulped down the frustration that threatened to bubble up inside me. I wasn't going to give Libby the pleasure of knowing that my plans—my entire future— were hanging in the balance because of Cassie.

Libby's curiosity almost crackled in the air, like a synthetic top pulled over your head on a dry day. Libby was dying to know what was in my letter. I didn't look up, focusing only on going through the motions of tea-making, a simple routine I could do on autopilot while my mind churned with thoughts about what the letter might say.

"You're up to something," Libby said.

I didn't answer.

"You've applied to university without telling anyone."

"So?" I said, not making eye contact with her.

Libby shook her head. "How are you going to do that on your own? Where are you going to live? How are you going to support yourself?"

"I'm not an idiot," I snapped. "I've thought it all through. Georgie and I ..."

"Georgie?" Libby said, her lip curling. "So, she's behind all this."

"She's not behind anything," I said. "I'm doing this for myself." It wasn't exactly the truth. Yes, this was what I wanted more than anything, but without Georgie's encouragement, I wouldn't have had the guts to act on it.

"You need to stay away from her. There's too much going on and you can't trust anyone right now."

"Georgie is my friend and I trust her completely," I said.

Libby pulled back as if I'd said something dangerous. I couldn't help but wonder if she'd ever been able to call someone a trusted friend.

"And yes," I pushed on. "I applied to university. I need a life, Libby."

"What you *need* is to be here right now. With all that's going on, now's not the time to be trying to save the world."

I bristled. Only Libby could make wanting to do good seem like something dirty. "Mum said I should," I said.

"Mum?" Libby said, looking surprised. "I am sure she did not."

"She said it was time I started my life, and she's right."

She shook her head, flustered. "Mum's not herself at the moment. Now *isn't* the time." Before I could respond, she added, "It won't bring Cassie back, you know."

"What won't?" I asked, realizing in that moment that Libby already knew my plans for my career. "Have you been snooping through my stuff?"

She stopped then and turned to me. "I know you, Abby. Maybe better than you know yourself. I don't want you to get hurt."

My teeth crunched as I ground them together, trying hard to bite down on my anger toward Libby. But mixed in with my rage were little flecks of truth, like dust you don't see until the light shines a certain way. Was she right? Was I trying to make up for losing Cassie? Were my career plans, my purpose, less to do with helping other children and more to do with making myself feel better, compensating for my guilt about Cassie? Did it even matter?

In my pocket, the burning letter turned cold. Maybe a rejection would be the best thing. Maybe I was an idiot to pursue a career helping others. I would always be chasing Cassie's ghost, always trying to make things right. But if I didn't follow my heart, then what? I had no other plans. Without this path to a different life, I was just a girl stuck in a cage.

"You didn't warm the pot," Libby said, sliding up behind me and peering over my shoulder.

"What?"

"The teapot. It's cold." She reached across to where the electric kettle was just beginning to steam.

I pushed her arm away. "I know how to make tea," I snapped. The hot water splashed from the spout onto Libby's uniform skirt. We both watched as it spread, turning the teal fabric black. The image of the red splash on my mother's white blouse blossomed again in my mind.

"Apparently not," Libby said.

"Well, it's not easy with you breathing down my neck, looking for every little thing I'm doing wrong."

Libby raised her eyebrows in surprise. She moved half a step backward, out of my space. "Just trying to help," she muttered.

"Well don't."

I grabbed the kettle and sloshed hot water into the teapot, splashing it over the rim and right onto my hand. "Dammit," I yelped. "Look what you've made me do."

"I made ...?"

"Just ..." my voice cracked and the next second I was choking back angry tears. Everything was suddenly too much—Cassie, my dad, Inspector Siddiqi and her manipulation, everything out of my control. And Libby always trying to push me around. I needed to box. It was the only time I ever felt in control. "Just leave me alone, all right?"

Libby grabbed my scalded hand and ran cold water over it from the tap. I tried to breathe, to get the knot in my chest to loosen. I wiped my eyes, trying to at least appear as if I was pulling myself together. Libby said nothing, but I could tell she was watching me.

"It's going to be all right," she said at last. She touched my arm with such a tender gesture, just light enough that I worried it might start the tears again. I needed to trust someone who understood, and right now, Libby was all I had.

"I'm scared," I said before I could stop myself.

"Of what?"

"I hate that I can't do anything to help her," I said. "I was there. I was probably the last person to see her alive. Why didn't I hear anything? I could have saved her."

Libby grabbed a tea towel and began rubbing the dishes as if she were trying to wear away the pattern. "You were just a kid. You were tired. You slept through the whole thing."

"Or maybe my brain shut down that part of my memory like a protective mechanism to save me from something I couldn't handle."

"What?" said Libby.

"That's what Inspector Siddiqi said."

Libby's face fell. "That's ridiculous."

"No. It's a thing. And if I could just remember—"

"You don't want to dredge up something like that. Not after all this time."

"I'm not a child anymore. I know something terrible happened to Cassie. I have the tools to handle it now."

"No, you don't. This is personal. It's not like hearing a story about a stranger. You don't want to relive that now you're doing so well."

"That's what Mum said. She said I should let it go."

A frown passed across Libby's face as if this was the last thing she expected Mum to say. Then she gave me a Libby smile. "She's right."

I dabbed my scalded hand with a towel. The skin was red but not burned. It was sore but wouldn't scar. Not like the rest of me had after Cassie. I might have healed in the years since she vanished, but the scars would always be there.

"That night," I said. Libby sighed. "When you came back to the cabin that night, did you see anything unusual?"

"Abby."

"I remember a stain on Mum's shirt."

"What?"

"A red stain."

"It was wine, Abby. Yes, they'd had a drink, but they weren't drunk if that's what you're implying. Don't start believing all the lies people tell."

"One of us must know something, though. What if we saw something that could be a lead? I don't understand why you wouldn't want to help."

Libby exhaled as if she were gathering her composure to talk to a very willful and possibly stupid child. "You were six years old, Abby. I was eleven. Even if you saw something, you would have been too young to make sense of it. And now your mind has been filled with other people's stories, whether they're true or speculation. Mine, too. There's no way to differentiate between our memories and the stories we've heard. It's all mixed together, fact and fiction."

"That doesn't make sense. Of course I'd know."

Libby stirred the tea around and around, and then she said. "Okay, here's an example. Think about a memorable event from when you were small."

"Cassie disappearing."

"Another event."

"My sixth birthday."

Libby frowned but went on. "Okay, tell me about it."

The memory was seared in my mind. It had been the last birthday Cassie and I had ever celebrated together. "We had a party. Our friends were there. We both got new bikes and Mum made a huge chocolate cake."

Mum had counted to three for us to blow out the candles together, but Cassie had cheated. She'd blown on two, and when Mum had us make a wish, I hadn't because Cassie had stolen my wish and taken it for herself. After, I wished I could have my birthday all to myself. I never imagined that wish would come true. After she was gone, my birthday was a somber affair, always tinged with Cassie's absence and the guilt of my wish. This year, Georgie and I had planned to take back the day, but how could I celebrate my life now that we knew Cassie had lost hers? Cassie had hijacked my birthday again.

But I couldn't tell Libby all this. Instead, I said, "Uncle Dave was there."

"I remember that," said Libby.

"He turned up uninvited and brought me and Cassie each a teddy bear." Bear and Ollie. We had loved those bears and loved

Uncle Dave for making our birthday special. But he'd almost ruined the whole party. It hadn't been quite like the fight he and Dad had that Christmas, but the result had been more final. I never saw him again. "They argued about money like they always did. That was the last time Uncle Dave came."

"You remember that?" Libby said, her voice guarded.

"Yes."

"You heard them?"

"Yes."

"Where were they?"

"What's your point?" I asked, growing frustrated with Libby's roundabout conversation.

"Just tell me where they were arguing," Libby said.

"I don't know. In the house, I suppose. The living room."

"And where was your party?"

"At the house."

"It was in the garden."

"Okay."

"So, there's no way that you overheard that argument. Mum told us it was about money. It's what they always told us. But it wasn't. You think you remember that because you heard it so many times, it's become real for you. We tell ourselves stories until they become a reality." She looked away, adjusting her expression until it was composed again. "If you start trying to remember something you didn't even see, you'll have no way of knowing what you really remember and what you *think* you remember. The things you told the police right after Cassie disappeared are going to be more accurate than anything you could tell them now."

"I suppose," I said. Except I had the feeling I *should* know something more, that I held a piece of information that could change everything. If Inspector Siddiqi was right, and I had locked some important detail deep inside a part of me that I could no longer tap, how could I retrieve it? If I had seen something that night, I would have been scared. I would have been sleepy, maybe, if I'd been awoken in the night. Frightened. Maybe surprised to see someone in our room. Maybe I could ask Georgie to jump out at me to see if it would shake loose a memory.

I brushed away the ridiculous idea. Libby was right. I was just a little kid, so exhausted from a day in the sun and water that I had slept through the worst night of my life. I would always have to live with that.

"I feel so helpless," I said, leaning toward Libby, needing to feel the touch of someone who truly understood how I felt.

Libby reached out first and took me by the shoulders, holding me at a distance. "We have to keep our chins up and trust the police," she said. "We have to accept that we may never find out what really happened."

I nodded, feeling like a lost little girl again. I willed my big sister to pull me into her arms and make me feel safe. But she didn't. There was a thin glass wall between us, and Libby would never let it down. To an outsider, we looked like two sisters brought together by tragedy. But although we had presented a united front to the world, there was an invisible distance between us that could never be bridged. And Libby would always keep it that way. My family had protected me and kept me safe from others, but Libby had never kept me close.

"I'm tired," she said. "I think I might go home soon and get some rest. Will you be okay here?"

"I don't see why not," I said, stretching the distance between us even further.

"I'll bugger off, then." She pulled on her uniform jacket and slipped on her shoes. The water stain on her skirt had already dried, and when she tucked a loose strand of hair back behind her ear, she looked perfect again.

I gave her a tight little smile that barely curved the corners of my mouth. "By the way," I said as Libby reached the kitchen door. "What was the argument about?"

"What?" said Libby.

"You said the argument Dad had with Uncle Dave wasn't about money. So, what was it about?"

Libby turned away, but not before I saw the change in her expression. My question had flustered her. "I don't know exactly. I just know Mum wasn't telling the whole truth. It doesn't really matter. My point is that you couldn't remember details from so long ago."

But the little worm of truth had started wriggling again and I wondered if Libby was wrong about it not being important. Dad and Uncle Dave had argued about something, and Mum had lied to us about it. Perhaps that was the most important thing of all.

Alone in my room, I opened the letter from the university. It wasn't a rejection, not exactly. It was worse. I closed the door and called the number given in the letter.

"Oh, yes," said the woman on the other end when I'd explained the letter. "It shows here that we made a conditional offer, but you withdrew your application."

"I don't understand," I said.

"Let me see." The woman rustled some papers. "You did school at home, is that right?"

"Yes." I'd done school with Mum, then taken online courses

to get the qualifications for university. I'd done everything right. Or so I'd thought.

"Our records show you withdrew."

"But I didn't."

"Perhaps there's been an error." She gave me a number to call and said she'd flag my application for now. "I'm sure it will all be resolved," she said. But I wasn't.

I hung up the phone and tore down the stairs. "Libby?" I yelled, but there was no reply. The house was quiet. Libby had already left.

Maybe this was just an administrative error that could easily be fixed, but given the way Libby had behaved when she handed me the letter, her insistence that I open it right there, and her knowledge of my plans, I had the feeling she had something to do with my withdrawal.

"Now's not the time," she had said about my going to university. Had she done something to make sure I didn't leave, didn't carry our family's story too far from home? Libby wasn't my favorite person in the world, but I couldn't believe she would sink so low as to sabotage my future. I would have to quietly unsabotage it on my own.

Keeping secrets was starting to be hard work, at least for me. Everyone else in my family seemed to be a pro.

Eighteen

More than two weeks after Cassie was found, another condolence card arrived. I snatched the pale-gray envelope from the mailbox as if it might explode in my hands. The cards had come in a thin, intermittent stream, uneasy notes of sympathy from Mum's friends and Dad's colleagues. We opened the first ones to find pale watery images of lilies and weeping willows, the insides printed with equally watery messages about our "loved one"—verses crafted in an attempt to say in ink what people could never quite put into spoken words. All of it was sincere, but none of it was ever enough to soothe the deep wounds left by Cassie's death. With every card that arrived, a little piece of my heart teetered and fell away, like a boulder that had clung to a cliff face for millennia, only to finally erode and fall. My family and I had put Cassie's disappearance behind us. Together, we had pulled through and kept moving, survived the unimaginable. Only once Cassie was found did I understand what a slippery grip I held on my acceptance. Now I was back at the beginning, losing Cassie all over again, pulling forward and slipping backward, and somehow ending up right back where I started.

I flipped the pedal on the kitchen bin and dropped the latest arrival inside. It fell onto the yogurt and fresh strawberries that were supposed to have been my breakfast, Libby's determined efforts to mother me. As the lid dropped closed, I caught the briefest glimpse of my name.

I popped the lid back up and retrieved the envelope, reaching for a paper towel to wipe away the goop. On the front of the pale envelope, in unfamiliar neat purple writing, was *Abigail Kirkpatrick* and my home address. I hesitated, not sure who would send something to me. Nervous that the contents might not be friendly, I slid my finger under the flap.

Dear Abby,

I was so very sorry to hear the news about Cassie. I can't imagine what it must feel like to lose her all over again. I only hope this news will somehow be the beginning of your and your family's healing.

Please know that I think of you often and should you ever need an understanding ear, I am here.

Your friend,

Paula

Below the signature were a phone number and email address.

I stared at the name and read the words over again. *I think of you often ... an understanding ear.* My stomach tightened at the shallow words. Paula had "thought of me often" but never bothered to keep in touch. And how understanding an ear would I find with someone who'd shut me out when I needed her most? I flipped open the lid and dangled the card back over the strawberries and yogurt. I paused, then let it drop.

Still, it called to me. Maybe it was unfair to judge Paula so harshly; we'd been children when Cassie went missing. I hadn't been equipped to deal with my grief and I was sure Paula had had no clue how to deal with me either. I couldn't blame her for not reaching out to me. But she was reaching out now. *I am here*, she wrote. *I am here*. The words shone like a beacon from the depths of the kitchen bin. *I am here*.

I retrieved the card and called the number.

It rang once. Paula had been my first and best friend.

Twice. The one person who hadn't been afraid of me after Cassie went missing.

Three times. She'd stayed in touch for a while, hadn't she?

Four times. She'd tried.

And then a woman's voice, soft, pleasant, polite.

"Hi there. Paula speaking. I can't get to my phone right now, but please leave a message."

At the beep, I opened my mouth to speak. But no words would come. I needed to know Paula was there for me. I needed to hear it from her. And until I did, I couldn't risk trusting her and being hurt again.

———

I left early for Project Talk that afternoon. I needed to get away from Paula's meaningless note and clear my head, so I walked to the bus stop via the path along the moors, the way I'd come home the day Cassie was found.

I wanted Paula's note to mean something. Like her, I had also hoped Cassie's discovery would bring answers and be the beginning of my family's healing. Instead, it cracked open my grief and created a million questions.

But tomorrow would be Cassie's funeral, my chance to finally say goodbye. Maybe that would be the catalyst we needed. Maybe things would get better from there.

It wasn't fair of me to dismiss Paula so quickly. After tomorrow, after it was all over, I would try her again, give her a chance to be there for me. It was perhaps the thing I needed most of all.

Danielle hadn't arrived by the time Claire was ready to start the meeting. I swore under my breath, frustrated that I couldn't get through to her, that she kept pushing away the one person who really understood what she was going through. But as the first kid in the circle began to talk, the door cracked open, and Danielle slipped in. She mumbled an apology to Claire and took her seat next to me. She didn't look up, didn't meet my gaze, and when it was her turn to speak, she shook her head and made the agreed-upon signal that she wanted to pass.

She avoided me at the break and sank deeper into her chair for the rest of the meeting. I had failed her completely. My history would always follow me. But I wasn't going to give up on her. As Claire brought the discussion to a close, I leaned over to Danielle before she could escape.

"I'm here for you," I said.

She nodded and slipped away. My insides sank. Words didn't mean anything unless they were followed up with actions, but I didn't think I would ever get through to Danielle. I wanted to, so much, for both our sakes.

As Claire stacked the chairs and I put away the few leftover cookies, I felt a presence behind me. Danielle stood shyly, staring at her feet.

"Chocolate chip was my mum's favorite," she said. "That's why I always pick them."

Her words reached inside me and clutched at my heart, a brief moment of connection between someone in pain and someone who cared. I held still, letting her know I would stay if she wanted to say more. She wrapped her arms around me then and pressed her face to my chest.

"I miss her," she said, her voice small.

"I know you do," I said, holding her tight. "I know you do."

NINETEEN

As the funeral car wound up the hill to the small chapel, my mother gasped. I looked up from where I'd been worrying a small pill in my scarf to see what had caught her attention.

"So many people," my mother whispered.

My mother had been adamant about attending Cassie's funeral. Her doctors had made her as comfortable as they could, and we'd promised to return her right after the service. Despite our request for a small family affair, we'd expected the media to attend along with a handful of nosy parkers curious to see the funeral for a girl who'd been dead for close to two decades. We hadn't expected the forecourt outside the chapel to be full of people. Mum's book club friends were there, all dressed in the good black wool coats they kept for funerals and rare fancy events. There were a couple of nurses from the hospital and a group of Dad's colleagues from work. It was so unexpected. I wasn't sure if it was an outpouring of love, curiosity, or obligation that had brought so many people out. All I knew was that my anonymity was dead. Everybody would know now that I was Cassie's sister.

The hearse stopped at the chapel door and our car pulled up behind it. I scanned the crowd and spotted Claire with a couple of mentors from Project Talk. Beside them, Georgie gave me a nod of acknowledgment and a hint of a smile, all the occasion would permit. My heart swelled from that one small gesture. I wouldn't be alone today.

We sat in nervous silence as the pallbearers opened up the hearse's tailgate. From the forest of flower-covered crosses and wreaths, teddy bears and bouquets, the four men in black mourning suits slid out the impossibly small white coffin and carried it to the chapel door. For the first time since my sister had vanished all those years ago, it suddenly felt real. There was a finality I hadn't anticipated. Cassie was no longer missing. Now, Cassie was dead.

In choreographed unison, the driver and usher slipped from the car and opened the doors, lifting my mother and her drip into the hospital's wheelchair and draping a dark blanket across her lap. Beside her, Dad stood to attention in the smartest suit I had ever seen him wear. The urge to laugh rose up in my chest, the ridiculousness of the rituals of death, the formality of it all. What would six-year-old Cassie have made of all this? Would she have giggled at these somber men dressed like butlers, treating her like royalty? I swallowed my laughter, but it bubbled up again, finding escape as tears.

Libby shot me a sideways look and narrowed her eyes at me. She had dressed in a neat black suit, a monochrome version of her usual unruffled self. Even with the adjustments Georgie had helped make to Mum's old suit, I felt untidy and uncomfortable. Libby, though. Libby looked like a china doll, her pale skin smooth and unblemished, a faint round glow of pink in each cheek as if it had been painted there by a master craftsperson.

Her hair hung like a blonde silk frame around her face. Even the chilly breeze that whipped up the gentle slope of the cemetery hadn't moved a single hair from its place. I had the vague, suffocating sense that my sister wasn't real, that no one in my family was who they claimed to be.

Libby handed me a tissue, the smallest of kind gestures, just enough to force my tears over the rims of my eyes. I wiped my nose, already feeling the rawness of flaked skin and the stickiness of damp makeup around my eyes. I had an urge to scream, to let out all my sadness, my frustrations, all the unanswered questions, to cry until they washed away. But today, we were on display, the crowds, the media, the people who'd watch the news tonight, mindlessly forking food into their mouths. This funeral wasn't for us to say goodbye to Cassie; it was for them to decide: Did we look like a family in mourning, or did we look like a family with secrets? We were both, but today we had to choose one.

Libby dabbed the corners of her dry eyes with a tissue and lifted her chin. If the public wanted to judge the Kirkpatricks, we would not be cowed. I followed Libby's lead. It was showtime.

The doors of the chapel opened, and our assigned minister appeared on the top step. As the pallbearers lifted the tiny coffin onto their shoulders, a flicker of movement passed along one end of the crowd. I turned in time to see four cameras drop from the faces of photographers. Cassie was still a sensation. She would have enjoyed the fame.

We followed Cassie's coffin into the chapel and took our seats on the front pew as the pallbearers set Cassie on the dais. To one side, a small shrine had been set up. Cassie's teddy bear Ollie was there. He had once been identical to Bear. But while

Bear was now threadbare in places, his limbs loose and his belly squashed from a lifetime of love, Ollie looked almost new.

Behind Ollie, an enlarged version of Cassie's photograph, the one the media had run—the one cropped to show only a sliver of my arm—stood on a simple wooden stand. In pixelated print, Cassie had been a pretty, dark-haired child with wonder-filled eyes that, even in black and white, were obviously crystal blue. Enlarged, the details of my sister's face became familiar to me again. Cassie's chin and mine were almost identical, our mouths a similar shape, but Cassie's smile was like Mum's and Libby's. Her nose was the small, freckled nose of a five-year-old, but if I had to compare it to anyone's, I'd put it closest to Dad's, although actually, it was more like our grandmother's. Dad's eyes were blue but paler than Cassie's, and none of us had the straight black hair that complemented Cassie's eyes and took her from pretty to beautiful. She'd gotten that from our grand-mother, too.

I only half listened as the minister worked his way through the script we had provided. I felt a pang of pity for him for drawing the short straw to conduct this service. What could you say about a girl everyone knew about but only her family had ever really known? How did you commemorate a life that had been too short and ended too long ago? The poor man did his best.

After the service, we shuffled outside. Despite the recent summer heat, a chilly wind whipped up the hill, filtered by the rows of headstones until it arrived in the chapel forecourt in thin pointed fingers of cold. I moved with my family in a tight clump along the line of mourners, shaking hands and thanking people for coming. The Kirkpatricks, a united front, the family that survived the unimaginable.

Near the end of the line, a young woman in a smart wool coat stepped toward me. She gave me a small, sympathetic smile and lowered her eyes. "I'm so sorry for your loss, Abby," she said in a vaguely familiar voice.

Dutifully, I pushed the words past the tight knot in my chest and out into the cold air. "Thank you for coming," I said. But as I looked into her face, I realized who she was. "Paula?"

She nodded. "I had to come."

My mind scrambled to match this sophisticated woman with my old friend and the lost little girl I had been.

"You came all this way?"

"Only an hour," she said.

An hour. She seemed to have come so far from where we'd grown up, years and miles, a lifetime. But all this time, she'd been an hour away.

"I missed you," she said sheepishly.

"You stopped calling." It wasn't an accusation, just a fact.

"I wanted to. I wasn't allowed."

I nodded, hurt but not surprised that her mother had wanted to keep her away. It wasn't Paula's fault.

"I never stopped thinking about you," she said. "I just didn't know if you'd want to hear from me."

She reached out and squeezed my arm. The touch was jolting. Instinctively, as if clutching for a lifeline, I grabbed Paula's hand. Her skin was cool and dry, her hands so thin that I could feel the bones beneath her fingers. It was almost fragile, a hand that I could crush if I squeezed hard enough. But the warmth of human contact radiated through my body, and before I could stop myself, I leaned into her. She was here for me. My forehead came to rest on Paula's slight shoulder, and a small sound like the whimper of a frightened animal jolted from my mouth. Her hands moved to my back with tentative pats.

"I wrote to you after you moved," she said in a soothing voice. "But my letter came back. And you weren't on social media. You weren't *anywhere*. I was afraid something bad had happened to you, too."

I stiffened at the word "too," the implication that whoever had killed Cassie could have hurt me, too. Paula kept patting and my mind caught up. Paula had written to me? Then why had the letter come back? Someone had interfered. Someone had sent it back.

I glanced at my family. Libby was shaking hands with someone I didn't recognize. My mother was staring right at Paula and me, a hard expression on her face.

"Why wouldn't your mother let you talk to me?" I asked quickly, bracing for the answer.

Paula hesitated and pulled me closer, so she could whisper in my ear. "Your mum asked her not to. I wrote again anyway, but ..."

Before I could ask anything more, someone yanked me away, letting cold air fill the gap left between Paula's body and mine.

"You must excuse her," I heard Libby say. "She's very upset."

"Of course she is, Libby," said Paula.

Libby froze at the sound of her own name. Her eyes flickered wide for a second as if she recognized Paula, then she gripped my arm and pulled me away. "Pull yourself together, Abby," she said, her expression not changing from the delicate, sad face she'd maintained all day. "People are staring."

I looked up at the sea of faces, but no one was staring at me.

No one except Paula, my mother, and a man standing alone beneath a tree away from the crowd.

That man. I looked again. Something about him was familiar.

"Who's that?" I asked Libby, but before my question was out, Libby moved in, pushing me against Dad, clumping our family back together as if we were antelope surrounded by a pack of lions. No one touched me. No one reached to squeeze my hand. No one wrapped me in their arms. I struggled to lift my head from the press of my family, searching for the man I was sure I knew, looking for Paula, a friendly face. But before I could find them again, I was smothered in my family's protective huddle.

"Why are they here?" I whispered, looking at all the people. "What have they come to look at?" I turned back to the group and shouted, "Show's over. I hope you got what you came to see."

"Calm yourself," Libby said. "You need to breathe."

"I don't want to breathe," I said.

Libby grabbed my arms and spun me around. Her eyes burned into mine. "Look at me, Abby. You need to calm yourself. Now. You need to breathe."

A wave of heat rose inside me. Libby must have sensed it too, because she tightened her grip on my arms. Even now, even in the one place I was supposed to grieve Cassie, Libby wanted me to keep it all inside. I wriggled to get free, but Libby held tight. My knees faltered and Libby pulled me to her. I soaked in the brief moment of connection, the flash of compassion. And then Libby stood me upright, nodding her approval at my change in mood.

A small hedge of tears sprang up along my lashes and I

blinked them away. Through the haze, I saw a friendly face. Georgie stood away from the huddle of mourners, her eyes locked on mine. Beneath her black jacket, she wore a gold-colored blouse that shone like a beacon. I took a breath and broke from my sister's grasp. I strode across the gravel forecourt.

"Where are you going?" Libby called behind me, but I didn't stop.

Georgie saw me coming and her face furrowed in concern. I kept moving. I knew my family was watching, half expecting to feel Libby's hand on my arm pulling me back. But I wasn't going back. I was moving forward now.

"Get me out of here," I muttered before I'd even reached Georgie.

"Gladly," she said, wrapping a protective arm around me.

My mind raced to piece together all that had happened. Bit by bit, pieces of the puzzle I'd been struggling to solve my whole life began falling together. But the picture was fuzzy, unclear, except for small dots of color, images I struggled to understand. Why had we moved away? Why had my mother cut me off from my friends? What was my family really hiding?

Something turned inside me, a tiny truth wriggling to be noticed. My family *knew* who had killed my sister. It was a terrible truth, too terrible to bear, and when I grasped for more details, they disappeared again.

We hurried down the driveway toward the cemetery gates. I didn't want to look back to see who had watched me go, to see if anyone in my family would come after me, but I had to look. I glanced back toward the tree where the man had been standing. He was gone. Only the feeling of familiarity remained.

Down the gentle slope of the cemetery, row upon row of

gravestones rolled into the distance. *So many secrets. So much knowledge lost with the dead.*

I had always been proud of my family. We had stuck together through the worst tragedy imaginable. But we were hurting ourselves. I could see that now. The only way any of us would get through this and be able to move on was to get answers. Cassie had taken her secrets with her, but I was determined to retrieve them, no matter what.

TWENTY

Coffee & Vinyl was mercifully quiet, but still, I chose a table in a far corner where the outside world couldn't find me. My mind grasped for one solid fact, one little detail that made sense, but already the scene at Cassie's funeral was blurry, the colors mixing until nothing seemed real.

"Well, that went well," said Georgie, sliding what appeared to be a Coke across the table. "You want to talk?"

"No," I said. "Yes." And then, "No."

I pushed my drink away, knowing Georgie would have slipped in a shot of something to calm my nerves. I needed to keep my head clear. Someone in my family was lying. Or maybe *everyone* in my family was lying. My mother was hiding, Libby was stage managing, and my dad? I didn't know what to believe about him. Somebody knew something and had decided not to tell for all these years. Their secrets had cemented us in the past. Without knowing what had happened to Cassie, I would never be able to put that part of my past behind me. I would always feel compelled to bring Cassie's killer to justice. I owed my sister the truth, no matter what.

"It was Paula that set me off," I said, clutching for one solid thought. "All this time, I thought she didn't want anything to do with me. But she wasn't allowed to call me. My mother said she couldn't."

"That's messed up," said Georgie.

"My mum was so ashamed of what happened to Cassie."

"Kids can be cruel, though. You know that. She was probably just trying to protect you."

"Or herself."

I understood my parents wanting to protect us from cruelty. But shame? I had never felt shame about Cassie's disappearance. But apparently, my mother had, and she had uprooted her family and our whole lives to avoid it. What was it that had made her so ashamed? Or afraid?

And what about Libby? What did she know? She must have her own suspicions. Was she acting from shame, too? Trying to hide behind her mask of normalcy?

And Paula. She must know now that something else was going on. If she was suspicious, how many others looked at us and saw something not quite right? Were my mother and Libby right to feel ashamed?

I was suddenly exhausted. After a day filled with people and questions, I wanted to be alone. I couldn't just abandon Georgie after she'd been so good to me and rescued me from Libby, but I needed a few minutes to myself. I wanted to hide and just let the quiet wash over me a while. Exhausted, I excused myself and went in search of the ladies' room.

Alone in the coolness of the tiled room, I tried to calm my racing mind and let my confusion fall away. But one dark knot of thought wouldn't budge. Something I had seen today held the answers I needed. I sifted through all the images from the day, trying to catch the one I couldn't quite see. But nothing would come.

I rinsed my gritty eyes and went back to Georgie. But when I pushed open the ladies' room door, a dark-haired man in a slim-cut suit had taken my seat. He was a regular at the café, a bit of a slimeball, but Georgie liked him. He had one elbow propped casually on the table and the other hand on Georgie's slender thigh. She laughed, her head thrown back, exposing a pale slim neck, her silvery curls bouncing, her body open and exposed. My stomach sank. I needed Georgie. I needed someone I could trust, but now even she was about to let me down.

"Georgie?" I said. "We should go. We're meeting your brother, remember?"

It was our code for "this guy's creepy," but I hoped she'd get the hint that I just wanted some time with her.

Georgie hesitated, and in that moment, the man reached up and stroked her hair.

Something snapped and the dark knot in my mind shifted. I saw a flash of glossy black hair across a pillow, a man's hand pushing it aside.

I bolted for my coat. "I need to go."

"Wait," Georgie said, pushing the man's hand away. "What happened?"

I didn't know. Only that something had clicked in my mind and I had to get out of the coffeehouse, out into the fresh air, out where I could breathe again.

Outside, I searched for a taxi to flag.

"Abby!" Georgie was beside me in seconds. She held my shoulders and moved until our gazes met. "What happened? What's wrong?"

"I don't know," I said. "That guy. The way he touched you."

"He's just flirting. It's okay."

"I know. I ..." But I couldn't make my thoughts line up and make sense. "I was being weird. I'm sorry."

"You're not being weird." Georgie wrapped her arms around me. She understood why I was overprotective, and she appreciated that I worried about her. But that's not what happened this time.

As Georgie drove me home, I rehashed my reaction in the café. I had overreacted. I hadn't really been worried about Georgie. The guy had seemed nice enough, maybe a bit touchy-feely, but not threatening. Quite the opposite. But the way he had stroked Georgie's hair. It was such an intimate gesture, the kind reserved for someone you knew well, not someone you wanted to get to know. It was a loving gesture, and yet it had made me squirm. It reminded me of something. Of *someone*.

As the sea of half-familiar faces from the cemetery washed over my mind again, one suddenly came into focus. The man beneath the tree. He'd stood away from the crowd of mourners, too far for me to see his face, but something about him had been familiar. Now the full memory came rushing back. The last memory of my uncle and the reason he'd gone from our lives.

We were five the Christmas he and my dad fell out. Uncle Dave's visit had been fun at first. He played with us, letting us ride him around the living room like a horse. He got down on the floor and played Hungry Hippos and let Cassie put ribbons in his hair. When he took out a palm-sized video camera, Cassie had hammed it up, performing for him, and pulling out her best tricks, while Libby looked on with her typical disapproval.

Mum gave Cassie and me our baths, and Uncle Dave squirted us with our bath toys and shaped our hair into spikes with soap bubbles. While Mum blow-dried our hair, he started a talcum powder fight. When we finally settled in bed, we begged Uncle Dave to tell us one of his wild stories. He obliged with a story of how he'd once had to hide in the hold of a fishing boat to sneak from one country to another and how a cluster of cats had followed him around for days after. He tickled us with pretend cat paws and made us squeal with delight until Mum came in and said it was time we all calmed down and went to sleep. Uncle Dave kissed us good night, and I felt jealous because he lingered the longest with Cassie. He pulled the covers up to her chin, tucking her in and making her cozy. He sat by her bed, stroking her hair long after she'd fallen asleep. I wished it had been me. I wanted to be the object of Uncle Dave's special attention. I wanted him to stroke my hair. I wanted to be Cassie.

Dad and Uncle Dave had argued that night, a physical fight that I'd heard from upstairs. I never knew if it was related to Cassie or just the result of too much drink, but Uncle Dave never visited again—at least not until he barged in and ruined our sixth birthday party a few months later. And then my mother had lied to Libby about the cause of that falling out. It wasn't about money. I was sure it was about Cassie.

After Cassie went missing, Uncle Dave's video ended up on the news, the perfect image of a little girl, happy and playful. The media gobbled it up because the murder of a child is all the more tragic when she is beautiful and perfect and adorable like Cassie was. And I got to replay that last perfect memory over and over again.

In the initial investigation, the police questioned Uncle

Dave. Presumably, they'd come up with nothing. But now that I'd seen him at Cassie's funeral, I wondered. Had they looked hard enough at the man with a physical resemblance and genetic similarities to my dad? A man who had been besotted by Cassie? A man who had risked attending a funeral where he knew he wasn't welcome?

The more I thought about Uncle Dave and Cassie, the more things didn't feel right. It wasn't just the intimate moments with Cassie or the fact that he had disappeared from our lives. Inspector Siddiqi had told us that someone had taken their time, wrapping Cassie's body in a blanket, making sure she wouldn't be found. Her killer had acted quickly, leaving no other marks, no prolonged pain. Cassie's killer had loved her.

"Pull over," I yelled to Georgie. I reached for the door just in time to vomit in the gutter, the images of Uncle Dave dancing in my head, the ones of us all fooling around, of Cassie and me in the bathtub, of that intimate way he had smoothed Cassie's hair. An innocent moment of a kindly uncle playing with his nieces. Innocent until it wasn't.

Twenty-One

Libby read me the Riot Act about fleeing Cassie's funeral. I let her words wash over me while she vented, and the next day we all went back to our lives. Libby was flying again, and Dad threw himself into a nonstop routine of working and visiting Mum. I caught up on Mum's bookkeeping work and made sure Dad and I were fed every day. I kept up the appearance of normality, but I put my time alone to good use.

There was no sign of the box of prescriptions in Dad's office, but it didn't take long for me to find something I could use—a tiny, battered address book in a drawer in my mother's desk. On its flimsy pages, my mother had updated addresses by crossing them out and adding new ones. Libby's address had already been crossed out four times, but Uncle Dave's had only one update. The newest address was not too far away, but I had no clue if that was where he was now.

A quick phone call gave me my answer. I had not heard Uncle Dave's voice for a long time, but I recognized it immediately, a deeper, rounder version of my dad's.

"Hello," he said when I didn't speak. "Hello? You need to

stop calling here." He muttered something unintelligible under his breath and hung up the phone.

I learned two other things from that call. One: Someone was harassing Uncle Dave for reasons I didn't know. And two: Although my dad claimed he had no knowledge of his brother's whereabouts, my mother knew his current address. Something about that did not add up.

When Wednesday rolled around, I convinced Dad I couldn't miss my shift at Project Talk. He barely fought me, even when I told a small lie that I'd be home later than usual due to a staff meeting after the group. Georgie didn't blink an eyelash when I told her of my plan and asked her to come along.

Uncle Dave's house stood in the center of a long row of terraced houses. Each had a front door that opened onto a small square of walled garden, but most people didn't use their front doors. Instead, they entered through the narrow passageways between every fourth house. Uncle Dave lived at number seventy-four. Through the frosted glass panel of his door, a large, dark shape loomed, a piano maybe—something heavy and immovable barricading the entrance, keeping Uncle Dave in or everyone else out.

"Is this it?" Georgie asked.

"I think so."

"Are you sure this is a good idea?"

"No," I said. "But I have to find out. Just give me an hour."

"That's too long," Georgie said. But when she saw I wasn't going to budge, she nodded. "I'll be right here."

I squared my shoulders and stepped into the dark, damp passageway leading to the back of number seventy-four.

The door opened on the third knock, and a tall man peered down at me. I forced myself not to run. He was thinner than my dad but wiry and strong. He'd aged since I had last been around him, and yet much about him looked the same as I remembered. His collar-length hair was still dark, with only a few streaks of gray at the temples. He had the same blue eyes as my grandmother. But his face looked worn, more so even than Dad's. He looked like he had lived life hard and wore every battle on his skin. I was here to find out how those battles related to Cassie.

He looked at me warily as if he didn't recognize me. It had been almost twelve years since we'd last spent time together, but he had seen me at the funeral, looked right at me. Apparently, I was not memorable.

"Uncle Dave?" I said, aiming for a confident smile I didn't feel. He seemed to search his own memory and finally came up with a name.

"Elizabeth?"

I shook my head, stung that he thought I was Libby. "It's Abigail," I said. "Abby."

Uncle Dave looked surprised. A sad look passed across his face. Was it guilt? Resignation? Or something else? Warily, he opened the door to let me in. Now it was my turn to hesitate. I searched his face, waiting for my instincts to tell me I shouldn't go inside. No warning came. I took a breath and stepped across the threshold, the door closing firmly behind me.

Uncle Dave turned off his music, a funky guitar rhythm with a catchy beat. "I'll make tea," he said.

I thanked him, needing a few minutes to regain my composure and guessing he might be doing the same. I didn't exactly feel like a welcome visitor from his past.

Uncle Dave's living room wasn't what I'd expected. I'd imagined some kind of scruffy bachelor pad with cheap temporary furniture and a hodgepodge of belongings. The neat, sparse room didn't fit the person I remembered. The place was clean and organized, the furniture not new but nice quality and in good condition. Across one wall hung countless framed photos of exotic destinations—all the places Uncle Dave had claimed he'd visited in his wild stories. Not so wild, after all. My gaze drifted to the white arches of an oceanside mosque, the rocky islands jutting from turquoise waters, the deck of a wooden fishing boat, and I imagined what a life like his would be like. I'd expected disarray, the trappings of a man who lived in disorder and disregard for social norms, so different from my dad. I had not expected to find the sort of man who had a neat rectangle of a Persian rug in front of his fireplace and an antique mantelpiece clock flanked by two Chinese dragons. I hadn't expected mint tea to be poured into matching glasses from an ornate silver teapot.

"Settles the stomach," he said. "You'd better sit down."

As I twisted to sit on the sofa, something caught my eye. On a bookshelf in the corner was another collection of framed photographs, just like the ones Inspector Siddiqi had of her daughter. Except these were of me and Libby and, most of all, Cassie. Seeing her face there, in his house, felt wrong. No matter the clean, pulled-together image Uncle Dave presented, I needed to stay on my guard. Years of living with Libby had taught me that.

Uncle Dave poured the mint tea and followed my gaze. "I've been following the news about Cassie," he said. "And your dad." He didn't appear surprised that Dad had been questioned again, but unlike me and anyone else who knew my dad, he didn't seem upset either. His expression was tight, almost a smirk—not exactly pleased that his brother was a murder suspect, but as if he believed it was perhaps deserved.

"I saw you at the funeral yesterday," I said.

Uncle Dave nodded. I said nothing, letting him talk.

"I first heard she'd been found when the police turned up at my door. Bit embarrassing that was. Your dad didn't even tell me." He shook his head. "This family and their blasted secrets."

His words prickled. He knew something.

"Why were you there?" I asked.

He looked surprised. "She was ... my niece," he said. "Whatever happened between your dad and me, that never changed. One of my biggest regrets in all this is that I didn't get more time with her. I wasn't there to see you girls grow up."

The way he spoke was so gentle and heartfelt. I recalled how he'd stroked Cassie's hair that night. Gentle, yes, but perhaps something else.

"Did you ever ... hurt her in any way?" I asked.

"What? Of course not."

"Then what did you and Dad fall out over?"

He shook his head.

"It was to do with Cassie, wasn't it?"

He sighed, resigned. "Your dad ..." He ran his hands through his hair and looked like he might change his mind again, but then his eyes hardened. "Your dad was always jealous, you know? Always thought the worst of people, like any good deed had something bad behind it. I helped your mum out when Libby was just a little one. Your dad didn't like it."

"Helped out how?"

"When she was on her own, I helped her with some jobs around the house, took Libby out to the park so she could get some rest."

"Where was my dad?" I asked, trying to understand why my mother had needed so much help.

Uncle Dave narrowed his eyes at me, then his face fell, and I knew he had let slip something big that I wasn't supposed to know.

He sighed. "I'm going to tell you this, but only because it will come out sooner or later with that policewoman sniffing around."

I braced for what Uncle Dave was about to tell me, that he had somehow been involved in Cassie's death.

"Your mum and dad went through a rough patch. It happens. They were young, probably not ready for a family. Who knows? They separated. Libby was three or four, maybe. It wasn't for long, six months or so. Your dad went to stay with our mum."

I tried not to let any emotion show on my face, afraid that Uncle Dave would realize I knew none of this and stop talking. But inside, I was reeling. Why had I never heard about this? And did Libby know? Maybe it was no big deal that my parents had split for a while—as Uncle Dave said, many couples do—but each new secret felt like a piece of stone chipped from the rock that had once been my family. Each chip changed our shape until we were almost unrecognizable as the family I thought I knew.

"She's a good one, your mum," Uncle Dave said. "I felt bad for her, left alone with a little one, so I helped out where I could. Your dad didn't like it. Accused me of taking sides. It was all childish, really.

"Anyway, they patched it all up, your dad moved back, and next thing you know, she was expecting. Everyone was happy, more so when they found out you were twins. I came around often after you were born. I loved being an uncle. But your dad, he couldn't let it go. He'd make these comments whenever I said anything nice to your mother. Petty stuff. Finally, it all came to a head."

"The big argument that Christmas."

"Yeah. Your dad had a bit to drink. So did I, I suppose, and he said some things that weren't nice. We both did."

"Was it to do with Cassie?" I ventured.

The way his head snapped up gave me my answer. I inched back in my seat, hardly believing that the very thing I'd dreaded was true after all. "You didn't ... you didn't do anything to Cassie, did you?"

"Me?" he said, shocked. "Why would you even ask that?"

I shook my head. "I'm just trying to understand."

"Your dad was a little bit drunk, and he got some ideas into his head, that's all."

"About what?"

Uncle Dave pushed his hand across his forehead as if trying to wipe away all my questions. "Look," he said. "You know how Cassie looked so different from you and Libby. Your dad got this idea, couldn't let it go that maybe she wasn't his."

"That's stupid," I said. "We were twins. If she wasn't his, then neither was I."

Uncle Dave shrugged. "Your dad got this idea in his head that something had gone on while he and your mother had been split up."

The ground wavered beneath me. My dad thought Cassie and I were someone else's daughters? Was that why he had treated me differently than Libby? Had he killed Cassie because of this? Had he planned to kill me?

"Was he right?" I asked tentatively.

"About you not being his? Of course not."

"About Mum," I said. "About her seeing someone else when they were separated."

Uncle Dave sighed and turned away. His silent answer made me feel dizzy. My parents had separated, and my mother had met someone else? None of that matched up with the people who had raised me, the couple who had stuck together through the worst tragedy imaginable.

"Do you know what happened to Cassie that night?" I asked.

Uncle Dave shook his head as if trying to clear his thoughts. "Some things didn't make sense. That story about your mum driving out to fetch Libby that night. Why wouldn't the girl's parents have just brought her over? Why would your dad have sent her out alone?"

Even with this new information about my dad and his jealousy, even fueled by the weight of infidelity, I didn't want to imagine my dad harming Cassie. But jealousy could be a powerful fuel. Had something happened to finally flip that switch?

"My dad," I said. "You don't think he had anything to do with it, do you?"

I'd been hoping for a resounding "no," but Uncle Dave shrugged in a noncommittal way. The gesture might have been casual, but the effect was devastating.

"Depends what you mean by 'anything to do with it.'"

"You don't think he ... you don't think he could have killed Cassie. Do you?"

He gave the smallest shake of his head. It was a "no" but still not a convincing one. "For all his faults, I don't think he'd be capable of that." He paused, his gaze drifting into the distance as if he was looking way back into the past and following a thread of something from then to now. "But I always had a feeling he knew more than he was letting on."

"What do you mean?"

"I don't think anyone took her. I think something happened."

"An accident?"

"Maybe." He paused. "I think something happened to her and they panicked."

"They?"

"Your mum and dad."

My insides hollowed as a scene unfolded in my mind. An argument between my parents, fueled perhaps by one too many drinks. Dad, lashing out, as he'd done once before, his jealousy coming to the surface again. And Cassie, an innocent bystander caught in the rage? And then what? A decision to hide the truth, to cover my mother's shame, my dad's uncontrolled temper? What were they so afraid of? What could have been worse than the accusations that followed? An accident might have made the news for a brief time, might have brought charges of negligence or manslaughter. But Cassie going missing had piqued the public's desire for drama. It had stuck in people's minds for years and catapulted us back into the headlines with her discovery. Had this been driven by my dad's illogical jealousy, or was he protecting some other secret?

And where was I through all this? Had I slept through this disaster? Had I dreamed of a man on a dock, a bundle falling to the water? Or had I seen it all?

"It ate away at her, didn't it?" he said.

I frowned, not sure quite what he meant.

"What happened to Cassie. It ate away at your mum."

His frankness surprised me. But he was right. Not finding Cassie meant I'd never been able to put her loss behind me. It had been a constant shadow, a small hole that could never be filled. But for my parents, it was a loss they'd never been able to face. The dark shadow of Cassie's disappearance had hung over them all this time. I didn't know how my dad had dealt with it, but Uncle Dave was right. It had, quite literally, eaten away at my mother, changing her body chemistry until her cells had turned on themselves, that dark shadow slowly working its way inside.

"Did you tell the police any of this?" I whispered, barely able to get the words out past the dark tangle of lies and deceit that tussled inside me.

"Of course not. Like I said, it was just a feeling. I'm not going to point the finger at my own brother just because of a *feeling*. No matter what happened between us in the past, we're still family, and I'll always have his back. You too. You're still family to me."

I smiled my thanks, grateful for a real conversation and a morsel of honesty, something I couldn't recall ever having with my dad. But a creeping feeling passed through me, a feeling I hadn't felt since Cassie had first been discovered. It was a feeling that, finally, I was getting close to hearing the truth and that maybe I wished I wasn't.

Twenty-Two

"There you are," Georgie said when I emerged from Uncle Dave's. "I was worried. Your sister's called me three times."

"Libby? But she's flying."

"She left a message, said she wanted to talk about your birthday."

"She doesn't even know you."

"Super weird, I know," Georgie said.

I didn't like this. If Libby had found Georgie's number, it meant she'd been snooping around my phone. What else had she been up to?

"Anyway, the main thing is you're not dead."

"Not dead," I said. "Very good."

"Was it him?"

I mulled the question. My gut told me no, but there was something about his story that wasn't quite right. "I'll tell you everything and you can decide."

"I can hardly wait," Georgie said.

On the drive home, I told her all that Uncle Dave had said, leaving out nothing. "Whoa," was all she said. "So now what?"

That was the bit I didn't yet know. I turned over everything from my visit with Uncle Dave. I'd learned more about my family in half an hour with him than I had from twenty-two years with my parents. If only they had talked openly with me like that, not treated me like a small child. I'd felt more comfortable in this near stranger's home than I ever had in my own.

All my life, I'd believed my parents had done the best they could for me. I didn't know if they'd always made the best decisions. Like Inspector Siddiqi said, our parents don't always know what's good for us. My parents had tried to shelter Libby and me after Cassie disappeared. They'd moved us away from the neighborhood where everyone knew us, tried to keep us in a bubble, tried to help us forget Cassie's disappearance. Libby had fought against it and sometimes won. But I'd always gone along with their plans, trusting that they knew best.

But what if they weren't just trying to protect us? What if they did have something to hide? They'd hidden their breakup from me all this time. What other secrets had they managed to keep?

"So, what do I do about your sister?" Georgie asked as we left the outskirts of Uncle Dave's town.

I was about to tell her to ignore the calls when my own phone rang. It was Libby.

"Where are you?" I could tell from the tightness in her voice that her jaw was clenched in rage.

"Out. What's the big problem?" I said, trying to keep the frustration out of my own voice.

"The big problem? The big problem is that they've arrested Dad."

"What?"

"What?" Libby mimicked. "Yes. So, you need to get yourself

back here ASAP. We've got a reporter coming to do an interview at seven and you had better be here."

My mind spun to catch up. Dad arrested? A journalist coming? I glanced at my phone. It was six thirty. There was no way I would get home for the interview. But I couldn't tell Libby that. Not unless I wanted her to totally lose it.

"I'll be there as soon as I can," I said.

"Make it sooner," said Libby, and the phone went dead.

———

Georgie had a lead foot and a thing for small windy roads. She reached our house so fast I barely had a chance to think through everything that had happened. Why Dad had suddenly been arrested. What they had found. And why on earth Libby had agreed to an interview after all this time.

In all the years after Cassie disappeared, my parents had never done a single interview. They had attended press conferences and stood together solemnly as some police superintendent or local official gave updates on the investigation. Mostly they amounted to, "We have nothing new to report."

At one point, Dad had been advised to make a statement to the media with all the family in attendance. He refused at first until his lawyer hinted that it would "look bad" for him to say nothing. After considerable pressure, Dad agreed to read an approved written statement, but he'd almost crumbled right there on camera. The emotion in his voice terrified me and I clung to Mum while he spoke. You could see me clearly in the footage because a camera operator had spotted me and zoomed in to grab the scene of devastation. The news outlets loved it, and so

I'd seen the clip of that awful moment over and over again.

As the five-year anniversary of Cassie's disappearance approached, a reporter had asked to interview us for a piece about missing children. My parents talked about it and discussed if it was time to tell our side of the story. But Libby threw an absolute fit. She was finally settled in school, she said, and no one knew anything about us. If we were in the paper, everyone would know, and her life would be ruined. It was typical Libby theatrics, but my parents caved. We said no to the interview and the topic never came up again. So, it made no sense to me that Libby had said yes to an interview now.

"Get upstairs and make yourself presentable," Libby snapped before I was barely in the door.

"What's going on? Why have they arrested Dad?"

"Never mind that now. Go and brush your hair and put on some different clothes," she said, following me up the stairs.

"Does Mum know?" I asked.

"I'll handle it."

"Libby, what's going on?"

"We need to put up a united front for Dad. But for once, if you can manage it, I need you to keep your trap shut and let me do the talking."

I stopped on the stairs and turned on her. "What exactly are you going to say?"

"I told you; I'll handle it," she said. "Just hurry up and get back downstairs."

"But why have they arrested Dad?" I asked.

"They say they've found new evidence, but they won't say what." She narrowed her eyes at me. "You haven't done anything stupid, have you?"

Going to see Uncle Dave would definitely count as stupid in Libby's book. But what if my visit had prompted Dad's arrest? What if Uncle Dave really believed his brother was hiding something and had decided to turn him in?

"Why do you always assume that?" I snapped. "When have I ever done anything stupid?"

Libby didn't answer, but one eye and the corner of her mouth twitched as if she wanted to say that my whole existence was stupid. Her face softened. "Abby, you need to be careful right now. I can't watch over you all the time."

"Watch over me? You? You must be joking." I could recall one time—one time!—when Libby had stuck up for me. That day before we moved away, when she'd threatened those boys, my tormentors. That day, Libby had been fierce. That day, Libby had been my protective big sister. Apparently, that equated to "watching over me all the time."

I stomped up the stairs to get ready for whatever Libby had cooked up.

In my room, I pulled a brush through my hair and stared at myself in the mirror. I was what my grandmother would have called "plain." Mousy hair and pale skin, gray-blue eyes, and unremarkable features. I was the kind of girl who blended in. Georgie had offered makeovers, a little sprucing up to make the most of my attributes, she said. But my mother always told me not to worry about my looks. She said it was what was inside that counted. I knew she only said that to make me feel better.

But now I was about to go public. I was about to talk to a journalist who would put my picture in the newspapers. What would the world see when they looked at Abigail Kirkpatrick? Would they see a freak and a weirdo, a girl who didn't fit in anywhere? My parents had protected me from the ugliness of the world, from the stares, the taunts, the prying questions. But in saving me from the stigma of being Cassie's surviving sister, had they given me a stigma all of my own?

And what was Libby going to say to this journalist? Libby, who was deluded about watching over me when her biggest concern had always been herself. What story would she choose to tell the world now? The sound of the doorbell jolted me back from my pity party, and moments later, I heard the voices of Libby and a woman. I was about to find out.

The reporter sat in Dad's chair, a notebook and mini recorder perched in her lap. She was way younger than I'd expected, maybe not many years older than Libby. She wore distressed jeans rolled up at the ankles and combat boots. She had a collared shirt and a casual suede jacket, like a stylish city version of the correspondents that reported from distant wars. Her long auburn hair fell past her shoulders, and she'd scooped it to one side and twisted it into a long curl. I felt frumpy and childlike compared to her.

The reporter smiled at me. "You must be Abigail," she said.

I nodded. "Abby."

"Abby. Thanks for agreeing to talk to me today."

I gave her a friendly smile and resisted shooting Libby a look. *Agreeing* to talk to her? Like I had a choice. I took a seat where I could easily see Libby, knowing she would be hurling cues at me if I said anything she didn't like. But when I looked at my sister, I was shocked. She wore jeans and a shirt that looked as if she'd slept in it. Her blonde hair hung in messy tangles and her mascara was smudged. She looked like she'd been crying. She looked like a woman with a murdered sister. I had never seen her this way before.

"We appreciate the chance to tell our story," Libby said,

putting a brave smile on her face. It was all I could do not to laugh. She was so obviously faking it, but the journalist took notes and nodded earnestly. She was buying the whole charade. "Whoever did this took Cassie's life and ruined ours," Libby said.

I sat quietly as Libby poured out a sob story of a ruined childhood, our move to escape cruel gossip, and Dad's persecution as a suspect when there was no evidence against him. Whenever the journalist turned to me, I nodded in agreement. Everything Libby said was true, but even though I had lived it, coming from her mouth, it sounded made up.

At last, the journalist said she had all she needed for her story and asked if she could take some pictures of us. I couldn't believe it when Libby said yes.

"Maybe sit together in the chair," the journalist said. "And do you have a photo of Cassie?"

"Of course," Libby said, getting up from her seat and reaching for the bookcase behind me. On it was a collection of family photos I'd never seen before. There was a portrait of Grandma Kirkpatrick as a young woman. She had the same dark hair and bright-blue eyes as Cassie. Uncle Dave had it all wrong. Cassie might not look like me, but looking at this photo of our dad's mother, it was obvious she wasn't someone else's child. In the collection Libby had so obviously set out for show, I recognized photos of my grandparents, my parents on their wedding day, and the three of us girls with our arms flung around one another as if we hadn't a care in the world. And right in the middle was a large framed photograph of Cassie. I shot Libby a questioning look, but she glanced right past me as if I wasn't there.

"This is one of our favorite photos of Cassie," Libby said

and settled into the chair next to me as if squeezing together was something sisterly we did all the time.

I forced a neutral expression onto my face as the journalist took a photo, made adjustments, and took another. But inside, I was churning.

I'd always assumed Libby's facade was her way of protecting herself. As long as everything looked good from the outside, nothing was really wrong. Libby was a master manipulator. I never blindly accepted anything she said or did. But now I had questions about the things she didn't show.

Why had we never had this picture of Cassie out before? Why had we never had any photos of her on display? Why had my parents packed away her things? Why had they never let any evidence of her into this house? Why had we *really* moved?

"This family and their blasted secrets," Uncle Dave had said about the foundation of our family, and he was right. My jealous, irrational dad was suspected of murder. My quiet, unassuming mother, who had dealt with the tragedy of losing her child, had also hidden the secret of an affair. My twin sister, who had carried the identity of her killer to first one and now a second grave. Even Uncle Dave himself hovered in the background of his family, kept away from us for reasons that still weren't clear.

And Libby, so perfectly put together with her veneer of composure that it locked her true self inside. Was Libby carrying the biggest secret of all? Did she know something important about the night Cassie disappeared? Did she keep a clear and terrible memory hidden inside that shell of control? Was she afraid to ever show her true self because of who she knew she was?

I thought about those boys who had taunted me that day.

They weren't boys who were easily scared, but they had been afraid of my sister. That look in her eyes— "as if she might kill them"—those boys had seen it, too. Had she really had the look of someone who could kill?

My grandma always used to say that the quiet ones are the worst. Could my quiet, composed sister be capable of murder? Could she have been capable of harming her own sister? Was she the secret my family had been keeping?

"Now that your father's been arrested," said the journalist, as she packed away her camera, "does this change anything for you?"

"It changes everything," Libby said.

"Of course," said the journalist, pulling back. I could tell she was reframing the question to get at what she really wanted to know. "What I mean is that neither of you remembers seeing anything unusual that night. Now the police believe Cassie died in the cabin. Is it possible your father could have killed Cassie?"

I opened my mouth to object but then closed it again. I wanted answers, too, and maybe Libby had them.

Libby was silent for a long moment, and then she lifted her head, a section of messy hair falling pathetically across her face. "I don't know anymore," she said. "I don't know what to believe."

The second the journalist left, I turned on Libby. "You owe me an explanation," I yelled.

Libby didn't respond right away, as if she'd somehow sensed this coming. "No," she said, finally. "No, I don't."

"You all but told that woman you thought Dad was guilty."

She turned her head slowly as if she was going to look at me, but then she turned it back. Slowly, she shook her head from side to side to let me know I was wrong. "This was his idea."

"What? Why?" I asked, my voice shaking. Then I under-stood. "You know something. You know something and you're keeping it from me. I need you to tell me. You can't keep secrets from me forever."

"I know what I'm doing," Libby said. "And you need to let me."

It wasn't a request; it was a threat. I felt my rage grow again. It blossomed in my chest, a tightening, like the collar on a steam pump, designed to keep the pressure in. I clenched my hands tight, stopping them from reaching out for Libby. But, oh my God, I wanted to feel my hands around her neck, feel the pres-sure as I squeezed, see her smug expression change to fear, knowing that, for once, I held the power. I pictured the scene unfolding and I felt a switch inside me waver. I urged it to flip to the "off" position, to send a message to my brain to keep my arms by my sides, to breathe, to walk away, to punch something I could not break, could not harm.

"Go ahead," Libby said, looking me dead in the eye. "Go ahead and do it. Give our parents two dead daughters. Go on."

Her taunt only tempted me more, but I was not the dangerous one in our family. My switch vibrated, then flipped to "off."

As I turned and walked away, I wondered if Libby would have stopped had our roles been reversed. That switch that kept her cool and in control, at what point would it flip? Maybe Cassie had found out. The question was: would I?

TWENTY-THREE

About a year after we'd moved to the big stone house on the edge of the moors, far away from our old life, I saw Cassie.

We were in the market in town, Mum pushing the cart and reading from her list while Libby grabbed items from one side of the aisle, and I gathered things from the other.

"You stay where I can see you," Mum warned. She never let us get more than a few feet away. I couldn't run up the aisle to grab a box of Sugar Puffs—mine and Cassie's favorite cereal— or circle back to another aisle to pick up the dish soap Mum had forgotten. We were attached by an invisible web that never stretched beyond my mother's sight. I hated being treated like a little child, but I never argued. Other mothers scared their kids with warnings about stranger danger. My mother didn't have to.

As I turned to pick up two tins of baked beans—Cassie's least favorite food—a tall, blonde woman in a stylish green rain-coat crossed the end of the aisle and reached for a loaf of bread. Beside her, in pink polka dot Wellington boots, was Cassie.

I knew it was her. Cassie had a distinctive look—dark hair,

pale skin, eyes the color of the summer sky. Even her bone structure was different from mine—a sharp, heart-shaped face with wide cheekbones and a small, pointed chin. I recognized her immediately.

From the moment Cassie disappeared, I'd imagined what had become of her. I had pictured her living among the fairies and woodland creatures in the forest, where she would have fit right in. Or perhaps she had joined the circus and spent her days riding around the ring on a jet-black horse, her dark hair flying out behind her. Sometimes I pictured Cassie on an endless vacation, building sandcastles on the beach and fortifying them against the sea, the way Dad used to for us. I hoped Cassie would send postcards telling me about her travels and how she'd been spending her days. But the postcards never came.

In another twisted fantasy, Cassie had been kidnapped and put up for sale, bought by a beautiful, wealthy couple unable to have children of their own. Cassie, whose name would have been changed to Cordelia or Veronica, would have her own room with a huge soft bed and all the toys and dolls she could ever want. Although Cassie would have missed her real family terribly, she would be happy and safe in her new life. That's what I wanted to believe.

And then there she was, in the bakery section of the supermarket, with her adoptive mother.

Abandoning the beans, I bolted down the aisle, tearing around the corner to where Cassie had gone, my mother and Libby's shouts fading behind me. Cassie was nowhere to be seen. I sprinted along the ends of the aisles back toward the supermarket entrance, but I couldn't find Cassie anywhere. Frantic, I ran down the freezer aisle, calling Cassie's name, hoping she'd hear me and remember.

I turned another corner and there was Cassie, standing in front of the shelves of yogurts, pointing to the Yum Yogs, another of our favorite brands.

"Cassie," I shouted, running toward her.

Cassie and the woman both looked up.

"Cassie, it's me. Abby."

Cassie shrank away, close to her fake mother. It had been too long; she didn't remember me.

I glared at the woman who had clearly told my sister lies. "Cassie," I said to the girl again. "Don't you remember me? I'm your sister. I'm Abby."

Cassie started to cry, and the woman pulled her behind her body. She held out her hand to keep me at bay. "Stop," she said. "You're frightening her. This isn't who you think she is. Her name's not Cassie."

The woman was lying. This little girl was my sister. "Cassie," I said again, pleading with the girl to remember.

"Where's your mum?" the woman said.

On cue, my mother's screech snatched my attention. "Abby!" Mum hurtled down the aisle with Libby close behind. She grabbed my arm and yanked me close. "What do you think you're doing? I told you never to leave my sight."

"She's okay," said the woman. "She just came running up. She thought she knew my daughter, that's all."

Mum's hand gripped firmly around my arm, but I could still feel her shaking. "I thought she'd gone. I didn't know where she was."

"She's okay," the woman said, her voice soothing.

"What were you thinking?" Mum said to me. "You've upset this lady and her daughter. I think you'd better apologize."

"I thought she was Cassie," I whimpered, pointing to the little girl hiding behind the woman's knees.

My heart felt like a pincushion spiked with tiny shots of pain. This was so unfair. I'd been trying to do something good and all I'd accomplished was to get myself in trouble ... again.

"Apologize now," Mum said.

"I'm sorry," I said to the woman, my lip beginning to tremble. "I'm sorry," I repeated to the girl.

The girl stepped out then and blinked her damp eyelashes up at my mother. My mother's hand dropped from my arm and the color drained from her face. She looked as if she'd seen a ghost. She knew it was Cassie, too.

I looked back and forth between my mother and Cassie, waiting for the realization to dawn, for my mother to spring into action and grab back my sister. But she didn't. In a second, my mother's face regained its composure. She grabbed my hand so hard I winced. "I'm sorry to have frightened you and your little girl," she told the woman. "My daughter made an honest mistake."

The woman looked as if she was going to ask something, but Mum didn't wait to hear. She marched me to where Libby was waiting, a look of horror on her face, and we left the store empty-handed.

My mother got a headache and went to bed as soon as we got home. Dad made us cheese sandwiches for dinner that night. No one mentioned the incident at the supermarket. No one mentioned seeing Cassie. Even Libby passed over the chance to tell me what an idiot I'd been. I took a crumb of comfort at the thought that Cassie's childhood tumbles and scrapes were being dealt with by a gentle, caring person like the woman in the long coat and not with the coldness my mother had displayed. I vowed to look for Cassie every time we went to that supermarket, but my mother shopped somewhere else after that, and I never did see Cassie again.

Now that Cassie had been found, I wondered again at my mother's reaction that day. I'd been so sure she thought the girl was Cassie, even if only for a split second. For months after Cassie went missing, my mother had kept putting up posters and making pleas for Cassie's safe return, seeming to never give up hope. But the way she'd shut out any possibility that day made me wonder if perhaps the unacknowledged truth had eaten away at her all these years. Perhaps her mother's instinct had long ago told her she wouldn't see her daughter alive again. Or perhaps she'd known all along that Cassie was dead.

As for Libby? Libby hadn't said a single word.

TWENTY-FOUR

Georgie had a new hanger-on when I arrived at Coffee & Vinyl. She was wiping the bar in broad circles; he was hypnotized.

"Still going to see your brother later?" I asked her pointedly.

She looked up, smiling. "Absolutely."

She tossed the cloth into the sink. "Show's over," she said to her audience of one, who looked duly heartbroken.

"Complete lech," she said as she led me to a quiet corner table. "Thanks for the save."

"I have something to tell you and I just need you to listen and tell me if I've completely lost the plot, okay?"

Georgie shrugged, as if to ask if I'd expect anything else from her.

"I think someone in my family killed Cassie," I said.

A flicker of shock passed across Georgie's face, but all she said was, "O-kaay."

I reminded her about Uncle Dave's suggestion that Cassie's death had been an accident and that my family had covered it up to protect the guilty party.

"Think about it. All these years, two investigations, and the police haven't turned up even one good suspect. They just keep looking at my dad."

"They always do that."

"That's right. When there's no other obvious suspect, they look at the family. Why? Because seventy-five percent of murder victims are killed by someone they know. Listen to this," I said, pulling out an article I'd found online. "Characteristics of a psychopath. Psychopaths are callous and manipulative but come across as charming. They are organized in their behavior and are able to maintain the appearance of being socially connected. Whereas a sociopath may exhibit random bursts of violence and know they are doing wrong, psychopaths do not feel changes of emotion, even in the most extreme of circumstances." I looked at Georgie, who listened in silence. "Sound like anyone you know?"

"Yeah," Georgie laughed. "It sounds a bit like me, but I definitely did not kill your sister."

I gave Georgie a hard stare. "This isn't a joke, Georgie."

"I'm sorry. It's just weird to be having this conversation."

"It's not exactly a picnic for me," I said.

"Go on."

"What if something happened—an accident, or a sort of accident, a fight perhaps. What if someone hurt Cassie, not deliberately. I mean, what if someone meant to hurt her? Maybe they didn't mean to kill her, but something went wrong?" I pictured the tap shoe Inspector Siddiqi had shown me, recalling how Libby had hated Cassie's tapping. I saw the stain on my mother's shirt. I saw my dad on the dock and the bundle he dropped in the water. It all lined up. "And then what if my family decided to cover it up to protect that person?"

"You're talking about major premeditation. I mean, your

family doesn't strike me as ruthless killers. To cover up something like that and not get caught, they'd either have to be brilliant or really lucky."

"Or expert at putting on a facade," I finished.

"Libby?" said Georgie.

"Libby."

Georgie glanced at me with her mouth open. "Do you think it's possible?"

I did. I told her about the journalist, about Libby all but blaming my dad, about the way that she could lie and manipulate to make herself look good. More than once, Libby had provoked me to the point of fury. Once, she had even pushed until I snapped. That time, she had laughed. It had been cold and cruel, and even as I'd lost my temper and flung myself at her, she had never lost her cool. Even the day before, when she'd taunted me, she had stared at me, her gaze hard and emotionless, her eyes never leaving mine. I had erupted in an outburst of emotion that had scared me. But even more frightening was that Libby had shown none.

I didn't want to believe she was capable of harming Cassie, but Libby had a cruel streak. She could taunt and provoke, then be charming and manipulative. She had done her best to convince me that my feelings and memories couldn't be trusted, but now I felt manipulated. Because I did believe Libby had the ability to harm someone. What I struggled to get my head around was that my entire family had kept the secret and now Libby had pointed her finger at my dad. That was the cruelest thing of all.

"Okay," said Georgie. "For the sake of argument, let's say that's what happened. Let's say Libby went too far. Let's say your parents, who were young, panicked and decided to cover it up to protect her. Libby was, what, ten? Eleven?" I nodded. "So, she's kept that secret all this time? She never said a single word about it to anyone, including you?"

"Right," I said because that was something I could completely see Libby doing. "She's all about her appearance, how she looks to the outside world. She was trained to act calmly, no matter what, but honestly, she's always been that way. I mean, even through all this with Cassie, she's gone to work and acted like nothing's up. That's not normal."

"Well, if she's carried that secret her whole life, there's no wonder she has issues. That's a big secret for a kid to keep."

"Not if she doesn't feel any remorse."

"But why would your parents cover it up? I mean, if it was an accident, it would be terrible, but accidents happen all the time. And even if it was deliberate, Libby was a minor. She wouldn't have been charged or anything."

"I don't know. There was that case a few years ago with two boys who killed their neighbor. Remember? They were taken away from their parents and put into care. Maybe my parents were afraid they'd lose Libby. And lose me, too."

Georgie and her brother had done several spells in foster care when their parents got into trouble. Even though she'd mostly landed in clean, safe homes with caring families, being taken from her parents—no matter how much of a train wreck they were—had been shattering. She understood what my parents were afraid of. "But wouldn't they want to get her help? I mean, they still had you in the house. I'd be worried she'd harm you as well."

"Maybe that's why we moved away. Maybe someone in the neighborhood spotted a problem with Libby, so we moved to a place with no neighbors. Maybe that's why she went to that private school instead of the local secondary school. Maybe she *did* get help. And now that Cassie has been found, Libby is frantic about keeping it quiet. I'm sure she's the one who withdrew my application, too. What better way to keep me quiet than to keep me at home?"

"Except for the interview she set up," Georgie said.

I shook my head. "It was all about looking right. The photo of Cassie, the fake tears, the sad pose. It was all orchestrated to make us look like a normal, grieving family."

As I spoke this out loud, so many pieces of my family's puzzle dropped into place.

"But why Cassie?" Georgie asked. She didn't need to add, "Why not you?"

I told her about my conversation with Uncle Dave and my dad's obsession with the idea that Cassie was not his child.

Georgie looked skeptical. "That makes no sense. If Cassie ..."

"Then neither am I. But if Dad was making a thing of it, maybe he and Mum had an argument, and Libby picked up on it, got it stuck in her head. For someone who's all about appearances, having two illegitimate sisters would be a nightmare. And maybe Cassie provoked her, and Libby lost it."

"Jesus," said Georgie.

"Or that girl she was staying with that night, maybe she made a comment about Cassie not looking like me and Libby. Maybe that's what flipped the switch and pushed Libby over the edge."

"She came home mad ..."

"Embarrassed."

"And what? Put a pillow over Cassie's face?"

I shook my head. Inspector Siddiqi had said Cassie had a

head injury. "Hit her. With a shoe." Cassie's tapping had aggravated Libby from the first moment Cassie had slipped her foot into those shoes. And Libby had finally silenced her.

"Jesus," Georgie said again.

"And then my parents panicked."

My mind flashed again to the image of the man dropping the bundle in the lake. It had always been a terrifying dream, but maybe it hadn't been a dream at all. Maybe I had seen something—seen my own dad—and my six-year-old brain, unable to process such a horror, had shut it out. Until now.

I shook my head, unable to acknowledge, even to my best friend, that this could be my reality.

"Jesus," Georgie breathed again, her face now white. "What are you going to do?"

"I don't know."

"Are you going to tell the police?"

"No."

"But if your dad is charged with murder and it wasn't him …"

"No," I snapped. "Not yet. I don't even know if any of this is true. And if my family has kept this under wraps all this time, there has to be a good reason. I can't just go blurting out some harebrained idea until I'm sure I'm right."

I'd hoped talking this through with Georgie would help it all make sense, but instead, the picture grew murkier. "I don't know what to believe anymore. Something is telling me I'm right, but I can't make the pieces fit."

Georgie scraped the froth from the inside of her cup. But she didn't move.

"All right, all right," she said. "Let's say you're right. Let's say this is all some big cover-up. So what?"

I sank back into my seat. She had a point. What would change if this was true? It wouldn't bring Cassie back. And it wouldn't bring me any peace. I might have found the answer to the question that had dogged me my whole life, but it would open up a million new questions.

"I'd have to go to the police," I said at last.

"Turn Libby in?"

"What if she did it again, Georgie? What if she got jealous of me one day?"

Georgie swallowed. "You can't go home. It's not safe."

"I can't go to the police until I'm sure, though. I need more to go on than this."

I didn't know what would happen if the truth came out. Maybe my sister would be charged with killing Cassie. But Libby had been just a child, too. Maybe she'd be committed for psych care? I had no idea. What I did know was that Libby would have to bear the stigma of violence for the rest of her life. Everyone would see right through the mask she'd so carefully constructed. People would look at her differently, knowing that she was capable of harming another human being and, perhaps even more frightening, that she had been able to keep her secret so easily for so long.

And my parents. What would happen to them if people knew what they had done? They had hidden the body of their daughter and faked her disappearance. And they had kept up their facade for more than a decade. If the truth came out, it would kill my mother; she would literally die of shame. Uncle Dave said Cassie's death had eaten away at my mother, but perhaps the real damage had been done by carrying the knowledge that her daughter was capable of violence. No wonder my mother had chosen to hide her family away.

As for me, would I somehow be an accessory in all this? Even if I wasn't, I could kiss my plans to work with children goodbye. Even if I sorted out my application and the university decided to accept me with all my psychological baggage, the fallout from this would be huge. I'd have to pick up the pieces of a shattered life and start all over again. And I'd have to live with the knowledge that I had been the one to break open my family's terrible secret.

I felt sick. My family had put me through hell: changing schools, losing friends, standing like a performing monkey while they lied. My whole life, I had carried around a dark hole left by my twin. Over time, it had shrunk, but not knowing what had happened to Cassie, always wondering if she would one day come back, meant that hole had never been allowed to close.

And now it had torn open again.

"Where will you go?" asked Georgie, her voice low now. "After it all comes out?"

My head shot up, the silence between us buzzing in my ears. Georgie was right. If I turned Libby in, what would become of me? I couldn't stay, but how would I survive without my family? I couldn't support myself, and my plans for a career were crumbling. "Not far," I said, trying to think fast. "But I can't be around them now that I know this. My whole life is a giant lie." I shook my head. "I always thought we were a strong family. I was always proud that we'd stuck together through all we'd been through. But now, if this is true, it changes everything."

Now we really would be The Killer Kirkpatricks.

TWENTY-FIVE

When I got home, Libby wasn't there. She'd left a note stuck to the fridge door: "Flying. Back Wednesday. Smoothies in the fridge. Want to talk when I get back." So typical of Libby to be cryptic. Well, I wasn't going to worry about our "talk" now, at least for the time being.

I opened the fridge door. Libby had lined up three glass jars, prefilled with frozen fruit and protein powder. All I had to do was add water and blend. Drink my little milkshake like a good girl. I slammed the door shut. I didn't need anyone mothering me, especially not Libby. I could fend for myself. But, first, I had some things to do.

It took me ages to get through to the right person at the school accreditation office, and then she put me on the longest hold in history. I paced the kitchen, trying to relax. Even though I had the place to myself, I was still nervous about getting caught. I needed time to get some answers.

"Looks like you withdrew your application on August twenty-second," said the woman when she finally came back on the phone. "Does that sound right?"

I jotted down the date, trying not to focus on what it meant just yet. "It was a mistake," I said. "My mum's really ill and I've been preoccupied. I must have clicked the wrong button or something. Can I fix it?"

The woman said she would email a form for me to sign. She would do her best to get me reinstated before the university sent their final admission letters.

I thanked her for her help and hung up. I barely cared about the stupid application anymore. She had given me what I needed to know.

I took my mother's flower calendar down from the kitchen wall and flipped back to the previous month. I tapped on the date Cassie had been found. Libby came home the next day, and I was withdrawn from the application process the following Thursday. That was the day Georgie and I had gone to the lake, the day Dad had been questioned by Inspector Siddiqi. With my mother in the hospital, that left only one person in my family able to make that change.

My stomach sank. From my own mouth, I had told Georgie that if I truly suspected Libby, I would have to go to the police. I needed to be sure. I needed someone who would validate the very worst of my fears.

Paula's card was still in the back of my drawer where I'd hidden it. If Libby had been snooping, at least she hadn't found that. Paula never returned my call. Maybe she didn't want to stir up old memories for me, as Inspector Siddiqi had said. But I wanted my memories stirred; I wanted to uncover anything that would help me find the truth about what had happened to Cassie, no matter how close to home it came.

I texted Paula on the number she'd written in the card, thanking her for coming to Cassie's funeral.

> Great to see you again.

She responded right away that she was glad she'd been there and that she'd love to catch up. A few minutes later, we were messaging back and forth.

She told me about the old neighborhood, caught me up on people whose names I hadn't heard for years. I laughed when she reminded me of the time we let her rabbit escape. And then she wrote:

> I was really sad when you moved away

> Me too.

> I thought about you all the time, but I was afraid to contact you. Your mum didn't want it, and my mum said I shouldn't push it, but I missed my best friend.

I hadn't wanted to move. Looking back, maybe the best way for me to have dealt with losing Cassie would have been to be around people who knew me and cared for me, people like Paula. Instead, I had been swept away from a friendly community to an old house in the middle of nowhere.

> And then Libby found me.

> What? When?

> Few years back. I sent another letter. She said I should leave you alone. She asked me to stay away after the funeral.

I pictured Libby having this conversation. It would have been more of a threat than a suggestion.

Asked?

Told.

She added a laughing emoji, though I doubted she found this funny.

Another message came in.

She was always pushy, wasn't she? Always telling you what to do. Bit terrifying, really. She was jealous of you.

Me?

You were everyone's favorite.

No way. Cassie was always the favorite.

Don't want to speak ill of the dead, but Cassie was a bit of a mare. So moody, always provoking people. I just wanted to play with you. Lot less fun with Cassie around.

My whole body tightened as a little truth fluttered around. A flash of a memory came to me, of Paula and me playing with our dolls and Cassie storming in. I had pushed her, not hard, but she had run to tell Mum. It was Libby who'd come up. I remember her face now, fierce with rage. "Run for your lives," Paula had squealed. Had she been closer to the truth than she'd known?

Everyone was shocked when Cassie went missing, especially when they arrested your dad, Paula wrote. But honestly, Abby, no one was surprised. Your family was like a ticking time bomb, and you were the only one remotely normal.

I didn't feel normal. I felt like I was slowly losing my grip on reality. I couldn't trust anything anymore, not even my own memories.

I had to tell someone what I thought I knew. But what I knew still wasn't enough. The answers were in this house somewhere. I knew it. But how could I find them if I didn't know what I was looking for?

I went to Dad's office first, pulled open drawers and thumbed through his shelves. There was nothing unusual there. My mother's study, where we'd done our lessons, was equally ordinary. On the top floor of the house, I opened the door to Libby's old room. The bed was made and the few possessions she'd left were neatly organized. Whatever it was I was looking for wasn't there.

I was about to give up when I noticed the heavy oak chest of drawers under the window. One of the round ball feet no longer sat in its original indentation on the carpet. Someone had moved it, and judging by the depth of the indentation and the way the carpet fibers had not bounced back, it had been moved recently.

I tugged at the dresser until it budged away from the wall. I ran my hand across the back as if I expected a secret door to pop open, but it was just a plain old dresser. I felt the edges of the carpet to see if they would lift, but they were firmly tacked down. As I stood, the trapdoor to the attic came into my field of vision. A tingle of anticipation prickled across my cheeks. I leaned my weight into the dresser, and it shifted across the floor. Hopping on top, I had just enough height to flip the trapdoor open and, thanks to my boxing, enough upper body strength to pull myself inside. The first thing I noticed was a wide track through the dust on the floor as if something had been slid away from the opening. I clicked on the flashlight and followed the path. It ended at a box ... the same box I had seen in Dad's office.

I hoisted myself up through the trapdoor and flipped open the box's lid. I'd been right about the slips of paper; they were prescriptions. I'd only been half-right about the patient, though. On some, the name scrawled across the top was my dad's, but on most, it was Libby's. I recognized the names of some of the more recent drugs from my Project Talk training: Antianxiety medications, antidepressants, and sleeping pills. My dad's change in personality could easily be explained by his medications, but my sister was a walking pharmacy and judging by the number of prescriptions, she had been for a long time. I dug down in the box, sifting through increasingly yellowed slips. I wasn't surprised to see the dates on the papers at the bottom. The oldest ones went back to the months after Cassie disappeared.

Libby and I had both been traumatized by Cassie's disappearance. I had struggled through my grief for years, often alone. But Libby had been granted medical help. Maybe she had demanded it. Like she'd demanded to go to school while I was schooled at home. Like she'd demanded we not tell my mother when Cassie had first been found. Like she demanded everything her own way and my parents gave in because it was easier than fighting with Libby. Easier to give a demanding child—or a demanding adult—what she wanted, especially if that adult had a history of getting things her way, no matter what.

Or maybe Libby's mental health care had been essential, the only way to calm an out-of-control girl who had harmed her little sister.

I thought about Dad and his militant routine of smoothies and cocoa. He had forced his "healthy habits" on all of us. Had he secretly been medicating Libby to smooth the dangerous edges of her personality? Had he ever slipped something into mine? Had this been his sick idea of getting us help?

Flicking the beam of the flashlight around the attic, I was surprised to see Libby's "Private" box still there, even though she hadn't lived at home for almost five years. It was pushed back into the farthest corner of the attic with the "Xmas Decos" box stacked on top. A peek under the flap of the top box revealed ancient tinsel and faded glass ornaments. I pushed the box aside and, sure I was inching closer to finding more answers, opened Libby's box.

Inside were the same old postcards and photos, a fuzzy-haired troll doll, and pictures of a favorite boy band. The photos were of Libby's old friends from the neighborhood where we'd grown up. The postcards were from Mexico, Algeria, and India, all over the world, and notes from pen pals chronicling lives far away. If Libby had made friends at her new school after we moved, there was no evidence of them in her box of memories. Her friendships had been distant, controlled, safe from spontaneous questions and dangerous answers.

There were two letters tucked under the bottom of the stack. I wasn't surprised when I turned them over and saw my own name above the address in Paula's once-familiar handwriting. If it had been my parents' idea to cut me off from my former life, Libby had made sure the past stayed far behind me. What else had she masterminded to keep me where she needed me to be?

Reaching down the side of the box, my hand found a yellow manila envelope. It looked newer than the other mementos. There was nothing written on the front. I squeezed it open and tipped out the contents. Five colored books slipped into my palm.

Passports.

There were burgundy passports from the United Kingdom and Germany, a navy-blue American one, a red one from Norway, and a black one embossed with silver feathers that had "New Zealand" stamped across the front. I didn't recognize the names of the owners, but the photos were startling. Every woman in them resembled Libby.

My tongue stuck to the roof of my mouth. I swallowed and wet my lips, trying to make sense of the damning evidence I held in my hands. My best guess was that the passports had gone "missing" from Libby's flights. My body turned cold at the thought of Libby flying around the world, responsible for the safety and well-being of passengers, smiling her practiced smile, and all the while stealing IDs and relying on drugs to keep her dark side at bay.

She was a disaster waiting to happen and it was time someone knew the truth.

TWENTY-SIX

"Okay, tell me again," said Inspector Siddiqi, tapping the end of her pen against the desk and looking like she hadn't understood a word I'd said. "Where were you that night?"

"In bed. Asleep."

"And Cassie was in the bed across from you?"

"Yes."

"But you said you were asleep, so are you sure she was there?"

"We went to bed at the same time. That's all I know."

"And where was Libby when you went to bed?"

"At a friend's cabin."

"But you say she came home."

"Yes. She phoned late and my parents, my mum, went to get her."

"And you saw her?"

I shook my head. "But I know she was there."

Inspector Siddiqi tilted back her chair, her hands clasped behind her head. She blew air through tight lips like she had more important things to do than squeeze useless information out of me.

"Tell you what," she said. "Why don't I get us some tea, and while I'm away, maybe you can put together a solid case for why you think it was your sister who killed Cassie and not the man we've arrested and charged. All right?"

My earlier conviction wavered. I had found evidence in the passports that Libby was untrustworthy, perhaps setting herself up to disappear at short notice. I had researched the prescriptions and confirmed that all the medications Libby had been given were used to treat behavioral issues specifically related to anger and explosive outbursts. Libby had manipulated my parents and manipulated me. She had threatened Paula, tampered with my application, and done it all with a calm demeanor and a cool smile on her face.

And yet I felt like an idiot because all the evidence I'd amassed against Libby was nothing more than speculation. I hadn't *seen* her hurt Cassie—I hadn't seen her at all that night —I just *felt* that Libby had something to hide. Everything she'd done was suspicious, but there was no way that would stand up in court. Still, with absolute conviction, I knew I was right.

As I tried to put my thoughts in order and build a more solid case, all hell broke loose outside Inspector Siddiqi's office door. The main source of the commotion was a woman whose ample flesh was barely constrained by her tight-fitting clothes as she flailed her arms and screeched obscenities at the officers attempting to calm her down.

"What kind of a man treats the mother of his children like this, eh? I ask ya. Not a real man, I'll tell ya that much."

From the holding cells down the hall, another voice boomed back. "He's not my effin' kid, and you know it. And you're nuffin' but a fat slag what dun't know what side 'er bread's buttered."

"You *are* 'is father, God 'elp me," she screamed back, then turned to me as she passed Inspector Siddiqi's door. "He *is* the father, but he won't hear it."

I nodded and looked away. I'd passed a small interview room on the way in, where two little boys were squeezed together in a chair, eating chips and watching cartoons. They were so close in age I thought at first they must be friends. Although one was dark-haired and the other blond, and their faces and body types quite different, there was just enough resemblance that they could have been related. The boys, I assumed, were the root of the screaming match.

I tried to clear my head, so I could tell the inspector calmly and succinctly what I believed about my own sister, but the argument down the hallway raged on, and I could barely hear myself think.

Two officers passed by the door of the office. "Hey, Siddiqi," the younger of the two called out, "fancy a bet?"

I didn't hear Inspector Siddiqi's answer, but the constable said, "Ten quid he's not the father."

"Paternity test says he is, but he claims it's his brother's kid," his partner said, tipping a stream of sugar into a mug of creamy coffee. "Don't fancy being at that family's Christmas dinner."

"Don't you two have bad guys to catch or something," said Inspector Siddiqi, shaking her head as she returned with two paper cups of tea.

"Quiet day for that sort of stuff," the younger policeman said. "Better than TV, this is," referring to the tabloid talk show host. "So, what do you say, Siddiqi? Bet me a tenner?"

"Not today," she said. "Saving for my vacation."

The policeman laughed. "Right. That'll be the day. Send us a postcard when you go."

"Yeah, you'll be first on my list."

She came back into the office, bumping the door closed with her hip. "Sorry about that. Things can get a wee bit stressful around here, and the boys like to blow off steam."

"They should try boxing," I said, accepting the cup of tea she offered. I forced a smile, but I couldn't help wondering if there'd been bets about Cassie or my dad or even me.

"Right," she said. "About your sister."

It was pointless. I knew what Libby had done and that Dad was protecting her, but until I had something more concrete, some real evidence, I was wasting the inspector's time, and we both knew it.

"Forget it," I said.

"Well, wait a minute. You seemed pretty sure you had something to tell me when you walked in here. What happened?"

What happened was I felt like an idiot. What happened was that she was in the serious business of solving crimes and she didn't have time for a foolish feeling.

"I'm sorry to waste your time."

I got up to leave, wanting to get out of there as quickly as I could, but Inspector Siddiqi stopped me.

"Before you go, would you be willing to give us a cheek swab?" she said. "Obviously, you're not a suspect in this case, but it might help us get the answers I know you're desperately looking for."

She gave me a warm smile that made me want to cry. I *was* desperate, so desperate I was willing to turn in my own sister based on a hunch. I needed all this to be over. I needed my sanity.

"Fine," I said. "I can do that. Can I see my dad after that?"

If I could get him alone, I would ask him for answers. But Inspector Siddiqi shook her head. "Not yet."

It wasn't until I was alone with the assigned officer that I wondered if I should have said no to the test. As she showed me how she would swab my cheek, I kept thinking about the argument and the bet I'd overheard. Two brothers arguing over the paternity of a child. A horrible thought put down roots inside me. Uncle Dave said Dad believed Cassie and I weren't his. Had Libby suspected too? Was I about to get my evidence, or was I about to deliver the motive that would implicate my dad?

I pictured Cassie's blue eyes, her dark eyebrows, and now the secrets that hid behind them. It couldn't be. It wasn't possible. Cassie and I were sisters. We were *twins*. And we were Dad's.

Too late, the officer ran the swab inside my cheek, my family's guilt and secrets clinging to the fuzzy white end.

When we were done, Inspector Siddiqi showed me out, ushering me past the two officers now exchanging money by the coffee machine.

"Sure you don't want to take that bet, Siddiqi?" the young one said.

"Trust me, it's his kid," she said. "Paternity tests don't lie, but frustrated wives do."

The policeman laughed. "It's the brother's."

She stopped then, glanced at me for a second, then looked away. "What makes you think it's the brother's, then? Paternity test says it's not."

I tensed. Had Uncle Dave told her what he'd told me about

my dad's jealousy? Had he divulged the secret of my parents' strained marriage and the specter of infidelity?

The policeman shrugged. "Those online tests are useless. A man knows these things. It's male intuition, innit? He might have raised that kid as his own, cos it's the right thing to do, like. He's got a kid of his own and they're like brothers. Don't want to split up the family and all that. But deep in his heart," he tapped his chest and gave Inspector Siddiqi a meaningful look. "A man knows."

My brain lit up like an old-fashioned telephone switchboard. I plugged in one line after another, trying to make a connection go through.

And then there it was. The missing link. Love, betrayal, jealousy, all the classic motives. But surely it wasn't possible.

Once outside, I ran to Georgie's car and hopped in. "I need you to look something up on your phone."

Georgie huffed. "We have got to get you a proper phone soon. How can you survive with that medieval machine?"

"Never mind that now," I said. "Just look up paternity tests. I need to know how accurate they are."

"What?"

"Please, Georgie," I said.

"Okay, okay." Her thumbs flew across the keypad. "This one says it's good to fifteen markers. That's about ninety-nine percent accurate."

"Keep looking. Add 'brothers' to your search and see what it says."

"Bro ...?"

"Please."

"Okay, okay." She went quiet for a minute and then she

said, "Huh. Says here that most at-home tests are reliable enough to tell apart two people who aren't related."

"But if they *are* related?"

"It says you'd have to get more matches than most at-home tests provide. Even then, it can be deceptive. What are you getting at, Abby?"

"Can you look for one more thing?"

"'Course."

"Search 'can twins have different fathers?'"

She laughed. "What?"

"Georgie."

She tapped at her phone, sounding out the words. "Can. Twins. Oh, look at that. Pops right up. *Can twins have different dads?*"

I waited for her to click through, dizzy with the anticipation of what she might find.

"Well, I never," she said at last. "I had no idea."

No, I thought. *But someone in my family does.*

TWENTY-SEVEN

"You're Cassie's father, aren't you?" I asked when Uncle Dave answered his phone. "Did you take her that night? Did you?"

I wanted him to say yes. I wanted to hear that a man who'd been a stranger for most of my life had been the one to harm my sister. I wanted to know that I'd been wrong about Libby, after all.

He didn't answer.

"I know about you and my mum. I know you think Cassie was yours. You knew it was possible we could have different dads. My parents knew too, didn't they? That's why they wouldn't let you see her. That's why you and my dad weren't speaking."

Uncle Dave said nothing and, in doing so, answered me loud and clear. "Did you take her that night?"

For an agonizing few seconds, I willed him to tell me everything, how he'd tried to get time with Cassie, how my dad had banned him from our lives, how my mother had sat by and let it happen, and how finally, Uncle Dave had reached his limit and decided to take matters into his own hands. How something had gone wrong, an accident, just like he'd told me. How he hadn't meant to kill Cassie. How he'd lived with the terrible truth all these years.

"She was my daughter," he said tenderly. "And I never got the chance to be her dad."

My chest squeezed around my heart as I imagined Cassie with this man as her dad, pictured the joyful, love-filled life she could have had.

"But I would never have hurt her," he said. "I would have done anything for her. I thought that someday she'd find out and come looking for me. I thought we would make up for lost time. As much as I hated your dad for keeping me away from her—and I did hate him, really hated him for that—I knew Cassie was better off with her mum, with you." He was quiet for a moment, then he said, "I was wrong."

The ache in my chest grew and spread as I understood why Uncle Dave had been so attached to Cassie. The resemblance was so clear, now I knew to look for it. No wonder my dad had been jealous. He had been forced to look at the truth every single day.

But now, my heartache curled up at the edges, hardening into anger. The secrets and lies my family had kept had eaten their way into everything like moths set free in an attic full of wool sweaters. Nothing was as it seemed.

One thing was clear though. If Libby had killed Cassie, even accidentally, my dad suddenly had a motive for wanting to hide the truth. So did someone else. Someone who couldn't stand the shame.

"There you are," said a breezy voice when I reached Mum's floor at the hospital. "We haven't seen you for a while. We were starting to get worried."

"Is my mother okay?" I said, feeling guilty. From her first diagnosis, we had made sure my mother hadn't gone through anything alone. When Mum had first become ill, we had worked together—Libby, Dad, and me—to make sure someone was with her for every doctor appointment, every infusion, every support group meeting, everything. We had created a roster and adjusted our schedules to switch off duties, adamant that Mum would never be alone. But with everything that had happened, my mother had been neglected.

"She's fine. Up and down, same as usual." The nurse sucked in a breath, and I could picture her biting on her bottom lip with a tea-stained tooth. "She was a bit upset this afternoon. I called your sister, but she never got back to me."

"She's flying. What's wrong?"

"Someone put the television on in her room. A volunteer. She didn't know she wasn't supposed to. Your mum was tired this afternoon, too tired to sit up, so the volunteer put the television on for her. It was one of those talk shows about missing children. They mentioned your sister. Your mum got upset."

"What did she say?" I asked, trying to keep the panic out of my voice. I hoped my mother hadn't blurted to a total stranger the secret I so desperately wanted to know.

"She was just blabbering," the nurse said. "Saying how sorry she was, that it was all her fault." She shook her head. "The poor thing," she said. "I can't imagine."

Something inside me, something small, hardened. My mother was blaming herself for what had happened to Cassie, something any parent might do. But I no longer believed my mother was entirely without fault.

"I'll talk to her," I said. "But please ... *please* make sure it doesn't happen again."

"It's getting harder and harder for us to keep her away from it."

"I know, but if you could just—"

"We're busy." Her voice rose. "You know how busy we are, and there can't always be someone watching her to see if she puts the television on. We can't control what everyone says or does. People talk and we can't protect her all the time." She paused, gathering herself back together. "We wondered if you'd thought about taking her home?"

Her question pinned me in place with the sharp point she had clearly made. My mother was dying, would die, and maybe it was time to take her home to let her do it in peace. But home was the last place she would find peace, and if what I had learned was true, I doubted she would ever find peace again.

"We'll think about it," was all I said.

My mother was alone in her room. Watching her sleep in her plain white bed, the hospital lights glaring above, the constant hum of activity all around her, my mother had never looked more pitiful. Her illness had forced her to sleep through the slow destruction of her family, but perhaps she'd been sleeping through it for a long time. At some point, she had chosen to shut out reality, to keep pretending that everything was okay. Meanwhile, the secrets, the guilt, the regrets had eaten away at her. Our family was disintegrating from the inside, and so was my mother.

She stirred from her sleep and looked at me drowsily. It seemed to take her several seconds to realize who I was. At that moment, I was glad Cassie and I had not been identical twins, barely resembling one another. What would it have been like for my mother to look at me every day for ten years and see a reminder of what she had done, what she had been a part of? But Cassie and I had not been alike in so many ways, and perhaps that was the real source of my mother's guilt and shame.

"Libby?" she whispered at last.

I flinched at her mistake. I was not like Libby, not at all, at least not in personality. A knot formed in my throat at the thought that my mother's life was coming to an end, that she no longer knew who I was.

"Libby's flying, Mum," I said softly. "She'll be back in a couple of days. It's me. Abby."

"Abby," she said, but she didn't smile. "I know." She seemed to sink into the bed as if gathering the last of her reserves. "I saw Cassie today. On the news." Her eyes shot toward me, her gaze suddenly focused and fierce. "They arrested your dad."

I scooted my chair closer. It would have been so easy to blame my dad and Libby, to tell my mother that I'd wanted to tell her everything from the beginning. "We didn't want to upset you, Mum. You need to focus on getting well."

My mother nodded, and I wondered how much she'd heard from the news and how much she had known all along. This woman, lying in her sickbed, did not look like someone who could have lived with this knowledge, an accomplice in the death of a child. It would take a monster to live that way.

"It wasn't your dad."

I nodded to say I knew that and waited for her to tell me more, to finally tell me everything. But her gaze drifted to the corner of the room, and I felt her drift away.

"Mum?" I whispered. "Mum, do you know what happened that night?"

She didn't answer. She reached for her pain button, but I got there before her and snatched it away.

"Mum," I prompted.

"We were so stupid," she said, her voice barely loud enough for me to hear. "We were young and stupid. And scared." Her eyes filled with tears and her fingers reached for the button that I held just out of reach.

"We thought we were doing the right thing, protecting you and Libby."

My stomach tightened as the horror of what she was telling me hit me. My mother had lied and fabricated a story. She had kept up her act for years, harboring a killer in her own family. She had created a child capable of harming another human being. Like a Greek tragedy, she had spawned one child who had killed another, the child of another man. She had created Libby, and then she'd tried to hide us all away.

She shook her head. "It will all come out now. You'll find out everything." Her voice broke, and tears rolled down her temples as she closed her eyes. "You'll have to be strong, Abby," she whispered. "You'll all have to be strong."

You'll have to be strong, she'd said. *You*, not *we*. My mother would take her secret to her grave. And she would leave her children to face the consequences of her actions. The knot in my stomach turned to fury. I wanted to tip my mother from her bed and watch her suffer for what she had done to me. My hand bunched into a fist around my mother's pain drip.

I had to go. I couldn't be with this person any longer. But as I turned, something caught my eye in the doorway. A flash of blonde hair and cool blue-green eyes boring into me. Maybe I imagined it. I must have imagined it because she'd told me she was working. And yet I was certain that I had seen her. I had seen my sister Libby.

"What's the matter?" my mother said, her expression placid. "You look like you've seen a ghost."

Not a ghost, I thought, running for the door. I had seen a killer.

Twenty-Eight

I raced from my mother's room, dodging dawdling visitors, my shoes squeaking against the polished floor. The fluorescent lights cast patches of light as I ran beneath them. I brushed by a group of doctors and rounded a corner to a bank of closed elevator doors. There was no sign of Libby. At the end of the hall, an Emergency Exit sign beckoned me. I pulled open the door and peered down the stairwell. Below me, the ground floor door banged closed. A sign on the wall caught my attention. "Have you washed your hands?"

I ran back to the elevators and pushed the button, willing it to hurry. My thoughts scrambled with all the things I'd learned in the past few days and all the gaps in my knowledge. But one thing I knew now with absolute certainty: Libby had killed Cassie. The person I had known and trusted my whole life had murdered my twin sister. My family had kept the secret from me, hidden me away from anyone who might know or guess. But I knew now. And Libby knew that I had worked it out. She had lied about being on a flight today, and she had come looking for me. With my mother fading fast and my dad in custody, I was the last possible witness—or at least link—to her crime. I had to face the possibility that Libby needed to wash her hands of me.

When the elevator arrived, I bolted inside and pushed the button for the ground floor. I didn't expect to catch Libby, but I had to try. Bit by bit, all the pieces began falling into place. No wonder Dad and Libby had wanted to keep Cassie's discovery from my mother. It wasn't because they didn't want to dig up the old pain; it was because they didn't want my mother to be scared that we might now be exposed, that my parents' role in the cover-up would come to light, that my dying mother, who should be cared for and nurtured, would suddenly be reviled.

As the elevator pinged its arrival, a terrible thought flashed into my mind. What if Libby had not been at the hospital looking for me? What if she'd come for my mother? In her drug-addled state, my mother had blabbered about it being her fault, not making sense to her nurses but making complete sense to the killer she was protecting. I hesitated, torn between saving my mother and tracking down Libby. But my mother was not going to be saved. For now, she was protected, but my mother was not going to get out of this alive.

I stepped from the elevator and ran for the hospital exit, hoping to spot Libby and planning what to do when I didn't find her.

Everything started to make sense now. Our moving away, the distance put between us and friends. It hadn't been a fresh start to protect Libby and me from gossip and stares. We'd been taken away in case we said something we shouldn't. And what about Uncle Dave? The rift between him and Dad took on a new meaning now. He had suspected, hadn't he? He speculated there'd been "an accident." He'd known that something wasn't right, and he'd been shut out.

And me? I had been brainwashed. All these years, I had believed my family was strong, that we had taken care of one another and protected each other from the outside world. But that wasn't the case at all. The protective shell wasn't to keep others out. It was to keep the truth in.

I texted Georgie.

She didn't respond. I called her instead, but still no answer. More pieces of this messy puzzle slotted into place. My sister would do anything now to keep her secret. And I had confided my suspicions to Georgie. I had a very bad feeling that Georgie's silence had something to do with Libby.

———

I stabbed at the doorbell three times before Georgie's roommate, Gary, opened the door. Even though it was already midafternoon, he looked like he'd just stumbled out of bed. I caught my breath from run walking the short distance from the hospital, told him I was looking for Georgie.

"Not seen her," he said unhelpfully.

"Has she been here at all?"

"Last night, I think. She went out early though. I think I heard her."

"I've been trying to get hold of her, but she won't answer her phone."

Gary ran a hand through his hair so that it stuck straight up. "Huh," was all he said.

My stomach sank. This wasn't like Georgie at all. Something was niggling inside me, telling me that this was all wrong.

"Now I think about it," said Gary, blinking as if his brain had just turned on. "I did get a weird message from her."

"What kind of message?"

He opened the door and indicated for me to follow him into the kitchen. It was spotless. Clearly, Georgie had been cleaning. A stack of pans and dishes stood on the draining rack. If Georgie left in a hurry, she'd made sure to clean up after herself first. Maybe I'd expected overturned chairs, a sign of a struggle. Or maybe that was just me being dramatic.

Gary moved like he was being chased by a snail. He found his phone under a pile of bills and scrolled through a thousand alerts until he got to Georgie's message. "Here. 'If you don't hear from me by nine, this is where I am.' And then an address."

He turned the screen to me so I could see Georgie's message.

The address Georgie had left was mine.

Outside Georgie's, I punched Inspector Siddiqi's number into my phone, my fingers trembling. But I wavered over the call button, dread churning my insides. The last piece of the terrible puzzle had dropped into place. And yet, it hadn't so much dropped as pushed. Even though the picture at first seemed complete, something was just a little bit off.

The picture I saw was that Libby had come home from her friend's cabin the night Cassie disappeared, upset about something. Maybe she'd thrown a tantrum, or maybe she was mad at Cassie for something. Maybe the friend had made a comment about Cassie's different looks and embarrassed Libby. Whatever it was, Libby had come home in a mood. Maybe she'd taken it out on Cassie, or maybe she'd been making a fuss and hit Cassie accidentally. But one way or another, Libby had killed Cassie. I didn't see her do it and I couldn't prove it, but every part of my gut told me I was right this time. My parents had hidden it for all these years, but then Cassie had been found. I had sniffed out that something was wrong, and then I had made the biggest mistake of my life. I had told Georgie.

It was so obvious now. Libby had told me over and over to keep it to myself, to keep Georgie out of it. She'd even called Georgie the day I'd been to Uncle Dave's, no doubt threatening her to stay away from me.

But I hadn't listened. I'd told Georgie everything and now my best friend—my only friend—knew too much.

I stared at Inspector Siddiqi's number, not knowing what to do. If a missing person wasn't found within the first twenty-four hours, the odds of finding them alive diminished quickly. Was Georgie actually missing? Or was this all an innocent mistake that I had overblown?

But it wasn't innocent. Libby had lied about being on a flight today. When she'd seen me at the hospital, she had fled. She'd called Georgie multiple times, and today Georgie had gone to our house, where Libby would undoubtedly be waiting for her. And now I knew what those stolen passports were for. Once Libby had silenced Georgie, she could disappear.

I had to tell Inspector Siddiqi. If I was wrong, I'd look like an idiot. But if I was right ....

Just then, my own phone rang, causing me to jump and my heart to race. I looked at the screen.

Libby.

I wasn't sure what to do. I didn't want to talk to her, didn't want to answer her questions or hear more lies. But it was the only way to get closer to the truth.

"Hello?"

"Hi, Abby," she chirped in a fake cheery voice. "Listen, my flight got canceled, so I went by the house and dropped off some groceries for you. I was going to make you a lasagna, but then the office called, and I had to pick up another shift, so I had to go in. But I think I left the oven on. Are you going to be home soon?"

"I don't know," I said warily.

"Are you close?"

I thought quickly. She'd seen me at the hospital around four, but that was more than an hour ago. I scanned the area, wondering if she was watching me. If she knew exactly where I was. I decided to take a chance on the truth.

"I went to see Mum," I said.

"Oh, really?"

Yes, really, I thought. *So, this is the game.* "I'm in town now. I can head back if you like."

"Oh, could you? That would take such a load off my mind. You can make the five-thirty bus if you hurry."

A flicker of apprehension flared in me. Libby hadn't lived at home for more than five years, always arriving by taxi when she visited. I couldn't recall the last time she'd taken a bus, but suddenly she knew the timetable off by heart? Clever Libby had the whole thing planned out.

"I'll pay you back," she said.

I bet you will, I thought. *I bet you'll pay me back.*

I had to think quickly. If I caught the five-thirty bus home, Libby would be waiting for me. I would be alone with her in that house on the edge of the moors. There was no one left to miss me if I went missing. My life had been set up perfectly to make me invisible.

But Inspector Siddiqi knew I existed.

"Can we talk?" I asked when she answered my call.

"I'm all ears." I could hear her rummaging on her desk, probably for her notepad and pen.

"Not on the phone," I said. "I think I've remembered something. I don't know if it will be useful, and I need to check one more thing before I say too much, but .... I know this is all a bit cryptic and I'm sorry."

"This isn't about Libby again, is it?" she asked.

"No," I lied.

"Is everything okay?"

Everything was far from okay, but I needed to move carefully. "I wonder, it's a bit tricky for me to get down to the station now, but is it possible you could swing by the house?"

"Um, I could," she said a little hesitantly. "It won't be until after seven. Will that be too late?"

"That'd be perfect," I said. But in my mind, I thought, *God, I hope it won't be too late.*

TWENTY-NINE

My plan was this: I'd go back to the house, just as Libby had asked. If the oven was on and everything was as it should be, I'd call Inspector Siddiqi back, tell her I'd made a mistake. But just in case my hunch was right, just in case Libby was there waiting for me, Inspector Siddiqi would arrive on the scene within an hour or two. Somebody would know I wasn't where I was supposed to be. Someone would care.

The house was dark. I stood at the bottom of the empty driveway, wondering if I was making a huge mistake. My gut said that Libby would be there waiting for me, but there was no sign of her. I took a breath and headed up to the house.

I was about to press my key into the lock of the front door when a thought came to me. I walked around the back of the house, and there was Georgie's car. Parked out of sight.

My first instinct was to leave, to get away from the house and .... And do what? Abandon Georgie? Call Inspector Siddiqi again? And tell her what?

How could I explain that I was afraid of my sister, that I had deduced what her professional detective work had been unable to crack? That my sister was a killer and that my family had been protecting her. That the search for Cassie's killer had come close but was off by one generation, one family member. And that family member would do anything to keep her secret safe. There was a tiny part of me, perhaps an overly hopeful part, that still wasn't sure. If I was right, my family would be destroyed. But if I was wrong. If I accused Libby of this terrible crime and I was wrong ... then what? I couldn't say anything until I was certain.

Steeling myself for whatever I would find, I slid my key into the lock. As I pushed the door open, my hackles rose. Something was wrong. The air crackled with tension. Fear was contagious. It could spread from one person to another, jumping vast gaps, but it was transmitted by living things. The fear that crawled up my back as I stepped into my own house was emanating from something alive. Something, or someone, was in the house, and they were nervous.

Keeping my phone handy, I leaned into the house, listening for signs of life.

Silence.

From the kitchen came the faint glow of the clock on the stove. The oven didn't appear to be on. Libby had set me up. She was here. And she was waiting for me.

I left the front door ajar and eased through the kitchen toward the living room, my senses sparking on high alert.

In a horror movie, this would be the point where the hapless victim steps right into the hands of the killer while the audience shrinks back in their seats, urging her back. But running wouldn't help me. This wasn't a stranger in my house. This was my sister. I could run as long as I wanted, but I would never outrun her. Whatever she wanted of me, she would find a way to get it.

My pulse thudded in my ears as I stepped toward the living room. My breath came in tiny puffs, in and out, so that my head felt light and fuzzy. At the door to the living room, I wet my lips, my tongue cemented to the roof of my mouth. I took a breath and reached into the room. My hand found the light switch. I held my breath and flipped the switch.

Light shone into the room, dazzling me. Right in the center of it all was Libby.

Inside me, something clicked. All my survival instincts snapped into place, and I lunged across the room at Libby. Her arm lifted as if she'd been expecting me, but I barreled forward. My fear exploded into rage. A familiar feeling blossomed in my chest, that vibration of a switch that could click over at any second. I pinned Libby against the table. She grabbed my arms, but she didn't fight. Her stare was cold and hard.

The room blurred around me, and I had the strangest feeling of déjà vu. My empty hand tightened, and my mind recalled something smooth and flexible grasped in my small fist. My arm swung behind me. Even though I knew it was wrong, I thrust my hand toward my sister, carried by the momentum of weight in motion.

But it wasn't Libby I saw. It was Cassie.

I should count to ten. I should calm myself down, the way Mum taught me. I should tell my parents that Cassie is being mean.

But I don't. I swing my arm and I hit her.

Cassie falls back in a way that doesn't look right. The buttons of her pajamas have been fastened wrong so that an empty button-

hole rests at her throat. But as I reach to fix it, the daffodil on the pillow by my sister's ear turns from pale yellow to red.

And then my mother is standing in the doorway, a splash of red wine darkening her shirt, her expression morphing from annoyance to fear. And I know I'll be in trouble again, that I will be blamed. And it won't be fair because it's all Cassie's fault.

In the living room of my home, my empty hand dropped from Libby's throat. My breath stopped, trapped in my lungs, shut in by the terrible realization as the last piece of the puzzle slotted firmly into place.

I had killed my sister.

I had killed Cassie.

THIRTY

I looked up from where my hands—my killing hands—hung by my sides. Georgie stared at me, her pale face stretched in horror as if she had never seen me before. Even from where I stood, Libby's trembling was visible.

In the corner of my vision, something flickered. A tiny, hopeful light. And then I saw the banner strung across the wall, the silver cone hat perched on Georgie's head. The small cake, enough for three. A single candle.

Georgie moved first. A small hesitant step, as if she thought I might bite. She touched my arm. "Abby," she said. "What happened?"

Before I could speak, before I could start to put into words the truth that now unfurled, Libby stepped between us, taking me by the arm, taking charge. I didn't have the strength to resist.

She led me to the couch and sat me down. "Stay here," she said. "Don't move."

Through the flurry of whispers between my sister and Georgie, I tried to grab on to a single complete thought, but my mind was a tank of eels, slithering and writhing, each thought too slippery to grab. Finally, flickers of images came back to me. Cassie and me squabbling. Mum sending us to bed. My protesting that it wasn't fair. A ringing phone. Cassie waking me, riling me up. Me, fuming. And then ...

The attack. Someone had attacked me, attacked us? And I defended myself. I had struck out and hit someone.

I squeezed my eyes shut, trying to picture my attacker, searching for the face I wanted to see: a man, ugly, cruel, hard, dark eyes, malevolent. But that wasn't what I saw. I saw Cassie, cruel, yes, malevolent, maybe, but Cassie, a child, an instigator, a tormentor, provoking me.

And I had responded. I had lashed out. Maybe not deliberately, maybe not with intent, but I had done the deed, nonetheless.

Georgie peered down at me now. She hesitated, the way a game warden might approach an unpredictable wild animal. "Are you okay?" she asked.

I shook my head. My chest spasmed a hiccup, and my face grew warm. Hot, scared tears flooded down my face. Georgie crept toward me. And as I sobbed, she wrapped her arms around me and kissed me lightly on the top of my head. "I'm sorry," she said. "We didn't mean to frighten you."

In the warmth of Georgie's embrace, I watched my whole history unspool behind me. The story I'd been told, the truth kept from me. My life had been a lie.

I wiped my eyes on the back of my hand and blinked through my tears, forcing my eyes to focus on Libby. She stood there, waiting for me to make the first move.

"You lied," I said, finally. "All this time, you knew, and you kept it from me."

Libby's expression was unmoved. I'd never seen anyone so cool and collected. But, just for a split second, her eyes darted to Georgie as if making the decision about which lie to tell next.

"Maybe you should go," she said to Georgie.

"No," I said. "She stays."

"What's going on?" Georgie asked. "What just happened here?"

Libby ignored her and turned her attention back to me. She let out an exasperated sigh and shook her head. "It all got away from us," she said.

Us. The word hit me hard. *Us,* our family. But not me. All these years, I had felt Cassie's absence, a part of me that could never be replaced, a loneliness that I could never fill. But Cassie hadn't been the thing that I'd lost that day. It was my family. They had pulled together in secrecy and had chosen to exclude me.

"Tell me," I said. "Tell me everything. And this time, don't lie."

Libby sighed again as if retelling the story of my life, revising the picture that had been painted for me, was all too much of a burden.

"It was an accident," she said.

"I said, don't lie."

She closed her eyes in a long, slow blink. "Georgie," she said. "It's better you're not involved."

Georgie looked at me for direction. She felt like the only real thing in my life anymore. I wanted her to stay. But Libby was right. It would be better if Georgie didn't know. Better she didn't hear the truth about me.

I nodded that she should go. "Thank you for my birthday," I said.

"Abby, I'm not going. I'm not leaving you here with ..." She glanced at Libby. "I'm not leaving you."

I believed her; she would never leave me, no matter what. But if I wanted the truth, I had to let her go. "I'll be okay," I said and looked away.

"If you need me," she said, but she sounded uncertain as if she didn't know who I was anymore.

I nodded, unable to watch my only friend walk away, not knowing when or if I'd see her again.

When the door closed, sealing me in with the weight of my past, Libby turned on me. "Okay. You want the truth?"

I nodded.

"Here it is. You didn't mean to hurt her. We never believed you did. But Cassie could push people's buttons. She was ... difficult that way. She would get you so riled up and you'd get angry."

"Had I hurt her before?"

Libby shook her head. "No. But when Cassie got that way, we'd separate you. It never got a chance to escalate. But this time ..."

"This time, what?"

Libby's face hollowed. She closed her eyes as if picturing the scene I had so easily erased, the scene she had never forgotten. She swallowed hard. "When I called to ask Mum to come and get me that night, I woke Cassie up. She started bothering you. You were upset. Dad sent you back to bed, and he fell asleep. Passed out, more likely. I could smell the booze on him the second I walked in. You were crying, so Mum went in to check on you. That's when she found Cassie. We thought maybe you shoved her, and she fell and hit her head. There was blood. You were crying, trying to wake her up. But she didn't."

I tried to picture the scene, the out-of-control child, her boiling anger spent, remorseful, but too late.

"And then what happened?"

Libby shook her head again as if trying to get the memories to land in a different formation to make a better picture.

"We found Cassie's tap shoe. Mum was hysterical and Dad was in a panic. They were frantic and arguing. They made me go to bed in their room and take you with me." She looked away, then back at me. "I was scared to be alone with you, but I did as I was told." Her voice wavered. "I always did as I was told."

I pictured Libby then, the good daughter, the perfect daughter, obediently taking this terrible secret and hiding it away, keeping it hidden her whole life.

"And then what?"

Libby shook herself straight. "It all went so fast. When they asked you what had happened, you said you didn't know. We thought you were lying, trying to pretend that it had nothing to do with you, but then we realized you were in shock. You didn't know what you'd done."

A newly formed image came to me, a memory. "I hit her."

Libby nodded. "Dad asked if you saw it happen and you said no. The more they asked you, the more you shut down. So, they made a decision. They thought they'd lose you if the truth came out, that they'd be found negligent and that you'd be taken away, put into care. Maybe me too. They were afraid they'd lose all three of us. So, they chose to protect you, to make you believe Cassie had just disappeared. They gave you a sleeping pill, put you back to bed, and in the morning, it was like you hadn't even been there."

"But all this time?"

"It was a stupid idea. It got out of control, and once they started the lie, they could never undo it. They had to keep it up. We all had to keep it up. And all these years, they just hoped you wouldn't remember, wouldn't start asking questions."

I let everything Libby told me sink in, trying to match the kind, sensible parents who'd raised me with the young, reckless couple who'd made a terrible choice. None of it made sense. And Libby, doing as she was told. Lying to protect both of us.

"And what about Cassie?" I asked. "What did they do?" But I already knew the answer. I had seen it in my dream. Somewhere deep in my subconscious, the truth had been hiding all my life. Maybe I'd heard the whispered plan as I half slept and stored the image for my dreams. From an imaginary rear window of our car, I had seen my dad. I had watched him carry Cassie's body to the end of the long wooden boat launch, and I had seen him drop the bundle into the water. Gently, lovingly, but dropped all the same, the truth was hidden at the bottom of a lake. Until now.

THIRTY-ONE

I sat in the darkness, my gaze washing across the uneaten cake, the gaudy banner, the living room wall covered in everything Dad cared about but no pictures of his broken family. From the kitchen came the sound of Libby's voice. On the phone, I assumed, maybe making plans for what to do with me now. Cleaning up the mess. My mind was full of new information and yet strangely empty. Every few minutes, I got up, determined to take some sort of action, but once I moved, I didn't know what to do next.

The outside of me, the bit that looked and felt like Abby, seemed to pull away from the inside me. In between was a dark, unknown space that hummed with fear and uncertainty. It blanketed the real me, the part I thought I knew. It was a place where I was capable of killing my own sister. All this time, I wondered what kind of person would have harmed Cassie. What sort of monster would hurt her? And all this time, I held the answer. The monster was me.

It felt like hours later that bright lights flashed across the living room and the sound of a car in the driveway snapped me back into the moment. Inspector Siddiqi had come to my rescue, just as I'd asked. Only now, she was the last person I wanted to see.

I ducked behind the curtain and watched as she crossed to the door. The doorbell sounded like an alarm jolting me into my new reality. I was the person Inspector Siddiqi was looking for; I held the answer to all her questions; I was Cassie's killer. My heart pounded in my chest, desperately pushing oxygen to my brain. *Th-think*, it seemed to say. *Th-think*. But I couldn't think. I didn't know what to do.

I could tell the truth. I could go to the kitchen and tell Inspector Siddiqi that I had remembered everything, that I had killed Cassie by accident and that my parents had hidden her body to protect me.

I could say nothing for now and give my parents the opportunity to do the right thing or come up with a better plan than mine.

I could do as Libby had done all these years and keep my mouth shut. I could go on as my parents had done, appealing for help in catching Cassie's killer and hoping the new investigation would go cold and slip back into oblivion.

Or I could run. I could bolt from the house and run for my life.

Four options, and not one of them good.

If I told the truth, Cassie's case would explode into the headlines. "Family hides killer for sixteen years." I didn't know enough about the law to know exactly what would happen, but I knew we'd be in a lot of trouble. There was no way the police would say, "Oh, it was just an accident? Oh, thank goodness for that."

My dad hadn't murdered my sister, but he had hidden her

body, disposed of the evidence of his own daughter's death—her pillow, her shoe. At best, he'd never be able to show his face in public again. At worst, he'd go to prison for hiding evidence, lying to the authorities, wasting police resources, and who knew what else.

And what about me? What would my future look like if I was branded a killer? Prison, psychiatric lockdown? Even if I went free, who would want to be around me? And how could I be around myself?

What happened with Cassie might have been the first time, but it wasn't the last. I boxed because Libby had provoked me, and I had taken her bait. That part of me had been there all my life. My family had done whatever they could to hide it. But it hadn't gone away.

I thought about Project Talk and how far I'd progressed with Danielle. I'd never be allowed to continue working with her, or with any child for that matter, once the truth came out. The future I had mapped out—university, Georgie, a career helping other children I thought were like me—all of that was impossible now. Even my freedom would be in jeopardy if the truth came out. The only viable option I could see was to keep playing the terrible game my parents had begun and, like my mother, take my secret to my grave.

In the kitchen, Inspector Siddiqi looked from Libby to me as if she sensed something was wrong but couldn't tell what it was.

"It's your birthday?" she asked. "I hope you saved me some cake."

We all looked at the cake box on the kitchen table. Blobs of rich frosting and chocolate shavings stuck to the sides, but I would never taste it now. It would be far too bitter.

"How can we help you?" asked Libby, stepping between me and the inspector.

"I came to see Abby, actually."

I searched her face, wondering what she saw in me, wondering if she would tell Libby that I had asked her to come, that I was ready to turn in my own sister. Would Libby now do the same to me?

"Now's really not a good time," Libby said.

Inspector Siddiqi ignored her, looking right past her to me. I couldn't meet her gaze.

I stared at Libby's back, her shoulders set to form a barricade between me and justice, me and my terrible future. I'd always resented her standing in my way, holding me back. But now I saw how she protected me, how she'd carried my secret for half of her life. My family had done terrible things, but they did them to protect me, to try and give me a chance at life. They had lost one daughter that night. They didn't want to lose another.

But they never looked ahead to the future. They did what was needed to keep their child safe, but they didn't think about what that would mean to the adult I would become. In protecting me, had they done me more harm?

My lips twitched around the words I needed to say, but I couldn't speak them. Just a few hours ago, I'd been willing to turn Libby in. I'd been so righteous about doing the right thing, about bringing Cassie's killer to justice, about finally having the truth be known. But now everything was different. My family had made a decision for my sake, and if I allowed them, they'd continue to keep me safe.

"I just have a quick question for Abby," Inspector Siddiqi said. I held my breath, wondering if she had made some connection that pointed the blame at me. She pulled out her notebook and flipped through some pages. "When we spoke before, you said you went to bed around eight the night Cassie disappeared?" I waited, confused. "Can you confirm that?"

She stared at me, not blinking. And then I understood. She knew I had something to tell her that couldn't be said in front of Libby. She was covering for me.

I breathed at last. "As far as I remember, yes."

She held my gaze for a long moment, and then she nodded. "That's all I needed. Sorry to take your time," she said to Libby before turning her eyes back to me. "But if you do think of anything else we ought to know, you know where to find me."

I nodded, silently thanking her for not ratting me out. "I will."

She gave me a last pointed look before turning to leave.

The second the car door slammed, Libby turned on me. "You want to tell me what that was all about?"

I shook my head. "It was nothing."

"Perhaps in the future, when I tell you to keep your mouth shut, you'll know that it's for your own good. Do you understand that now?"

I nodded.

"You need to stay away from Georgie, too. I'll deal with her."

"Deal with her how?" I asked, afraid that I had pulled my friend into harm's way.

Libby shook her head. "I'm not the dangerous one, Abby."

I slumped under the weight of her words. "What am I supposed to do now?"

"Nothing. You need to lie low and let me handle this."

"Like you handled my plans to go to university? Like you handled Paula?"

"It was for your own good."

I scoffed. "And what about Dad?"

"Dad knows what he's doing. He made a decision to protect you, and that's what he's going to do."

"But if we tell the truth ..."

"Your life will be over, and Dad will probably be charged anyway. Obstruction of justice, child endangerment, maybe even accessory to murder. Is that what you want?"

"My life's already over."

"They have nothing on Dad right now. They'll let him go."

"You don't know that."

"At some point, Abby, you have to start trusting that we know what's best for you. You'll be a lot better off if you do."

I was about to argue, but what was the point? I could no longer trust myself, so maybe she was right.

I went downstairs to box. I swung punches at the red vinyl, my anger building with every strike. How often had I tried to picture the face of Cassie's killer? How many times had I let out my frustrations on an unknown culprit? And now I could see the face clearly, and the face was my own. I had searched for the truth about what had happened to Cassie, and the truth I'd found was uglier than I'd ever imagined.

I clung to the bag, bile rushing up my throat. Who was I now? I was a monster trapped in a basement, no longer in control of any part of my life. Maybe I had never been in control.

Even boxing was one more thing my family had devised to keep me in check. They'd encouraged me to box to keep my anger at bay. They'd moved me away from my friends, not to protect me, but to protect themselves. They'd pulled me out of school and kept me isolated in the middle of nowhere, not to give me a better chance in life but because I was a shameful secret they needed to keep hidden. And Libby. She'd threatened Paula to stay away—no doubt under my mother's instructions —sabotaged my application, tried to stop me from breaking free. One more nail in the door that would keep me imprisoned. One more nail in her prison door, too.

But so what? Now I knew the truth about myself, what would my future hold, anyway? How could I go to university, how could I study mental illness, how could I pretend to help other people, knowing what I was and perhaps what I could be again?

My whole life stretched out in front of me, but I could no longer see any further than the four walls of this terrible haunted house.

Up in my room, I dug in the back of my drawer for the university brochure. It felt heavy in my hands. Not just the thick, glossy folder and the sheets of information. There was my future, my chance at a normal life. There was a new beginning, a chance to step out of Cassie's shadow and test my own light. There was a place without shame or guilt, a place to take a chance and make mistakes, to find out, on my terms, who Abby Kirkpatrick really was. I stared at the ivy-clad red brick building bathed in sunshine, at the images of students working in lecture halls, of carefree young people relaxing in the quad. That was never going to be my life.

I dropped the packet into the trash and leaned my forehead against the cool glass of my bedroom window. On the road below, a car's headlights approached. For a flicker of a moment, I hoped it was Georgie or Inspector Siddiqi, one of them coming back to free me from the suffocating prison of my family. But the car didn't slow at the crest of the hill. The lights flashed across our gates and kept going, lighting the way forward to the driver's destination.

"You have to trust us," Libby had said, "Trust that we know what's best for you."

I had trusted them, but I couldn't trust them anymore. I couldn't trust anyone, not even myself. I was a person capable of killing, and my family were people capable of living in nothing but lies. I was trapped inside a person, in a family, in a history from which I couldn't escape.

"Why do our families think they know us better than we know ourselves?" Inspector Siddiqi had once asked.

Well, I knew myself now. I knew what I was. And the only way I was ever going to be free of the past and of the lie my family had built to shelter me was to tell the truth.

THIRTY-TWO

On Wednesday afternoon, while Libby was out running errands, I caught the bus into town and huddled in a shop doorway near the corner of the street, waiting for Claire and the Project Talk group to arrive. It was almost four when Georgie jogged across the car park and up the stairs. She didn't see me.

Georgie hadn't stopped texting since that night. When I ignored her, she called me. When she threatened to come over to the house, I begged her to give me some time. My secret fidgeted inside me, desperate to get out. I needed to talk to Georgie, but Libby was right; it was better she didn't know. I had tried to distract myself by reading or pulling weeds in my mother's neglected garden, but the whole time, I kept glancing at the driveway, half hoping to see Georgie's car and half hoping I wouldn't. I didn't know what I thought she would do. Be a knight in shining armor and gallop away with me? To where? To do what? I had no money of my own and no skills to earn it. I had no future without my family. The doors of the house were not locked, and there was no fence around me, but I was as much a prisoner as if there had been. Mostly, I wanted to talk to

Georgie, to tell her everything, not because I thought she'd know what to do, but because I had to let my secret out. Georgie felt like a small, safe island in the middle of a turbulent sea.

When I was sure everyone was in the meeting, I slipped up the steps and into the building. I zipped past the meeting room door and around to the small window in the side corridor. Through a gap between the art therapy pictures stuck to the window's insides, I could see a small segment of the group. I maneuvered myself until I saw Georgie leading this week's talk.

Georgie had been my life raft. She had been the only real thing in my life. Georgie was flawed and messy. She made mistakes, lurching to the edge of trouble and back. She said the wrong things, drank too much and flirted with trouble when it came to men. But she was a fierce friend. When I'd decided to go to the lake, she'd taken me there. When I'd told her my fears, she had listened without judgment. She'd given me a place to stay, an ear that listened, and a shoulder to cry on. She was my best friend. She was my only friend. She, too, had a dark past—a brother in prison, a flatmate who was shady at best—but if I told her the truth about me, would she stick around?

Just then, Danielle arrived. She looked different today. She was dressed in slim jeans and a pale-pink T-shirt that almost made her look her age. She hesitated at the door before slipping into her seat. I should be there for her, but how could I now? I was supposed to be a safe person, someone she could trust, but how could she trust me when I was living a lie? Danielle had seen more life than most adults. She would see right through me, knowing that I was as bad as the people I was trying to shield her from. I shifted my position at the window until I saw Danielle. She slumped in her chair, listening to Georgie but flitting her gaze to the door every few seconds. She was looking for me.

What would my life have been like if my parents had made a different choice for me? What if they hadn't hidden the truth about me? What if they'd admitted what I was and got me some help? What if I'd had a Project Talk where I could be myself and talk to people without their judgment?

My family had made a decision about me. They had branded me a lost cause and hidden me away. What would become of Danielle if she was labeled the same way? I wondered if my family had really done the best for me.

If I kept my terrible secret, maybe I could redeem myself. I could help Danielle and other kids like her, like me. I was more qualified than any academic to understand how they felt, but without the proper credentials, I wouldn't be allowed, and as long as my family kept me protected, I could never branch out into the world.

Danielle's family had not protected her. Quite the opposite. They had taken away her childhood and left her behind. My family had done everything to protect me. Hers had done nothing. She counted on me and Project Talk for a safe place to talk. If I had to leave the group, I needed her to know it was not because of her. She needed to hear that none of this was her fault. I slipped into the room, taking care not to make eye contact with Georgie. The second she saw me, Danielle's face lit up, and she launched from her chair, wrapping me in a tight hug.

"I thought you weren't coming," she said, almost in tears.

I put my arms around her, glancing at Georgie and hoping she wouldn't pull me away. She must have figured out the truth about me. What if she had reported me to Claire, warning her that I was no longer safe to be around children?

"Nice to see you, Abby," was all she said. "Can you ladies take your seats?"

"Sorry I'm late," I whispered, trying to keep my voice even. I couldn't look Georgie in the eye. I was afraid of what I might see.

I sat down and Danielle took my hand. She didn't let it go for the rest of the meeting.

As everyone filed out and left for the evening, Georgie sought me out. "I'm glad you came," she said.

"I came for Danielle," I said. "This will probably be my last time, so I'm glad you let me stay."

"You're leaving?" Georgie asked.

"I'll have to. After what happened."

"Abby," Georgie said. "Nothing's changed."

"Everything's changed."

"No. Information has moved from one place to another, that's all. Nothing about you has changed."

"I killed Cassie," I whispered.

Georgie flinched but nodded. She knew. "You were six." Her voice wavered. "It was an accident."

"But it wasn't."

Georgie stared at me. A glimmer of fear flashed in her eyes. And then I saw concern, worry, and also trust. We were two messy girls, but we kept an eye on one another. My chest tightened, but it couldn't stop the words from flowing from me. "I remember now. I was so angry. I wanted to hurt her. Maybe I didn't mean to kill her," I choked. "But there's something dark inside me, Georgie, and I can't let it get out again."

"You need help, Abby. Just like all the kids here need help. You've helped them. You've seen the difference you've made."

"It's too late," I said. "We've hidden it for too long. To get help now means uncovering everything. It would do more harm than good."

"Your family has a lot to answer for," Georgie muttered.

"They did what they thought was best."

"If they'd got help like this for you ..."

"Maybe."

Georgie said nothing for a moment. I could see she was thinking, churning all this new information about someone she thought she knew. "You're an adult now. You can choose," she said. "You can live with me. I'll help you. I'll talk to Gary. He'll be okay with it. You'd have to get a job and contribute a bit, of course, but it would be a fresh start. You could get help, talk to someone. You can still get your degree, follow your passion. You're good at this, Abby. Look at how Danielle reacted when she saw you tonight. And with your personal experience, you could really help other kids."

"But what about my family?"

Georgie frowned, and then she said shyly, "I can be your family."

For a brief moment, I imagined throwing a suitcase into the back of Georgie's little red Ford, gravel from the driveway flying as she gunned the engine and whisked me away. I could be free, like Georgie, like Libby, living life on my own terms.

But then the guilt hit.

I shook my head. "I can't do that to them. We have to stick together, now more than ever. They took care of me ..."

"They abused you."

The words stung. I shook my head. Georgie was wrong. My

family hadn't abused me; they'd done what they believed was best. "If I turn my back on them now, I'll lose them forever. I'll lose everything."

"But you'll get to be your own person. For the first time in your life."

I pictured Libby flying around the world. She had packed her history away and re-created herself, put on a mask of competence and control. What if I could put the past behind me and, with Georgie's help, create a whole new Abby?

But Libby's secret was different than mine. She was running away from the killer in her family. No matter what, I would never be able to do that. The killer would always be in me.

"I need your help," I told Georgie.

She eyed me for a moment, perhaps wondering, as I was, if she'd be willing to do the thing I was about to ask her. "Okay," she said at last. "What is it?"

Behind us, a door opened. I turned to find Claire staring at me.

"Abby," she said. "What are you doing here?"

She was going to throw me out. She was going to tell me I wasn't welcome here anymore. "I'm sorry. I didn't mean to cause any trouble, I ..."

Claire reached for my arm. "You're not causing trouble. I just wasn't expecting you. After the news. Your dad."

"What news?"

Claire's face fell. She looked from me to Georgie and back again. She squeezed my arm tighter. Panic rose in my chest. "Oh, Abby. I thought you knew. It's all over the news. Your dad confessed. They've charged him with murder."

THIRTY-THREE

Georgie drove as if my life depended on it. In a way, it did. At yet another red light, she reached over and squeezed my hand. "You're doing the right thing," she said for about the hundredth time.

I nodded, keeping my eyes on the road. No more lies, I kept telling myself. No more lies.

When I looked at every possible path for my future, the only one that didn't run up against a brick wall was to tell the truth. Libby had warned me my life would be over if the truth came out, but perhaps that wasn't such a bad thing. So far, my life had been a book filled with other people's stories. Telling the truth—or at least my version of it—was my chance to rewrite that book, to start all over again from the beginning. There'd be a price to pay—a big price. My family would never forgive me for what I was about to do, and my future would be uncertain. But maybe I could finally get real help, and maybe I would no longer be trapped by the secrets of The Killer Kirkpatricks. And maybe someday, people would forget. With no more mystery, no more intrigue surrounding Cassie, people would move on.

At least, that's what I hoped.

The entrance to the police station was mobbed. Local and national news vans circled like covered wagons around a tribe of reporters, camera spotlights illuminating their grave expressions. I flipped up the hood on my jacket and followed Georgie. As she pushed her way through, I kept my head down, my face covered, and my eyes on the ground ahead of me. I made it all the way to the front door of the station before someone recognized me.

"Abby," a reporter called. "Abigail Kirkpatrick. Did you know your father was responsible for Cassie's death?"

I ignored her question, pushing at the door of the station. It was locked. I spotted Sergeant Nowicki standing guard by the door and signaled him to open up, but either he didn't recognize me, or he'd been ordered to keep me out.

"How do you feel now that your father has confessed?" someone shouted.

"What did you really see that night?"

"Did you know your father was lying about your sister's murder?"

The question stopped me. He had never lied about not killing Cassie. All these years, he'd told the truth about that. But he'd lied about everything else. He'd helped fabricate a box in which I could safely live, but the walls were built from deceit. The only way for me to escape that box was to finally tell one truth.

Georgie hammered on the door, shouting to be let in, but Nowicki shook his head. Finally, I pulled back my hood and waved to him. The buzz of the reporters built to a frenzy as they pounded me with questions. Sergeant Nowicki saw me then. He wavered for a second which felt like a lifetime and finally unlocked the door to let me in. Georgie pushed me inside, slamming the door closed behind me and flipping her fingers at the reporters as they surged forward, pressing up to the glass. She gave me an encouraging nod as Sergeant Nowicki locked the door behind us, shutting out the baying wolves, and hurried me away.

"Inspector Siddiqi," I breathed. "I need to talk to her."

"She's in with someone at the moment."

"I know," I said. "With my dad. But he didn't do it. I need to tell her he didn't do it."

Sergeant Nowicki gave me a tight smile as if he felt sorry for me and my pathetic attempt to save my dad. "Why don't we get you a cup of tea," he said, "and as soon as she's finished, I'll let her know you're here."

He didn't get it. He didn't understand. And I couldn't wait until he did. I dodged past him and took off down the hallway, hammering on doors and calling out Inspector Siddiqi's name. I'd almost reached her office when she shouted from behind me. She stood in front of the closed door of an interview room, frowning at me the way she probably looked at her daughter when she misbehaved.

"My dad," I said, running back toward her. "It wasn't him."

She held up her hand to stop me. Behind her, Sergeant Nowicki moved in to aid her.

"He confessed, Abby. It's over," she said.

"He's lying. I know what happened. I know who he's protecting."

Her eyes narrowed as if something I'd said had rung true.

"Give me five minutes and I'll tell you everything," I said.

She nodded. "Five minutes." She indicated to Sergeant Nowicki to take over in the interview room and led me across the hall to another. I prayed my dad hadn't heard me. I knew he would intervene if he had.

Siddiqi took a seat behind the table and indicated the chair opposite, but I was too agitated to sit. I had to get it all out now before I changed my mind.

"My dad didn't kill Cassie," I said. "It was me."

She raised an eyebrow in surprise. "A couple of days ago, you were convinced it was Libby. Forgive me if I'm a little skeptical."

"I remembered everything. It was an accident. I was mad at her. I lashed out and hit her. I didn't mean to do it, but I killed her."

"Okay," Siddiqi said. "And then what?"

If I was going to tell the truth, it had to be the whole truth. I took a seat at the interview table and looked her dead in the eye. "My parents panicked. My dad hid her body. He did it to protect me."

"He covered up the death of his own daughter?"

And nothing but the truth. "She wasn't his."

Inspector Siddiqi balked. "You told me you were twins."

"But when I was here last time, the bet you had about those two boys having different fathers? It all made sense to me. Cassie and I were fraternal twins. We didn't look alike."

"So, Cassie's father is ...?"

"My Uncle Dave. My dad's brother."

"And you are?"

"I'm my dad's daughter."

She shook her head. "And you killed your sister. Your *half* sister."

The word *half* stung as if Cassie was no longer fully important. But she was important to me and so was the truth about her death. "Yes. It was me."

Inspector Siddiqi sat back in her chair and scrutinized me. The corner of her mouth turned up, just the smallest movement, but triumphant, before she let it fall again. "I've seen a lot of things in my time on the force," she said, "but you Kirkpatricks are a breed of your own."

It wasn't a compliment.

"I'm not sure I've ever met a group of such competent liars. I don't think a single one of you has uttered a word of truth in this whole case. And now you sit here and tell me, after all these years, after all the hours of investigation, that when you were a sweet six-year-old girl, you took a swing at your sister and killed her."

"Yes."

"And your dad hid the evidence."

"Yes."

"And your mother and sister just went along with it?"

"Yes."

She snorted with derision. "I admire you for wanting to help your dad, I really do."

"I'm not trying to help my dad; I'm trying to help myself."

"Abby, he's confessed."

"What about a motive?" I asked. "Why did he do it?"

"You just gave me the motive."

I frowned. I didn't know what she meant.

"Jealousy. We couldn't get clean DNA samples for Cassie, but we got them from your dad and from you. We'll never know for certain if David was Cassie's real father, but she looked like him, and that alone was enough to drive your dad to kill her. He couldn't stand to be reminded that he was raising someone else's child."

"But he didn't do it. It was me. I was the one who was jealous."

"You need to stop, Abby. Maybe you believe all this, but you're sorely misguided."

"He's just trying to protect me. He's my dad," I said, desperate to make her see.

"But that's the thing," Inspector Siddiqi said. "We can't be sure about Cassie's parentage, but we're sure of yours. There's one more lie in your family's stockpile of deceit. Your DNA doesn't match your dad's. I don't know who your father is, but it's not the man in that room."

THIRTY-FOUR

The media vultures were camped outside the hospital, too. Just one news van, but it was enough. If Inspector Siddiqi didn't believe me, maybe they would. Still dazed by her revelation about my real father, I drifted toward the van. The reporter saw me coming. I braced myself, ready to give her the story of a lifetime, but she looked away as if I had suddenly disappeared. Invisible Abby.

I quickened my step, the weight of my humiliation pulling me forward. No one wanted to hear my side of the story. No one really wanted the truth. Well, I'd show them.

But the thought struck me again: Invisible Abby, a killer hidden in plain sight. Nothing about me was real; my whole life was a lie. Even the truth wasn't really the truth; there were still too many unknowns.

I turned and hurried inside the hospital. When I glanced back, the reporter was scrolling through his phone, bored.

My mother looked different today. She was thinner and her skin was a yellowish gray. But that wasn't the reason she looked like a stranger to me.

I thought back to the little girl I had seen in the supermarket that day, the one I had mistaken for Cassie. My mother had been so angry and upset that day. I thought it was because she believed, for a brief, wonderful moment, that we had found Cassie. Now I realized my mother had come face-to-face with her fear and shame. She already knew Cassie was dead and she was afraid that little girl would trigger some memory in me. That's why she'd reacted so strongly. And perhaps the girl had reminded my mother of her greatest shame, the child she had created—not Cassie, but me.

Everything pointed back to my mother's fear and shame. She had cut me off from my friends, moved us away, keeping me isolated from other children as if I had some contagious disease. All this time, I thought she was protecting me from the cruelty of other children, but now I knew she was protecting them from me.

But it was the lies that dug the deepest. Every time I felt I knew myself, felt my feet were finally on solid ground, someone in my family shook things up and knocked me off balance. I didn't know who I was anymore. I didn't even know who my family was. My dad wasn't my dad; my sisters were maybe half sisters. The only person whose role I knew with any certainty was my mother. And she, the one person I should have been able to trust, lay at the center of my confusion.

Beside my mother's bed, machines beeped and whirred, monitoring and controlling her final days on earth. Every hour, another machine clicked and hummed, sending another dose of morphine into my mother's bloodstream, keeping her comfortable, protecting her from pain.

My eyes locked on the machine's switch and my chest tightened with rage. How dare she numb herself from the pain?

There was no one in the hallway outside the door. If I flipped the switch off, would it trigger an alarm, or would the drip just stop until my mother began to feel again? I pictured her clicking her button, *click*, *click*, *click*, desperate for relief.

I wanted her to feel what I was feeling now. She had ruined my life and I wanted her to know how that felt.

"Abby?" her voice was a whisper, weaker than the last time I'd visited. She was slipping away, escaping from what she'd done.

My hand hovered over the switch. Why should I have to suffer for her decisions while she slept on, blissfully unaware of what she'd done?

But wasn't that my whole life? Thanks to my family, the truth had been hidden from me, keeping me blissfully unaware of what I had done. My mother felt the pain every single day.

The anger washed from me as I realized I would lose her. She had tried to protect me, paid the price for her choices, and all that would soon be gone.

"Libby came," she said. "She told me what happened to you."

"All this time, she knew the truth."

It wasn't a question, but my mother nodded anyway, her chin barely moving.

"You trusted Libby, but you didn't trust me?" I said.

"You were so young."

"But I'm not anymore. Why didn't you ever tell me? Why did you let me keep believing Cassie might come back?"

My mother closed her eyes, but she didn't answer.

I felt sick. It wasn't just that they had kept the truth from me. They had kept up the lies. All the times I'd talked about Cassie coming back and they had not once sat me down and told me that she wouldn't. All this time, I'd lived with that hope, albeit a tiny flicker, that my sister would be found. I had been brought up in a fake world, a fantasy created by my parents. I had grown up believing that girls could vanish in the night without a trace, that parents knew best and always did right by their children, and that I was just a normal girl who'd had something bad happen to her. I never had a clue that I was capable of hurting someone I loved.

"We were stupid," she said at last. "We thought we could protect you."

"By lying?"

"You didn't know what you'd done. You were in shock."

The memory came back in flashes. A feeling of sitting in a bubble while a world I didn't understand whirled around me.

Mum crying, trying to pick up Cassie. Dad holding her back.

"Ring for an ambulance."

"It's too late."

A sob.

Libby.

I stared at my mother in her hospital bed. "Why did you do it?" I cried. "Why did you hide her?"

My mother closed her eyes. "When we realized we might lose you, that you and Libby could be taken away from us, we knew what we had to do."

All this time she had stayed quiet about what had happened to Cassie, kept it all inside, and the secret had eaten away at her, just as Uncle Dave said. She had put on a brave exterior, wrestled with her grief and guilt, and all the while, the truth had wormed its way through her body, killing her from the inside out. I wouldn't let the same thing happen to me.

"I need to ask you something, Mum," I said. "And I need you to tell me the truth. I won't tell anyone else if you don't want me to, but I need to know this, and I need to hear it from you."

My mother nodded to tell me to go on.

"It's about my dad," I said. "My real dad."

My mother looked surprised as if she was going to ask how I knew. But we both understood that the truth had found a way out. My mother could plug all the holes she wanted in order to keep her secrets in, but sooner or later, the messy truth would come oozing out.

"Who is he?" I asked.

She shook her head.

I took a chance on the hunch that had settled in since that day I'd heard the argument at the police station.

"Was it Uncle Dave?"

She looked away. "It's possible, yes, but I never knew for certain. I never found out because I loved you girls all the same, and so did your dad. I told myself it didn't matter." She shook her head. "I made a lot of mistakes back then. A lot. I always thought that if I just kept moving forward, sooner or later, I'd leave my regrets behind. But it doesn't work like that, Abby. If you run away when things don't go right, sooner or later, you end up running smack into them again."

"So, what do I do now?"

"Let your dad help you," she said. She closed her eyes and seemed to sink further into the stark white sheets of her bed.

Was that the answer? To let my "dad" help me, to let him pay for all their mistakes? To stay quiet, let the police and the media believe what they wanted to believe? But was he really helping me, or was he anchoring me in a place he believed I'd be safe? And how could I really live knowing that truth?

I thought about Uncle Dave and the kind of dad he might have been if he'd had the chance, the kind of daughter I might have been if he'd raised me. But it was too late now. Wasn't it?

"Which dad, Mum?"

But my mother just closed her eyes again. "I'm cold," she whispered so that I could barely hear.

She wasn't going to answer me, but I no longer cared. I saw the possibility of an answer for myself. My mother had made mistakes and kept secrets, and it had killed her. I thought my parents had stuck together and weathered the impossible. But all they'd done was build a shell over us while the insides had crumbled. And as long as I played by their rules, I was still trapped inside that shell. I had to make some new rules.

I took a pair of knitted bed socks from the table at my mother's bedside. They looked like the kind of booties a baby would wear, pink yarn flecked with blues and greens, a crocheted flower on each ankle. I untucked the covers and touched my mother's pale feet. They were icy cold. I slipped on the socks and tucked her back in, adding an extra blanket around her frozen feet.

I handed her the pain button. Three clicks.

"I love you," I whispered as she drifted away.

THIRTY-FIVE

I arrived home to the welcoming glow of the kitchen light. I imagined walking in to find Dad making tea while Mum, back to her healthy former self, sat in her favorite chair with a book. I imagined Inspector Siddiqi releasing Dad, not believing his confession. The trail to Cassie's killer would go cold again, and this would all go away.

But it wasn't Dad in the kitchen; it was Libby. And she wasn't going anywhere.

The kitchen looked different. The table had been moved and set with two brightly colored mats and matching cloth napkins, folded and tucked into cherrywood rings. The counter was covered with plastic packages of fresh vegetables and herbs, and a rich, tomatoey smell filled the kitchen. In the back corner, where Dad's old blender had always been, a gleaming new machine stood in its place. It had a heavy chrome base and solid glass jug and looked as if it could turn anything into liquid with the flick of a switch.

Libby clipped around the kitchen in flip-flops, shiny blue toenails catching the light. She wore a crisp white apron tied twice around her narrow waist. Libby, making everything look pretty and normal, even when it was rotting inside. She beamed at me when I came in.

"Hungry?" she said with a cheery smile.

I was starving, but I shook my head, wary that Libby was up to something I wasn't going to like.

"Well, drink this for now," she said, flipping a toggle switch on the new blender. "We can have food later when you're ready."

She tipped the contents of the blender into a tall glass and handed me the pink frothy drink. "Your smoothie," she said. "Fix you right up."

I touched the glass to my lips, suddenly longing for something familiar, but before I could take a sip, I changed my mind.

"What's going on, Libby?" I asked. "What's this all about?"

"A fresh start," said Libby. "No more games."

I looked at her carefully. I liked what she was saying, but I didn't believe a word of it. "Go on," I said.

"I'm taking a few days of family leave until we see what happens with Dad."

"What happens with Dad is that he's confessed to a crime he didn't commit, and the police won't believe me when I say it wasn't him. So, we're stuck in the same mess as before."

"No," Libby said. "Because now *you* know the truth."

"So what?"

"I'm sorry, Abby," she sighed. "It shouldn't have been this way. We should have told you before."

"But you didn't."

"And I'm truly sorry for that. But we have to be smart now. It's better that you know the truth. It will help you understand.

But we can't go shouting our mouths off about this. We have to maintain control."

I shook my head, dismayed. "We don't have any control to maintain, Libby. Can't you see that? My life is ruined. There is nothing left to control."

"No, Abby," she said, grasping my elbows. "We're going to fix all this. I'm going to help you find a job, so you can have a normal life. I've talked to personnel, and you could fly on my crew. You'll have to go through training, of course. But that way, I can be there to help you."

"I don't want to fly. I want to go to university and help children. People like me. But you sabotaged that, too, didn't you?"

"We needed to keep you close. It's different now. I know how to take care of you."

"Take care of me?"

"I'm going to help you, Abby. Real help, not this." She wafted her hand over the glass I'd set on the table. "You can have a normal life. Put all of this behind you. We can even give you a new birthday, celebrate properly, your own day. You know?"

"A normal life? You mean like yours?" I thought about the box in the attic. "What's that, then? Flying around the world, stealing passports from strangers?"

Libby's face fell.

"Was that your plan *B*? Your getaway?"

Libby looked away. "There was no plan."

"So, the passports were what?"

She slumped. "A game. A way to pretend to be someone else. A way to be anyone but myself."

My mind struggled to keep up with what Libby was telling me. It sounded like more lies, more pretense, more doing everything *except* living a normal life. And I realized then that mine wasn't the only life my parents had ruined. My life had been one big lie, but Libby's had been a show, performing whatever tricks were needed to keep our secret safe. She'd lost her friends, changed schools, lived with my secret. No one had come out of this unscathed.

I was about to tell her as much when my brain latched on to something and wouldn't let go.

"What do you mean, 'not this,'" I said, passing my hand over the smoothie the way Libby had. "What exactly is 'this'?"

Libby's shoulders slumped, but she recovered quickly. "It's just a drink to keep you healthy."

"And?"

"And some supplements to help keep you balanced."

"Balanced."

"Calm, less anxious."

I stared at the glass with an awful realization. All those stacks of prescriptions. Not for Libby. For me. I had literally been numbed. "You drugged me."

Libby said nothing.

I thought back to all the mornings Dad had made smoothies for me, all the nights we had drunk cocoa together. Warm, cozy moments I'd cherished with my otherwise distant dad, moments that now turned sharp and dug deep into my heart. And Libby had been in on it, lining up my smoothies when she left, afraid of what would happen if I didn't take them. "How long has this been going on?" I asked.

"From the beginning. They took me to the doctor after Cassie went missing, got a prescription to help me cope. They gave some to you, too. It made you better, calmed you down. So, they kept taking me to the doctor and giving the meds to you. Eventually, the doctor refused to prescribe more, so Dad found another source. Then I flew with a guy who brought stuff in from overseas. We just wanted to help you, that's all."

I closed my eyes. I was such an idiot. I'd never questioned any of this, just drank my drinks and did as I was told. A good, obedient science experiment. "Well, I'm not doing it anymore," I said.

"Abby," Libby said.

"No."

"Abby, you can't just stop taking them. You don't know what might happen."

"Nothing will happen." I thought about the days I had skipped while no one was around to administer my medications. I'd felt fluey and maybe a bit more anxious, but mostly I'd seen things clearly for the first time in my life. "I'll get professional help."

"No," Libby said, lunging for me. "You can't tell anyone about this. We have to be patient until it all blows over. We have to stick together. We're family. You have to let us help you, Abby."

I stopped fighting then. "Let your dad help you," my mother had said. *Let your dad help you* ... And now Libby was offering her help, too.

I stood up from the table, feeling my feet firmly on the ground. "This job," I said to Libby. "Do you think I could do it?"

At last, her eyes lit up and a small smile crept onto her lips. "Drink up and I'll tell you all about it."

I reached for the smoothie and brought it to my lips. Behind the sweet scent of strawberry was a hint of bitterness. It wasn't just the taste of medicine. It was the taste of control. I tipped the glass so that it made a strawberry mustache above my lip and took a small mouthful.

I kept my eyes on Libby, trying hard not to blink. I needed her to trust me, to believe I meant it. I grinned and wiped the mustache from my face, and when she was done telling me all about *her* big plans for *my* life, I drank the smoothie for the very last time. From now on, I was in control.

Epilogue

One Year Later

I stepped aboard the plane. The ridiculous teal high-heeled shoes were already killing my feet, despite the cushioned insoles and "comfort" features. My uniform fit snugly around my body, making me feel sophisticated and confident and, at the same time, confined and trapped. I stashed my in-flight bag in the overhead compartment and worked my way through the preflight safety check, row by row, seat by seat. Everything appeared normal.

I took my place by the door as the initial stampede of passengers reached the end of the jetway.

"Welcome aboard," I chirped, pushing my face into a smile that caused my makeup to fold and smear against itself. "Welcome aboard, welcome aboard." *Welcome aboard this metal tube that will propel you through the skies. Welcome aboard the last flight Abby Kirkpatrick will ever take.*

From first class, Libby eyed me between forced smiles for her elite passengers. We'd been flying together for six months already, but I still caught her looking at me as if wondering when my switch might flip again.

The passengers filed past, eager to reach their seats and claim a spot for their oversized bags. They barely acknowledged me. Even dressed top to toe in teal, I was still invisible. They only saw a woman doing a job. They didn't see a person who'd already lived a thousand lives. That was fine by me. Disappearing was exactly what I wanted to do.

Robert Kirkpatrick, the man who raised me, got five years for involuntary manslaughter and perverting the course of justice. There were protests outside the courts on the day he was sentenced. Some thought the judge was too lenient on a man who killed and hid the body of his own daughter. They had no idea that it was an unfit sentence for a man who had done his best to save another child's life, a child who wasn't even his own. He had loved me in his own twisted way, but in the end, his love had ruined us both.

My mother didn't live to see him go to jail. She slipped away into oblivion with her two remaining daughters and a man she had once loved by her side. She didn't take all her secrets to the grave. She left them behind, bequeathed them to Libby and me to carry for the rest of our lives.

Danielle told her secrets, though. I sat in court, in her line of sight, as she testified against her stepfather, told all the terrible things she had seen that night. I hoped she found closure. I hoped the truth finally set her free.

True to her word, Libby stood by me. We sold the haunted house and I stayed with her until I found my feet. I got a real doctor, a proper diagnosis, and appropriate medication. A trustworthy therapist guided me through years of trauma, although probably not the most messed-up childhood she'd ever dealt with. I was stable, if a little fuzzy at times, and I had a future ahead of me.

I had visited Cassie's final resting place only once since her funeral. A new stone marker had been placed at the head of the small patch of freshly turned earth. The inscription on the stone read, "Cassandra Kirkpatrick, daughter of Robert and Theresa Kirkpatrick, sister to Elizabeth and Abigail. Our angel, taken too soon."

Even in death, the Kirkpatricks lied. I'd never know how many of those words were true. If Cassie was Robert's daughter or Libby's sister. Even my own relationship was in doubt—maybe sister, maybe twin, maybe half sister. But definitely killer.

"I never meant to hurt you," I told Cassie that day. I couldn't imagine feeling that anger, feeling that I wanted to harm her. But I had. "I wish things would have been different. It would have been worth it to have you with me. I would have been proud to call you my sister, no matter what."

Standing there at her grave, I'd had a fleeting thought of Cassie, how she would have been at twenty-two. She would have been beautiful and confident, strong-willed and opinionated. She would have been a pain in my backside, too, I was sure.

And what about me? How would I have been had I not lived the life my parents chose for me? Instead of quiet and fearful, what kind of woman would I have been? It was time to find out.

The flight touched down in Marrakesh on time and without event. The passengers trudged off, and I followed with the crew, pulled along in a sea of teal. I showed my passport to the uniformed immigration officer, collected my bags from a metal-fronted conveyor belt, and caught the crew shuttle to a hotel with two hundred identical rooms. We could have been anywhere in the world. Only the signs in Arabic hinted that we were in Morocco.

Within the hour, the crew was in swimsuits by the tiled pool, chilled cocktails in hand. From my arched balcony, I watched Libby chat and laugh, wearing her carefree world traveler mask. I wondered if anyone else saw through it to the wounded person beneath.

When the second round of cocktails arrived, Libby glanced in my direction. We shared a look for a moment, not long enough for anyone to notice. We both knew this was the end. Libby tapped her heart, an almost invisible gesture, then passed around the drinks. I closed the shutters and changed into jeans and a bright logo T-shirt, winding my hair into a bun. I slipped a small envelope of my meds into my pocket along with my wallet. Finally, I grabbed a bottle of water from the minibar and a white button-down cotton shirt. When they looked for me later, they would see nothing unusual missing. They'd assume I'd gone out to explore alone, as I did in every city we flew into. The crew had grown used to Libby's strange sister disappearing. It would be hours before they realized something was different this time. Libby would do her last, perhaps greatest, performance in her signature role of the anguished sister of a missing girl. And then she would be free.

At the front desk, I asked for directions to Jemaa el-Fnaa, the big tourist marketplace in town, making sure to mention my name. With the doorman, I double-checked the route I'd long since memorized and joked with him as I headed in the direction he pointed. He would remember me, too. When the questions came later, both would recall seeing me leave. At the market, I found a group of English-speaking tourists and chatted with them. One of them commented on my distinctive T-shirt, another witness for my collection.

I waved as I moved toward the entrance to the souk, disappearing among the crowded stalls. Amid the scents of spices, the chatter of shoppers, the bustle of transactions, I slipped on my shirt and buttoned it, covering my T-shirt. I pulled on my hat and sunglasses, veered out through a side entrance, and flagged down a taxi.

We bounced through dusty streets, away from the clamor of the city, until we reached a quiet neighborhood in a northern prefecture. By the river, I found Le Jardin Café and took a table in the corner. At two o'clock, a man arrived, ordered a drink, and slipped me a plain brown envelope. Out in the street, I turned the corner, walked a short distance, and ducked into an alley.

Georgie was waiting. She leaned against the side of a beat-up car, pretending to smoke a rolled cigarette as if she'd done it all her life. Her blonde hair was tied in a red rag and her lips were painted to match. We climbed into the car, and she kissed me on the cheek, leaving a greasy red lipstick stain on my skin. I didn't wipe it off.

"Hungry?" she said and tossed me a can of Pringles.

I caught it, feeling the dull thud of rolled-up notes inside.

"Birthday gift from Gary," she said.

She pulled out of the alley and drove away from the city. Neither of us said a word.

We rolled down the windows and sang along to the radio, even as it cut in and out. My hair blew all around my face and made me feel light and new. For a brief moment, my thoughts flitted to Inspector Siddiqi. Cassie's case was closed now, a conviction made, and the media had moved on to new territory. Had Inspector Siddiqi moved on, too, or would this case stay with her? Maybe someday, she'd recall my frantic confession and wonder if she should have believed me. Maybe she'd come looking for Abigail Kirkpatrick, but she wouldn't find her. All the Kirkpatricks were gone.

My mother and Georgie once said you can't run away from the past, that it always catches up with you. But there's a difference between running away from who you are and starting again with what you've got. I needed some time to discover who I really was, time to build a life on my own terms, time to create a new family of my choosing.

Finally, I opened the brown envelope. Inside was one of Libby's stolen passports. Adalene Martin looked a little like Libby and a lot like me. Tucked inside were hotel reservations and a visa, secured by a "friend" of Uncle Dave's, and an address in Casablanca where he would meet us. I looked for a note, but there wasn't one. Anything my dad—my *real* dad—had to say, he could say in person a few hours from now. We had years of lost time to make up for and the rest of our lives to do it.

A NOTE FROM THE AUTHOR

I hope you enjoyed *All Our Lies Are True*. I would be so grateful if you'd help spread the word to other book lovers. Here are some ideas:

Write a review. Even a few words posted on your favorite bookseller's website or reader community help readers discover an exciting new book. If you enjoyed this book, please consider posting a short review on Amazon.com, Goodreads.com, or your bookseller of choice.

Share this book. Please tell the book lovers in your life about this book. Post, share, pin, or text. Your influence matters.

Stay in touch. You can connect with me on social media and through my website. Be sure to sign up for my monthly newsletter to receive news of my upcoming books, get behind-the-scenes peeks into my work, see what I'm reading, or just to say hello. If you know other readers who might be interested in

what I have to offer, please share this information with them.
LisaManterfield.com

Also by Lisa Manterfield

Finalist 2018 American Book Fest Best Book Awards: Cross Genre Fiction

"A thrilling modern adaption of an important historical tragedy."

~Publishers Weekly BookLife

The very last thing Emmott Syddall wants is to turn out like her father. She's descended from ten generations who never left their dull English village, and there's no way she's going to waste a perfectly good life that way. She's moving to London and she swears she is never coming back.

But when the unexplained deaths of her neighbors force the government to quarantine the village, Em learns what it truly means to be trapped. Now, she must choose. Will she pursue her desire for freedom, at all costs, or do what's best for the people she loves: her dad, her best friend Deb, and, to her surprise, the mysterious man in the HAZMAT suit?

Inspired by the historical story of the plague village of Eyam, this contemporary tale of friendship, community, and impossible love weaves the horrors of recent news headlines with the intimate details of how it feels to become an adult—and fall in love—in the midst of tragedy.

ALSO BY LISA MANTERFIELD

"This bittersweet debut about learning how to live after loved ones are gone will captivate readers."

~Publishers Weekly BookLife

Kat Richardson isn't running away from grief; she's just hiding out in a gloomy Welsh university town until she's sure it's gone. Now, one year, nine months, and 27 days after the climbing death of her first love, Gabe, she thinks she's ready to venture out into the relationship world again. And Owen—a cake-baking, Super Ball-making chemistry student—appears to be a kind, funny, and very attractive option.

But the arrival of Kat's newly adopted niece, Mai, forces her home to northern England, where she runs headfirst into all the memories of Gabe she's tried to leave behind—and discovers that Mai stirs up an unnerving feeling of *déjà vu*. Before long, Kat's logical, scientific beliefs about life after death are in battle with what she feels to be true —that reincarnation is real and Gabe has come back to her through Mai. The question now, is *why*?

Taking on the topics of love, loss, and how we deal with grief, *A Strange Companion* is a twisted love triangle among the living, the dead, and the reincarnated.

Acknowledgments

This book has traveled a long and winding road to publication. Along the way, it was fortunate to meet many loving helpers.

I am grateful to my agent, Melanie Figueroa, who kept believing in this book—and me. Thanks to Kit Frick, Cady Owens, and Rosa at My Brother's Editor for their insights and attention to detail. Also, to Stuart and the Books Covered team for the perfect design.

Big hugs to Julia Clarke for providing the catalyst for the strange dream that inspired this story. Thanks to Teri Case for cheerleading from the very first draft. Stephanie Martin Rausch read the very first version of this book and still found something encouraging to say.

My gratitude to the early readers who helped guide this book to completion. Rayne Lacko, Marylee McDonald, Julie Sullivan, and Tess Canfield all lent their generosity and expertise. Special thanks to Steven Wolfson for getting into the weeds with me, and to Kathleen Guthrie Woods for reading many drafts and being a continued source of friendship and support.

I am grateful to the helpers who supported, cajoled, and opened doors for this book. My thanks to Natasha Yim, Ginny Rorby, The Mendocino Coast Writers Conference, The Inessential Workers, and The Uninventables, in particular Debbie DeVoe and Shirin Yim Leos.

A finally, more gratitude than I could ever convey to Jose, who first said, "You have to write this book," and then patiently supported and encouraged me until I did.

ABOUT THE AUTHOR

Lisa Manterfield is the award-winning author of *A Strange Companion* and *The Smallest Thing,* and two works of non-fiction. Originally from northern England, she now lives in Northern California with her husband and two cats. When not writing, she can be found hiking in the redwoods and daydreaming in her vegetable garden.

Learn more at LisaManterfield.com.